CW00431841

MINOTAUR IN LOVE

To John,

Many thanks

for your support,

Fraser

April 2007 Tokyo

Also by Fraser Harrison

The Yellow Book
The Dark Angel
A Father's Diary
A Winter's Tale
Trivial Disputes
Strange Land
The Living Landscape
High on the Hog

MINOTAUR IN LOVE

Fraser Harrison

Illustrated by Harriet Dell

FlambardPress

First published in Great Britain in 2007 by Flambard Press
Stable Cottage, East Fourstones, Hexham NE47 5DX
www.flambardpress.co.uk

Typeset by BookType
Front-cover image by Harriet Dell
Cover Design by Gainford Design Associates
Printed in Great Britain by Cromwell Press, Trowbridge, Wiltshire

A CIP catalogue record for this book is available from the British Library.
ISBN-13: 978-1-873226-89-6

Flambard Press wishes to thank Arts Council England
for its financial support.

Flambard Press is a member of Inpress,
and of Independent Northern Publishers.

To Sal, with love

Notebook 1

~~Anna~~

No, no, that won't do.

I'm so used to addressing you in the old, unadorned way that I've forgotten my manners.

~~Dear Anna~~

My dear Anna,

I owe you an apology.

I owe you an explanation too, so I'm going to use my stay here by trying to elucidate the dreadful events of the last few months. Let me be frank (about time, you're probably thinking): my ambition is to get back into your good books. No pun intended; as you well know, I abhor puns.

You have observed me at my lowest in two senses of the word, despicable and dejected; but I want to persuade you that the person you have tolerated and supported for most of our brief and calamitous acquaintance has not been representative of the true man. To coin a cliché that's impossible to better, I have not been myself. Myself is another person, related but different, as I hope to demonstrate. To that end I must burden you with a brief memoir. I should have confided in you all along.

I have another motive for winning back your respect, assuming I had it in the first place, but I must postpone revealing it for fear of putting you off before I've begun.

I know I have you to thank for arranging my stay here in Cynthia's chalet. As you're well aware, I'm no fan of hers, either as a woman or as a writer, but I have to admit the old tart has excellent taste when it comes to building love nests. At least I assume that's the purpose of this Pyrenean retreat. It has a double bed the size of a swimming pool, though the thought of her frolicking in it with one of her toy boys does not make for dreamless nights.

Have you ever stayed here yourself? The place is disgustingly comfortable and has a quite beautiful setting. It stands on one side of a Basque valley and looks out on the other. A stream, flanked by the road, runs along the valley bottom. Its name is *La Joyeuse*. Isn't that encouraging? Biarritz and the Atlantic are thirty miles to the west, and the Spanish border is visible from the valley rim above the house. Every afternoon the valley is patrolled by vultures, huge gliding creatures that never seem to beat their wings. The only other habitation in sight is a little farm worked by three generations of the same family. The old man wears a beret on the back of his head, like a black halo. At the moment I can see a yellow dog in the yard, the very one, presumably, that barked so tirelessly through the night. Despite the heat, it shows no sign of weariness this morning, but is chasing round, still barking. The family keep their sheep on the other side of the valley and twice a day they trickle like cream down tracks that lead to the farm so they can be milked. The result is a cheese which has the imaginative name of *brébis* (French for ewe).

I sit at a long table under the window that looks over the valley. My books, paper, pencils and notebooks are laid out in orderly fashion. Like you, I can't sit down, far less work at a desk that's not orderly, with everything in place.

I've bought three French notebooks specially for my purpose, red, green and blue. Surely three will be enough to confess my sins? Why does foreign stationery always seem much more stylish than our own? These notebooks are marketed under the bold trade name *Super Conquerant* and claim to have velvety (*velouté*) paper that is *douceur de l'écriture*. I hope it gives *douceur* to the reader too, because

I know my handwriting's abominable, though you must be used to it by now. Cynthia's typewriter, a monstrous contraption from which her indefatigable fingers must have conjured many a masterpiece, lies idle at the end of the table. I never learnt to type.

Thunder rolled through the valley last night loud enough to wake the dead. Not my dead, I hope. In any case, she is beyond resurrection, or rather reconstitution, since she is reduced to ashes. Having received no other instructions, the crematorium asked me if we would like her remains to be scattered, with all due reverence, in their Garden of Remembrance. I said yes, though I wondered if they also offered a Garden of Forgetfulness.

I remember, I remember . . . Is there a grimmer phrase in the whole of human communication? I long to be liberated from memory, to be free of its ghosts and ten-thousand-times-told stories. Children point forward in time; old people point backwards; and men, real adults, inhabit the here and now. I have been locked for too long in a museum of childhood, flesh-and-blood exhibit among the mummies (!), never growing up.

I woke this morning to find a thick mist rolling down the sides of the valley in slow-motion waterfalls, but it has cleared now, leaving the sun to shine in a blue sky. The terrace is buzzing with insects, mostly flies and a few wasps. A small lizard, a little jewel of a creature, has skittered onto the stone flags and is sunning itself beside my foot. Its skin is beautifully decorated in a zigzag pattern of black and sage-green. Cicadas scrape and strum in the grass. After two days of rain the valley has acquired a kind of emerald blush. The petals from the crimson rose growing on the corner of the terrace wall are dropping off in the heat.

I'm procrastinating.

To begin, I must go back to just before the beginning.

Let me present the facts objectively to you, Anna, as if I were a psychiatrist passing the case notes on one of my patients to a colleague.

The parents marry in 1939, husband in uniform; it is probably a love match. Two years later a daughter is born, and from the moment she draws her first, remarkable breath she is adored, especially by her doting, besotted papa. She is named Rosemary after his mother. The child thrives and shows every promise of becoming a beauty. Her father's love for her is extravagant: the girl is the sun that wakes him at dawn, the moon that sees him to bed at night. (For the moment, we will not ask where this left the mother, hitherto the object of his impassioned attention.) The little darling reaches the age of six. Her curls are blond, her eyes are just as blue as the bluest sky on a sunny day, her smile is entrancing, and though she has been spoiled by her infatuated Daddy her temperament is sweet and modest. The kid's a princess; a saint in infant form.

And then one Sunday afternoon in May, when both parents are at home, both working in the garden, so neither can blame the other, Rosemary climbs a tree. It is a venerable beech tree whose trunk has obligingly grown in a series of rough-hewn steps, allowing a delicate five-year-old girl to ascend and perch like a pretty bird on its lowest limb. No one understands how it happens, and it hardly matters, but the angel tumbles out of her heaven and falls on her golden head, snapping her neck as if it were a twig.

The parents don't realise it, but while they stand at the graveside watching Rosemary's little coffin as it is lowered into the grave they are not two but three, because the funeral is also attended by the dead child's sibling, in embryonic form.

My mother, always inattentive to the inner workings of her body, is already and unwittingly pregnant with me by two months. Am I a miraculous gift, a consolation prize, or a wooden spoon?

My father has the beech tree cut down, its stump burnt, its roots dragged out, and its site sown with grass. As a child myself I often play on that patch of lawn without knowing its significance.

My timing could not have been worse, for neither of my parents was ready for another child.

My mother never forgave me the agonies of parturition that my massive lump of a body put her through. Rosemary had slipped out of the womb like a graceful, gladsome fish, neither crying herself nor causing my mother to cry, whereas I came into the world in a maelstrom of pain and howling.

For his part, my father regarded my blundering intrusion on his grief as a gross impertinence. He could not forgive me, and his anger at my being myself and not his beloved daughter never abated.

I believe that whenever he looked at me, at least when I was a small child, he saw in my square, stolid form, my ungainly gambolling, my myopic groping, a disgusting mockery of the beautiful, airy seraph that had been so cruelly snatched from his embrace. I believe he saw a monster, a hideous changeling, sent by malign fate to tease him in his grief. Instead of leaving him alone to canonise Rosemary, he was obliged, before the darling child was cold in her grave, to turn his attention to a real child with fleshly needs, a child who was, however, a gross parody of his idea of children, a boor, a brute, a buffoon. I suppose I might have brought him some consolation if I had been a male alternative to Rosemary, a fair-headed, blue-eyed, graceful princeling. But I wasn't: I was swart and maladroit.

As you know, I've never been a parent, far less a parent who has lost a child, and I can't imagine the depth or sharpness of his pain, or of my mother's. Even though I was a witness at close quarters of their later grief, I still have no conception of the way they felt when Rosemary was so suddenly taken away from them. However, the point at issue here is not their grief so much as the fact that I was its innocent victim.

The notion that my father and I might sit in the presence of a therapist (a breed for which he has the utmost contempt) and give accounts of the years that constituted my childhood is utterly implausible. But if some modern version of the Inquisition extracted from him a truthful confession of his fatherly experience of me, I think the word 'despair' would sum up his attitude. He despaired of me; I filled him with despair; I was the symbol of his grieving despair. He had no hope for or of me; I was a hopeless case. The sight of me filled him with anguish over his loss; dejection at the idea of a future devoid of his beloved daughter; misery over the loneliness (and, I would interject, self-pity) that his grief had inflicted on him.

While I was an infant he dealt with these appalling emotions by ignoring me, but when I became unavoidably obtrusive, he resorted to the classic stratagem of his class and packed me off to boarding school.

None of this will make sense unless you understand my friendship with Nick Armstrong. (His name must be familiar to you, but did you ever meet him? I don't think so.) He has proved himself a real bastard, but so much of my life is intertwined with his that even though I despise what he's done I can't renounce him.

Our friendship is very old: it dates from the time we were sent as seven-year-olds (brings a tear to the eye, doesn't it?) to a preparatory school near Abergele in North Wales, a seaside resort on which the sun never shone. This gulag cowered in the shadow of a black mountain beneath a slate-grey sky. If I think of the place, not a habit with me, I'm always reminded of evening prayers when we droned hymns in the darkness while the masters in their gowns sat like crows on a branch, waiting to catch boys who whispered or yawned.

I was well into adulthood before I could put a name to my father's feeling for me. It's not easy to acknowledge that one is hated, especially by a parent, but my account will be unintelligible if you're not prepared to accept that I was the object of my father's hatred.

If you say you're hated by one of your parents, some well-meaning person is bound to insist that you've got it wrong, that you're exaggerating, or labouring under a delusion. Stony-hearted parents seem to be so gross an offence against nature that these sentimentalists cannot believe they ever occur. 'He does love you,' they protest, 'he just can't show it.' Or, 'He doesn't mean it.' Or, 'It's just his way; he loves you underneath.' They try to present him (or her – there's no gender monopoly on parental cold-bloodedness) as an old curmudgeon with a bark worse than his bite, who suffers from the emotional inhibitions of his generation, and so on and so forth. They will do anything to avoid accepting what they've been told in good faith, which is that some parents (ordinary parents, not monsters) fail to love their offspring, and that in rare cases they even hate them. It's an observable truth, and it only benefits the haters to deny it.

On my tenth birthday I was given a bicycle. This glorious machine was a Raleigh, for in my day there was no other make worthy of a boy's respect, and it was that magical thing in a child's life, which parents frequently aspire to and so seldom achieve, a surprise. I woke to find it gleaming and potent beside my bed. Its livery was scarlet, its white-wall tyres filled my bedroom with rubbery perfume; its bell was chrome and clangorous; and its lamps fore and aft were fired by a little spinning generator attached to its back wheel.

That morning my mother found me blissfully spinning the front wheel, content to listen to the intoxicating noise of ball-bearings rotating round their axle and watch the spokes melt and reform as they revolved and slowed. The machine seemed so beautiful to me, so satisfying as a sculptural piece that I had to be persuaded to remove it from my bedroom and put it in contact with the corrupting road, where its perfection was bound to be marred.

How can a man who buys generous presents be accused of hatred, I can hear you ask. Well, I dare say it was my mother who actually orchestrated my birthday surprise, but that's not the point. What is hard to grasp if you haven't experienced it at first hand is that hatred and duty are not incompatible. My father was a man who always did his duty, as he conceived it. He never failed, therefore, to do his duty by the institution of fatherhood, and if it required him to give bicycles at the appropriate age, the best that money could buy, he did so, regardless of his feelings for the recipient.

My parents ran their lives according to a changeless timetable, and their Sundays followed an order of rituals as rigidly prescribed as any church service. Lunch was invariably a roast meat, usually pork, and as my mother began to peel the potatoes, my father, dressed in a suit and dark tie, would discreetly leave the house. He would return an hour or so later, go upstairs to change his clothes and join her in the sitting room for a sherry. These solitary Sunday disappearances of his were never explained or referred to, but by some telepathic process available to children, I knew that he went to visit my dead sister's grave.

Being a strictly conventional man, my father had arranged for his daughter to be buried in the local churchyard, where her body lay beneath a stone of terrible simplicity. Its inscription gave her name, Rosemary Eleanor H., and her shocking dates, '1941–1946'. There was no epitaph, no design carved into the grey marble, which was itself plain and rectangular. At some point my mother must have shown me Rosemary's grave, though I have no memory of any such solemn visit. In the ordinary run of events she did not go near the place, and I was never invited by my father to join him on his Sunday pilgrimages. Neither parent encouraged me to entertain any awareness of my dead sister's memory or memorial.

I don't think my father held any Christian beliefs beyond a rudimentary acceptance of the Deity, and to my recollection neither he nor my mother ever attended a service inside the church itself. I'm sure he didn't believe in an afterlife, far less in a heaven where Rosemary might have enjoyed immortality, awaiting him at some paradisal rendezvous. But for all that, he could not let go of his beloved daughter; he could not finally consign her to oblivion. I've no idea, and I don't suppose my mother did, what passed during his weekly one-sided exchange with his dead daughter, but I'm sure that it was passionately intense.

One sunny Sunday, not long after my father had departed to keep his graveside vigil, I took my new bike and rode up the hill behind our house to the church. I can't recall my motive. Maybe it was curiosity, or a misconceived wish to provoke; maybe it was a desire to identify with my father by doing once what he did every week.

Panting heavily and standing on my pedals, I swung into the graveyard. When I spotted my father at the far end of a gravel path, his hands behind his back, his head bowed, I rang my bell and accelerated towards him, waving.

Nightmare has appropriated the memory of the next few seconds, adding all sorts of grotesque details. For many years I was tormented at night by visions of black figures, associated with my father, which descended on me, their mouths gaping in rage, before hurling me into the emptiness of mine shafts. I hasten to say that none of this accords with my father's behaviour, which was always tight-lipped and proper. I have no doubt he simply strode along the path, reversed my bike and set me back on my course down the hill towards our house. The only feature of the incident that memory has left intact, its impression indelibly sharp, are the words he spoke: 'Don't ever come here again. You have no place here. You are not wanted.'

Are you tempted to say there is ambiguity in that phrase, 'You are not wanted'? Maybe he was telling me that he didn't want me with him at the graveside. Maybe, but on that bright October day I knew what he meant, and nothing in his behaviour since has ever ameliorated the force of that meaning: as a human being, as a son, I was not wanted, at least by him.

In due course Nick Armstrong and I served sufficient time at our Welsh asylum to be sent on to the next institution in the middle-class penal system, a public school. (The usual thing: Victorian chapel, acres of playing fields for summer shadows to fall on, squalid accommodation, inedible food, mad masters and posters of Brigitte Bardot on the walls.)

The dread of every child in a new school is that he or she will be conspicuous and therefore the butt of teasing. I made an easy target for several reasons, not the least being my obsessive neatness, which was then at its most elaborate. (These days I'm all spontaneity, as you know.)

We were required to keep our clothes in trunks beneath our beds. Mine were folded and arranged with military strictness in little ziggurats, their edges aligned, their corners squared. Needless to say, they offered an irresistible temptation to vandals and it was not long after our arrival that my precious piles were flung round the room and dumped in the bath. I restored my ravaged trunk to its former orderliness, but a second assault was inevitable.

It occurred on a rainy March afternoon when games had been cancelled. You can imagine the scene for yourself, Anna: a circle of mocking boys with nothing better to do, the astute use of a nickname endlessly chanted, and a ringleader, stronger, older and stupider than the others. The lid of my trunk had been wrenched open, leaving its meticulous contents wretchedly exposed. The ringleader was making darting snatches, which I was managing to fend off, but my defeat was only a matter of time, especially since tears were welling in my eyes.

'I shouldn't goad him too hard or he may show you his real strength. Not a nice sight.'

This was Nick's voice, a drawling, laconic voice which suggested that he, for one, was rather interested to see what would happen if my 'real strength' was provoked. It was enough to deflate the ringleader for a critical moment, and the crowd, jeering and laughing as much at him as me, began to disperse. I slammed down the lid and sat on my trunk.

I know this is a story that might come from the pages of *Tom Brown's Schooldays*, if not a Billy Bunter story, and I tell it partly to show that, despite this being the 1950s, we did indeed inhabit a more or less nineteenth-century world. I also tell it because the anecdote marks the birth of a little myth, one of those mutually nourished myths on which friendships are founded.

Nick left the room without a word to me, but from that afternoon he got into the habit of implying that my strength was of such epic power that, for fear of the appalling conse-quences, I had to make it a rule never to unleash it. My strength, he hinted, was equivalent to nuclear weaponry: it was catastrophic and therefore unusable. Like all myths, this one drew on credible evidence, for I was indeed strong; but the truth was, as Nick surely knew, I was a timid child and much too fearful to get into fights.

There was a counter-myth, as there had to be. I reciprocated by showing Nick a flattering image of himself in the mirror of friendship as a great humorist.

Ever since our first term together in our Welsh Broadmoor Nick had been able to make me laugh, but the truth was that my laughter was not the result of wit on his part, or a humorous way with words, or even a gift for comical story-telling, though he had all these gifts in moderation. No, I found myself laughing because his own laughter was infectious. He had been blessed with a laugh that flowed out of his throat like sunshine and honey; it was a laugh so potent that his softest chuckle could reduce an entire chapel of small boys, solemnly bent over hymn books, to universal hysteria; a laugh that could rescue the dullest party; a laugh that could take off a girl's clothes without his touching a button.

Wherever Nick went people smiled and laughed, and for them to laugh so pleasantly, he must surely have said something funny; but it was not the case. As I knew from long experience, it was not wit, but charm to which they had been exposed, a magically genial, treacherously seductive charm.

Contrary to folklore, some adolescents (Nick, for example) undergo puberty with grace, gradually evolving from child to adult while exhibiting a kind of fleeting beauty at every stage. Most, of course, suffer from changes that seem to occur suddenly and catastrophically. There was a boy in our house who went to bed with flu and got up a week later to discover that he had grown two inches and none of his clothes fitted. In my case, it was not the pace of pubescent growth that was extraordinary but its direction: instead of growing upwards I grew sideways.

I had always been a solid child, and now I began to fulfil what turned out to be my laterally gigantic though vertically stunted potential. During this period of transformation I gained no more than a few inches in height, leaving me as an adult to stand in my stocking feet at five foot five inches. In breadth, however, I expanded enormously: my limbs thickened to great columns, while my chest and shoulders acquired Herculean proportions. My head, always large, swelled and rounded, and stood on the thick plinth of my neck like an enormous cannonball. To proceed from base to apex, I became large-footed, heroically-calved, mightily-thighed, barrel-chested, hugely-thewed, bull-necked and beetle-browed. I also grew a pelt of thick, black, curly hair. No ordinary shop could cater for my ever more unusual dimensions. The only clothes I could find that were sufficiently broad for me had been designed for men twice my height, and everything I wore had to be specially tailored.

Why am I telling you this? You're all too familiar with my peculiar dimensions.

My parents viewed my transmutation from infant to stunted colossus with differing emotions. My mother was horrified at the scale and seemingly relentless pace of my widthways expansion, though also a little proud, but her chief response was curiosity as to where my wild gene of gigantism had come from.

'Look at me and Carl,' she would say, 'we're perfectly ordinary, and so were our parents. I can't understand it, we've never had anything like it in the family before. At least he'll never starve. He can always work as a circus strong-man.'

'More likely as a freak,' my father would add. 'They can exhibit him in a cage and call him "The Ape Boy".'

This witticism stuck and it became his nickname for me; indeed, he virtually ceased to call me by my real name. I lived in terror of his addressing me as 'Ape Boy' in the hearing of someone from school, but fortunately it didn't happen and the dreaded insult never acquired currency outside my home where, as I say, I was already beginning to feel a stranger. (My school nickname was the unsurprising

'Bullock', of which more later. For extra laughs it was often corrupted into 'Bollock'.)

How did I feel about my freakish rebirth as a titan? Alas, I could not distinguish the achievement, if that's the word, from my father's reaction to it. I have no idea how I might have regarded myself in the mirror if my parents had congratulated me on my unique dimensions; I suppose I would have felt pride, tempered with all the usual teenage anxieties and self-consciousness. As it was, taking the cue from my father, I felt nothing but shame, and learnt to avoid my reflection in the glass, except when shaving my precociously vigorous and sable beard.

I took to hanging my head, my eyes on the ground, in a futile effort to disguise my unfurling size, and I tried, successfully I think, to make myself unusually precise and neat in my movements, so as to distract from the hugeness of the limbs that were executing them. I devoted very special attention to my hand gestures, hoping that their graceful complexity would mesmerise people sufficiently to blinker them from the ungainly remainder that began at my hirsute wrists. Today I can acknowledge that these stratagems were as pitiful as they were useless, though they have become habitual with me and are still a source of reassurance at nervous social moments, but as an adolescent I clung to them with all the desperation of a stammerer restricting himself to a few safe syllables.

From my earliest days I showed a lack of ball sense approaching imbecility, though it did not prevent several schoolmasters from seeing the sportsman in my sawn-off immensity and trying to turn me into a wrestler, weight-lifter, shot-putter and, in one near-disastrous case, discus thrower. (With a wild and premature release, which broke through the protective cage, I nearly decapitated my eager coach.) By contrast, my father saw my physique as a grotesque joke, but his mockery of it was nothing to the rancorous contempt he felt for the person whom I was becoming as my aberrant adolescence unfolded. If I had indeed taken up wrestling or even the discus I believe he might have set aside, or at least mollified, his hatred. But as surely as my body thickened, my mind grew more delicate and sensitive, more aesthetical and effete; or so it seemed to him, and he was disgusted.

It was true that my character and body had been playfully mismatched by the gods of human design. I had been equipped by nature to uproot trees with my bare hands and hurl back lightning bolts, but all I cared to do with my formidable frame was to sit and read, applying my strength to lifting nothing heavier than pages. I was Samson the bookworm; Hercules the swot; Goliath the geek. And by way of completing the joke, nature had endowed me with wretchedly weak sight. I was a bespectacled bull, a myopic Minotaur. Without my 'gig-lamps' I could hardly see my hand in front of my face.

To my father all this signalled but one thing: effeminacy. Like many men of his generation, he had a homophobic (a word which in itself would have filled him with disgust) horror of behaviour that failed to radiate adequate manliness, a quality he wouldn't have been able to define except on the robust grounds that you knew it when you saw it. Not only had he lost his darling daughter, but he had been cursed with a son who was more girl than boy. You only had to look at the way he waved his hands about. He might have the body of a grizzly bear, but who ever saw a boy, a proper boy, ponce round the place in that niminy-piminy way. (So much for my efforts at gracefulness.)

And what about your mother, I can hear you asking, dear Anna.

What indeed? A mysterious woman; a woman, you might say, of hidden depths, if in fact they were depths and not just unfathomably murky shallows.

To be frank, I find it difficult to write about her. On the subject of my father, I am fluent, clear and informative, but when I turn to my mother confusion sets in, and I begin to stammer, so to speak, on paper. This incoherence is not the result of excessive emotion; I am not clogged with feeling. On the contrary, I sense a kind of emptiness opening around me and engulfing me.

When I think of our house – the word 'home' never occurs to me – I think of a silent, vacant place, in which my mother moved about like a ghost. Not that she was insubstantial in herself, far from it, but the point is that ghosts come and go by impalpable means, melting through walls and vanishing into mirrors, and my mother had the same facility. She could materialise in a room apparently without having opened the door. Suddenly, there she was, cigarette on her lip, larger than life, and then, just as suddenly, there she wasn't. Perhaps all I'm saying is that she had a fast-moving, quick-silver manner, unlike my father, from whom I inherited my own plodding, methodical manner of walking. We were deliberate movers, he and I, plotting our course in advance and following it doggedly to our destination, whereas she was a sprite, a bat, a swallow – Ariel to his Prospero. (And I? Caliban, of course; Caliban.)

Even though my mother laboured in the garden as if fulfilling a punishment, I have no memory of flowers in the house, of their colours or scent. Her efforts were dedicated to keeping the place in order rather than encouraging growth; in fact, it seemed to me she only allowed plants to flourish so she could have the pleasure of burning them in autumn. Bonfires were her passion. My father never set foot on her territory at the back of the house, which she screened with conifers. They grew at an astonishing rate, enclosing us within a wall of dark green, through which neither light nor wind penetrated. This was erected in the name of privacy, but it had the effect of turning our garden into a kind of exercise yard designed for prisoners forbidden to see the outside world or feel the sun's warmth.

If my mother had been a politician, the feature all cartoonists would have fixed on, the equivalent of Thatcher's nose, would have been the cigarette that was invariably plugged into the corner of her vermilion mouth.

I have no particular memory of it, but our house must have reeked of tobacco, for she smoked in every room at all times of the day and night. She was one of those hardened smokers who could keep a fag alight on her lips without blinking as she read a newspaper or did the ironing. She would clamp one side of her mouth on her cigarette while speaking out of the other, gangster-style, and though she was forever driving me outside to benefit from the fresh air, she herself chain-smoked when working in the garden. There was always an ashtray beside her bed, full of stubs kissed with her lipstick.

I mention this, not only because it characterises her, but because I have a special memory of my own that illustrates her curious style of mothering. When I was a small boy she would draw my bath, leave me to splash about for a while, and then kneel down to wash me. During this part of the ritual I would have to take care to dodge the fiery tip of her inevitable cigarette; if I failed I would hear a warning hiss on my wet skin before feeling a sting of pain.

'Don't wriggle,' she'd say.

'You're burning me.'

'Nonsense.'

And there it was.

What did my mother feel when she discovered me, or at

least my tadpole self, securely lodged and frolicking in her womb while she struggled to absorb my sister Rosemary's death? Did she see me as a miraculous compensation, or a cruel trick designed to punish her still further for her loss? And how did she deal with my father's all-consuming, unforgiving grief? What room was left in their silent house for her own grief? These are questions I can't answer. She never confided in me, and I never had the courage to besiege that taciturnity of hers. I am certain of one thing alone, which is that she did not hate me. Her attitude bore no resemblance to my father's. Then did she love me? I can't say. Perhaps; after her own fashion.

My alleged aestheticism, my 'namby-pamby, bloody arty-fartiness', as my father called it, amounted to nothing more homosexual than a passion for books, because as a teenager I became a bibliophile, or, more accurately, a bibliomaniac. I was not only an insatiable reader, gobbling up books like sweets, but I developed an obsessional interest in the volumes themselves, both in their physical make-up, their jackets, binding, typeface, paper, illustrations etc., and in their bibliographic history. I rapidly metamorphosed from keen reader into compulsive collector.

It was typical of my perverse but dutiful father that, while ridiculing my bookishness and even jeering at my short-sightedness ('Look at him, the first teenager to go blind on Dickens'), he nonetheless allowed me an account at Young's, in those days Liverpool's best bookshop, and never queried the titles on the monthly bill or quibbled the amount, which was often considerable. He would even reimburse me if I bought books from second-hand dealers, as I did whenever I went into the city. His method of doing this was entirely characteristic. In order to ensure that no open acknowledgement took place either of my sickly habit or his indulgence of it, I was required to leave the bills in a silver tray on the hall table in the evening, and next morning, after he had gone to his office, I would find the exact sum in notes and coins lying in the tray. Most curious of all, he would have initialled and dated the bill, as if to indicate that the two of us had transacted some piece of business together.

I've no doubt that it was my mother who originally insisted that he paid for my book collecting, but later, when my acquisitiveness required not only my room but the spare bedroom to be walled with shelves from floor to ceiling, he made no attempt to restrain this profligacy but, on the contrary, encouraged it. He would wander round my stacks with a gratified look on his face, saying, 'What's this lot worth then? It must be a fair old sum.'

In those days his interest puzzled me, but later (thanks to Darling, of whom more later) I came to understand his motive, even if he did not. Books were the bricks that made the walls of a private prison in which his shameful son was busily incarcerating himself. The monster was building his own labyrinth. Not only that, he was voluntarily confining himself within its shadowy penetralia. Books were all the companions he seemed to crave, and so his parents, never sociable people themselves, were not required to expose him to public gaze or drag lads and lasses for sacrifice in his lair. True, the monster was on view at his school, but the place was a world away and therefore out of mind, which, let's face it, was the point of paying its exorbitant fees. At home their son was a happy Hess in his self-made Spandau of books.

As I said, Nick Armstrong was one of those schoolboys who breezed through the rigours and indignities of adolescence. (No doubt there are schoolgirls too, but my experience was exclusively limited to my own gender.) He was graceful, spotless, and untroubled by the angst that is the cruel birthright of most teenagers. He had the gift, not always an attractive one, of being able to stand back from the action and observe it while remaining neither involved nor altogether detached. He seemed to be leaning against a wall, ankles crossed, enigmatic smile on his lips, ready to flee or attack as the situation proposed.

Nick could not have been called sporty, far less 'hearty'; nevertheless, he batted for the school's first cricket team during three successive summers. His style at the crease was languid and elegant, his strokes wristy and smooth. He seemed to have no real interest in scoring singles or runs that called for actual running; likewise, he seemed to disdain the showy vulgarity of the six, preferring to compile his innings from fours only. He loved to strike balls that sped from bat to boundary by gliding along the grass, picking their cruel course between wrong-footed fielders. In truth, his scores were never high – he seldom knocked up more than thirty – but his lordly style provided such a tonic to his team mates and was so demoralising to the opposition that his contribution was worth far more than his actual total.

I was always acutely aware that my safety from teasing and bullying at school was precarious. It depended on maintaining my identity as an outsider who was both potentially dangerous (Nick's myth) and inaccessible to persecution. As a simple stratagem of evasion, I developed a kind of hurrying gait, which was neither walking nor running, but a laughable hybrid of the two. Well, I don't have to describe it to you, Anna, but I thought you might be interested in its origins. My scurrying was easily copied and I was often pursued by mimics winning themselves a little easy popularity. What these jokers failed to realise was that by making myself ridiculous I was also guaranteeing my escape: they were lampooning a vanishing man. Don't ask me how I did it, but at school I seemed to leave far more rooms than I entered; I was always on my way out – out of sight and out of trouble.

I became an outsider mostly by staying inside and taking part in as few school activities as possible. While the other boys were playing games or fooling around in their studies, I sought the protection of the library. This building was a gift from some grateful old boy and it was designed in neo-classical style as a little temple with a portico supported by six Corinthian columns. Its interior was lavishly furnished with polished oak tables and chairs padded with leather. Brass lamps were suspended, one to each table, by long chains from the ceiling, and in winter a coal fire was lit every morning by a school servant, who loaded the scuttles with fuel. Special permission was required to read the books in this sanctuary, and the librarian did not tolerate frivolous requests or unscholarly behaviour. As a result he managed to keep intruders to a minimum, leaving him free to pursue his own arcane studies. (Do you remember, I wrote to him about a possible monograph on Ovid's years of exile, his subject, but he replied saying his research was only at the embryonic stage? That was more than twenty years after I'd left school.) I was one of the few students whose academic sincerity he respected and, rather than have me interrupt him, he gave me the run of the place, allowing me to take whatever I fancied from the shelves. I became the Phantom of the Library; it was my home, my haven, my hermitage. Another labyrinth.

My parents shared one thing in common, and maybe it was enough, which was a malicious view of their fellow human beings. In my father's case, I believe this was the product of what could be termed an evil personality; he was a man of small evils.

In view of their hostility to their fellow humans, you won't be surprised to hear that my parents had no acquaintances who might be described, even loosely or indulgently, as friends. Neither of them ever thought of inviting people to the house, and I can't recall a single occasion when we sat down to a meal with a guest. In later years my father was driven by business ambitions to entertain clients in the evening, but he always took them with my mother to restaurants. It was these professional contacts who were the unwitting butts of my parents' malice, which mostly took the form of inventing cruel nicknames: 'Weary Willy', 'Moaning Minny', 'Droopy Drawers' and the like. My sharp-tongued mother was especially adept at conjuring up these damning playground sobriquets, but once she had coined them my father adopted them as his own, and never referred to their victims in any other way. (I should add that 'Ape Boy' was one of his rare unaided inventions. I never heard my mother use it; on the other hand, I never heard her try to discourage him.) For his part my father possessed a baleful skill for summing up people in terms of their misfortunes. Thus he would say to my mother, 'You know who I mean, that woman who's always having miscarriages,' or 'Aren't they the couple with the Mongol kid?' or yet again, 'Guess who I saw today – that chap who tried to bump himself off.'

My father was filled with malevolence, unlike my mother who was merely contemptuous. There was a time when I used to think that his bitterness concerning my sister's death was so poisonous that he wished the rest of the world to suffer as he suffered. Now I'm not sure. What sort of father was he to Rosemary? Was he tender and playful? Did he pull funny faces to amuse her, and turn his handkerchief into a white mouse? Did he take her on his knee and read Beatrix Potter to her? These pictures are fantastic to me because they are so remote from the man who was my father, the man who never smiled or addressed an unnecessary word to me.

The question I'm asking is this: what sort of man was my father before Rosemary died? Did he love his living daughter as keenly as he mourned his dead one, the only sister I knew? Did he love her so intensely that when she was snatched away from him his pain was correspondingly intense? Was his malevolence the result of love turned sour by misery, or was it already part of his nature? If the latter, how could such a man feel love for a daughter, whether dead or alive? How could a man capable of grieving so passionately for his dead daughter hate the rest of the world so spitefully? Or was that the explanation – that in truth his grief was a form of anger, a raw, childish, unquenchable anger?

I can't answer any of these conundrums.

In his day-to-day behaviour my father never took me by surprise; he was predictable and intelligible, a man without mystery despite these unanswerable queries about his past. My mother, on the other hand, was inscrutable, at least I found her so; she often shocked me, and I never learnt to understand her. Let me give you an example.

In an effort to demystify my parents, I used to look through my parents' drawers and desks and cupboards when they were out of the house. This was not a habit with me, just something I did occasionally, and I couldn't have told you what I was looking for, just some little clue that might throw them in a new and illuminating light, revealing their faults, their secrets, their other lives.

I should preface this by saying that my mother could not have been described as fashionable. Her invariable outfit – it could almost be called a uniform – consisted of a sweater and trousers, usually men's corduroys, which she bought at second-hand shops. In summer she exchanged her sweaters for navy blue Airtex shirts, a brand worn by schoolboys in those days. She kept her hair, which was blond and fine and potentially pretty, cut mannishly short; she never smelt of anything more alluring than Du Maurier cigarettes; and she never wore a trace of make-up, apart from her lurid lipsticks. I should also add that beneath her eccentric clothes she had a small, neat figure kept muscular and supple by gardening.

You can therefore imagine my surprise when, one afternoon, I spied a hitherto unnoticed cardboard box at the bottom of my mother's chest of drawers. It was one of those large, flat boxes that the dizzy heroine of a Hollywood romantic comedy would thrust into the arms of her reluctant beau (Cary Grant) while she continued her shopping: a shiny, frivolous, outrageously extravagant box. Naturally, I lifted it out of the drawer and eased up its lid. Like champagne gushing from the bottle when the cork is popped, an eruption of silk and nylon lingerie frothed from the box, slithering over my hands in a slippery stream. Beyond recognising some of these things as bras and pants and stockings, I couldn't name or identify the function of most of the other garments, though with their bows, frills, straps, bold colours and general filminess it was clear they were under things not designed for warmth or practicality. I ran them through my hands like liquid, holding them to my face to feel their coolness fade on my cheek. Impossible to believe that these exotic items belonged to my mother, whose underwear displayed twice weekly on the washing line was grey and serviceable. It was unimaginable that my mother costumed herself in these outré undies for my father's amorous stimulation; equally unimaginable that my mother might put them on for some solitary auto-erotic purpose. I was out of my depth, and at that moment could only think that my mother had been invited to take part in a fancy dress event, or perhaps was storing the stuff for another woman.

I hastily crammed them back in their box, rammed on the lid and pushed it into the drawer, at the same time pushing this disturbing discovery to the back of my mind. The next day I looked again, and thereafter made regular checks. The box was always there. Sometimes a new garment would be lying on top, still wrapped in its tissue paper chrysalis, but it would lie dormant along with the others, never unfurling its wings, its colours forever interred.

I was in the last month of my seventeenth year when I had my heart broken. The circumstances were not without a modest glamour. My parents, most uncharacteristically, had decided to take a ten-day cruise for our annual holiday. The ship, called the *Marije*, was Dutch and she sailed from Rotterdam, collecting her English passengers at Southampton. Our voyage, if that is not too grandiose a term for the pottering little pleasure trip we embarked on, took us to Casablanca, Madeira, Lisbon and home again.

During the first couple of days we gained our sea legs, explored the ship and, in my parents' case, spent many contented hours leaning on the rail and disparaging our fellow sailors. In the evenings, after dinner, the passengers gathered in the saloon to drink at the bar or dance on the little dance floor to music produced by a venerable five-piece band. My parents would try to attach themselves to people they hoped would be socially or financially helpful to my father's career, and I would be left more or less to my own devices. The first couple of evenings, embarrassed by their flagrant behaviour, I withdrew to my cabin and the company of the small library I had brought on board with me.

Before embarking, I had given much thought to books appropriate to ten days seafaring and, after several visits to the library and the bookshops, I had loaded my suitcase with such literary salts as Conrad, Stevenson, London, Childers, Hemingway and so forth. However, it was Herman Melville's *Moby-Dick* that I opened first, lying on my bunk and feeling the pitch and sway of the ship as she began to negotiate the Channel. I won't bore you with my enthusiasm – fanaticism might be the word – for this most extraordinary of novels; I will only say that had I not stirred from my cabin throughout the entire ten days, never deserting the *Pequod*, I would have staggered down the gangway at Southampton a wholly satisfied customer.

And that might have been the story of my holiday if on the third night, when I was sitting moodily at the bar wondering how to sneak away to my cabin for further whaling adventures, a girl of my age, a girl with an astonishingly long, white and slender neck, had not slid her elegant haunch onto the stool next to mine.

And now, dear Anna, I'm going to take you into my confidence and tell you something I have never before told to a living soul.

It was around the time of our cruise, perhaps a year or two earlier, that my father had taken to amusing himself by calling me 'Ape Boy'. As is often the way with people who are being persecuted, I learnt to laugh along with my tormentor when the jokes began to fly. I recall – and now we are opening the door on a very dark place, which I have kept locked up all these years – I recall that I even played up to the joke, capering in our sitting room, scratching my armpits, dragging my knuckles and making apish noises. Without thinking it through properly, I hoped that by teasing myself more cruelly than my father I would appease him and make his teasing redundant. It goes without saying that my calculation was utterly misconceived. All I managed to do was convince him that I was a bigger fool than he'd taken me for; the victim had vindicated his own victimhood.

I soon realised my stupidity, and I don't remember trying this tactic more than twice at the most. Yet, believe it or not, I had a reason, a very secret reason, for being grateful that my father saw me as a monkey. The fact is that I nursed a fear, which sounds laughable now but in the toils of adolescence seemed all too real. I feared that I was indeed metamorphosing, not into King Kong, but into the bull of my nickname. I feared I was turning into a modern Minotaur.

How is your Greek mythology? I'm sure you won't be insulted if I refresh your memory (this story is engraved on mine). All you have to know is that the Minotaur was a monstrous creature with a bull's head and a human body. His mother was married to Minos, the king of Crete, but she fell in love with a white bull – don't ask – and by means of disguising herself inside a hollow wooden cow specially made for the purpose she succeeded in seducing the brute. In due course (how long to gestate a monster?) she gave birth to the Minotaur. (Congratulations! It's a little minotaur.) His stepfather, the king of Crete, was so horrified by the bull-bastard his wife presented to him that he arranged for the freak to be imprisoned in an inescapable labyrinth. Here, in secrecy and darkness, the misshape grew into a living metaphor: a man with all the strength and savagery of a beast; a man with a bull's mind in his horny head. He became a monster and his appetites were suitably monstrous. Every nine years the city of Athens was required to send a tribute to King Minos, seven youths and seven maidens who were sacrificed to the Minotaur trapped in the black heart of his puzzle-prison. The myth is silent on the subject of what the monster actually did with these virgins, but once they had been thrust into his labyrinthine lair they were never seen again. The Minotaur was finally killed by Theseus, who escaped from the maze with the aid of a magic thread supplied by Ariadne, the daughter of Minos. No one, not even his zoomorphic mother, seems to have mourned his death.

You might say it was preposterous of me to imagine that I was turning into a mythological beast, but the evidence seemed overpowering. My head, already over-sized even by the measure of my colossal body, had become thickly capped with coarse, curly, woolly hair. My body remained smooth and only moderately hairy, as befitted my human half, but a tuft of coarse bristles had begun to sprout at the base of my spine. Night and morning I struggled to peer at it with the aid of a hand mirror, convinced that I was examining the forerunner of a *tail*. A thousand times a day I would run an anxious palm over my fleecy forehead and imagine that I could feel the swelling of a pair of horn buds. I was a boy-bullock, rapidly transmuting into the bull-monster itself.

No wonder I was grateful that my father ridiculed me as an ape, since my increasing resemblance to the Minotaur seemed unmistakable to me. I was certain that even if my parents were blind to my unnatural growth, no girl would fail to recognise me for what I was becoming. This was a more or less theoretical fear, since girls on our school site were as rare as giraffes, and during the holidays I took care to avoid the very few (girls) that might have crossed my path. Yet, like any teenager, I was tormented by sexual desire, which I assumed would be forever frustrated because of my monstrosity. Who would want to kiss a bull?

I tried to comfort myself by spinning daydreams on the theme of Beauty and the Beast. I would dream that a gorgeous woman – a film star of the day, usually Brigitte Bardot, Claudia Cardinale or my particular favourite, Gina Lollabrigida ('*La Lollo*') – would perceive beneath my bovine exterior an inner man of such spiritual and intellectual beauty that she would immediately dismiss her current lover (a handsome cretin), take me in her lovely arms, undo several buttons and . . . What came next was always cloudy and unspecified, yet fervid. However, these little home-made movies brought only brief consolation, and I reached my eighteenth year certain that I could expect nothing from girls but disgust and rejection.

Convinced of my beastliness, I was ready to flee when the girl with a long neck perched beside me at the ship's bar, and yet I hesitated for a fateful moment. Glancing at her sideways, I was emboldened by her air of disconnection from the world and her indifference to the social mores, which are at their most stringent on cruise ships. She didn't look at me, or order from the barman. Neither uncouth, nor 'bolshy', she was aloof. She was so aloof she seemed barely present on the ordinary material plane occupied by parents, pursers, waiters and the rest of humanity. As I continued to observe her, it occurred to me that such a girl might be blind, or at least indifferent to my taurine ugliness.

I have no idea how we fell into conversation, since we were both as shy as we were arrogant, but somehow we did, and spent the rest of the evening together. This represented a double miracle: for the first time in my entire life I spoke at length with a female other than my mother, and this same female showed no signs of finding me repulsive.

Her name, I discovered the following day by consulting the passenger list, was Régine; she was Dutch and travelling with her mother.

I suppose our friendship could be called a shipboard romance, but it fell into a rarefied category, for we only got together in the evenings. During the day we had virtually nothing to do with each other. I was absorbed in my reading, note-taking, and diary-writing, while she was required by her mother to attend various remedial classes at the gymnasium and swimming pool in order to improve her allegedly poor posture. My own mother made the tart comment that if 'the merry widow' (my parents' nickname for Régine's lone and melancholy parent) thought the poor girl's chances of hooking a husband were going to be improved by doing a few physical jerks the woman was even sillier than she looked. She could not have known how far from the mark she was. The fact that adult consensus looked on Régine as a physical aberration (pigeon-chested, pigeon-toed) made her both approachable and irresistible in my eyes. We were kindred spirits.

Looking back, I see that in fact her only abnormal feature was her slender, pale, curved, elongated neck (not an ugly duckling's, still less a pigeon's, but a swan's) of which I still dream.

If there were other young people on board the ship, I have no recollection of them; if I had a rival for Régine's attention I was unaware of him. When we met in the evenings we were exclusive and inseparable. While the adults gathered round the bar we sequestered ourselves in a dark corner at the back of the saloon, sitting face to face at a small table. Naturally, we disdained the buffooneries of the dance floor, preferring to smoke packet after packet of cigarettes (happy days of ignorance) and drink expensive cocktails, which we put down alternately on our parents' bills. We entertained ourselves by talking. We talked interminably, continuously, unstoppably, and every evening we had still more to say to each other. We discussed such topics as existentialism (having read Camus' *L'Étranger*, we were experts) and the ghastliness of rock and roll when compared with the infinitely more sophisticated music of Juliet Greco, Edith Piaf and Jacques Brel. We expatiated on the bottomless vulgarity and insensitivity of our parents. We jeered at the barbarity of the other passengers. In short, a more pretentious pair would be hard to imagine.

With my willing consent a large part of these marathon conversations was devoted to Régine's memoirs. Despite her slender seventeen years, she was able to describe at epic length the handful of incidents that thus far comprised her autobiography. (Though now I marvel that all those hours of self-examination have left no record in my memory beyond a faint perfume of prolixity.) For my part, I was no less loquacious, though I mostly restricted myself to literary confessions, telling her about my favourite books and the lives of their authors, which seemed to engross her. I may have touched on the topic of my unusual dimensions, but I didn't breathe a word concerning my Minotaurine nightmares. There was one topic on which she too was silent, and that was her father, or rather his death, for he had only recently succumbed to cancer, the very reason her mother was taking them on this recuperative cruise.

Régine's hair was the colour of cream, so blond it was white, but with a hint of buttermilk; her eyes were the exact blue that the sea acquired in the southernmost port we visited, Funchal on the island of Madeira. She was not tall, perhaps an inch shorter than I, she was wretchedly slight, and, despite her mother's callisthenic regimen, her posture was incurably shy and shrinking. Her English was faultless, though she spoke with a marked Dutch accent that gradually charmed my ear until I began whispering words to myself with her special intonation. I remember she said the word 'mouse' with what I learnt to think of as an adorable hushing noise at the end: '*moushe*'.

At the end of these evenings, long after our parents had repaired to their cabins, after the band had played the last waltz and packed up their instruments, after the barman had refused to serve the last belligerent drunks, after the stewards had turned out the lights and locked the saloon doors, we would go on deck and keep ourselves warm by huddling close to a ventilation pipe while we watched the moon chopped to pieces on the black Atlantic. Still talking, we would begin to yawn at last, a signal to make our final inspection of the empty, throbbing ship. We would walk hand in hand to the lower deck where our cabins were located and at Régine's door we would solemnly say good-night. I would kiss her lips and lingeringly kiss her swan's neck; then we would part.

Why did I kiss her neck? And, having kissed her neck, why didn't I go into her cabin, lie down on her bunk and kiss the rest of her? At that time of night there was no one awake to monitor our behaviour and all three of our several parents seemed content to leave us to behave as we chose. I kissed her neck because it exercised an irresistible fascination over me: it was the most erotically graceful thing I had ever seen. On one occasion, I did place my hand on her breast, or rather on that part of her dress that lay outside the bra that protected it – one might almost say fortified it, such was the formidable wiring, padding and general bullet-proofing that went into the construction of even teenage bras in those days – but she did not respond, and the instinct that had brought me this far suddenly deserted me, leaving my hand clinging to her front like a damp leaf on a pavement. I can't say I was frustrated; on the contrary, by kissing her neck and throat, which I did with passionate tenderness, being careful not to mark its pristine, silky, milky whiteness, I reached the limits of my sexual ambitions. The truth was I didn't know what to do next, and she gave no indication of knowing either.

I had no experience of 'falling' in love and therefore did not understand what was happening to Régine and me; at least, I think I speak for her too. All I knew was that I had discovered love and dread simultaneously. At breakfast on the morning of the eighth day of our ten-day voyage, I suddenly realised that it was essential, a matter of life and death, that Régine and I spent every remaining minute together. Just as Melville himself had jumped ship to linger in the Marquesas with a native maiden, I deserted the *Pequod* in mid-voyage, jumping off my bunk and leaving the book face down and open, a thing I never usually did or do. I ran to the ship's gymnasium, where I found Régine bandying a medicine ball with a listless boy in a singlet. My mere appearance at the door was enough to make her turn tail and join me, leaving the forlorn ball to complete its trajectory uncaught and thump on the floor.

From that moment, apart from a brief few hours when we were alone and asleep in our separate cabins, we were not parted. And what did we do with this inestimably valuable time? We smoked more cigarettes and stared miserably over the ship's side, watching the sea turn from blue to grey as it bore us closer to Southampton. I studied my watch a hundred times an hour to see exactly how many minutes, how many seconds remained before I was sentenced to be separated from my now infinitely precious Régine.

I did not know what to do with my feelings, did not recognise them, could not name them. I only knew they were tumultuous and all-consuming, that they were more intense than anything I had previously experienced. Nor can I tell you if they were reciprocated. I was so overwhelmed by the turbulence of what was taking place within me, I never paused to wonder if Régine was similarly overwhelmed. I assumed she was, for although I drove the pace of our relationship, she showed no reluctance to spend those last agonising hours in my company. As far as I can recall, neither of us invoked the word 'love', which in any case would not have described the emotion that was consuming me. What I felt for her was not love, but a terror of deprivation: I was facing the prospect of her loss, and it had reduced me to a state of frantic despair.

The day of our parting dawned all too quickly. No need to retail the miserable details: you can imagine for yourself the exchanges of little gifts, the frantic hand-holding, the tears bravely but unsuccessfully fought back, the endless looking into each other's eyes, the impassioned kissing as if to imprint oneself forever on the very soul of the other and to receive her impress forever on your soul. Finally, there was a last tragic embrace followed by a long, tottering walk down the gangway as I disembarked, leaving Régine at the rail (the Dutch passengers were due to sail on to Rotterdam) waving, waving, waving.

Twelve hours later I was back in my bedroom, ignoring my mother as she shouted up the stairs that I should stop moping and come down to eat supper. I sat at my desk, pen poised over a sheet of paper, preparing to write my first love letter. 'My darling Régine . . .' Tears were falling on the paper, and my hackneyed heart felt as if it had been broken.

My hand was shaking so badly that I was unable to write.

A single emotion – missing her, longing for her, yearning for her – had overtaken my being. 'Régine! Régine! Régine!' I cried out her name, and feeling I could no longer control the urge to howl, I opened the window at the back of my bedroom, which overlooked the garden, so my bellowing would go unheard. 'Régine! Régine!' I thrust my head into the uncaring night and, like an actor in a silent film, held out my arms in an empty, histrionic embrace. I howled to the moon and begged it to transport me to Régine.

We exchanged letters, of course; indeed, they became the very meaning and substance of my life, for when I was not writing mine to Régine, or re-reading hers to me for the thousandth time, I simply suspended myself like a fish in a bowl between feeding times and waited out the limbo that separated one postal delivery from the next. My letters were passionate and lengthy declarations of undying love (I was nothing if not a verbose lover) and hers, if shorter, were no less agonised. But though we howled our misery across the North Sea, we felt no relief from the tortures of separation. In fact my feelings seemed so unendurable that I swore, even as I was calling out for my beloved, that I would never again allow myself to be vulnerable to this agony.

Nor did photographs bring any consolation. I kept one in my wallet, taking it wherever I went, and I put another in a frame and stood it on my desk. When I was not writing to Régine, I would stare and stare at it, occasionally even kissing her image. But the face in the picture, with its changeless smile, its idiotic unresponsiveness, began to mock me. Here was I, tears streaming down my face, beseeching her, and there was she, in her blue dress, apparently smiling at my anguish.

It was torture to recall her hundreds of endearing little ways: her habit of tapping a cigarette, tobacco end down, with two brisk knocks on the packet before lighting it; her quaint mispronunciations; the moustache of sweat that used to appear on her upper lip on hot days, tiny diamonds sparkling among the otherwise invisible hairs; and so on. Yet as each grief-laden day succeeded the last, a subversive thought began to preoccupy me: surely there had been more to Régine than this miscellany of traits and tricks, charming though they had been and heartrending though they were to recall? What had been so exceptional about her that she was able to shatter my world and leave me exiled in my own life? To my dismay I couldn't answer these questions.

And did my feelings for her really qualify for the term *love?* Somewhere at the back of my fevered mind, I knew they didn't.

In due course my pain abated, but before leaving the subject I'd like to add a little anecdote.

One evening following our return from Southampton, at the very nadir of my despair, I had resorted for the fifth or sixth time to the window, tears gushing from my eyes, when to my horror I heard the door opening as someone (mother? father?) came into the room. I withdrew my head from the window space, banging it sharply on the frame. Then, realising that whoever was now in the room would see my reddened eyes and wet cheeks, I pushed it out again, inflicting another blow.

'What the hell are you doing?' asked my father, always blunt.

I cleaned up my face, still keeping it outside.

'Is there someone in the garden?' he asked.

I tried to retract my head into my collar like a tortoise and turned away from him.

'No. No one. I was looking at the stars. They're so bright.'

He snorted sarcastically and left the room, but later I overheard him reporting the incident to my mother. My crying had not escaped him.

'What's the matter with him, now?' he demanded of my mother.

'Can't you see? He's in love.'

'Love!' said my father in tones of disgust. 'Who on earth is he in love with?'

'That girl on the ship. You know, whatsherface, with the drippy mother. Surely you must have noticed him mooning over her?'

'Do you think he poked her?'

'I very much doubt it. Can you see him poking anyone, as you so delicately put it?'

'I should bloody well hope not. I don't want to start paying out for some paternity suit.'

'You can be grateful he isn't queer.'

'Well, does he know how to use a frenchie?'

And so on.

I am making this up, but I can assure you that a conversation along these lines did take place. I particularly remember my mother's scathing reference to Régine's 'drippy mother'. How typical of her to hit on such an accurate but horribly derisive way of describing the poor woman, who did indeed have a rather ineffectual manner, but was doing her best to face the world after the death of her husband. Grief, the keynote of their lives, was not an emotion in others that drew charity from my parents.

What then did I learn from this early lesson in my sentimental education? I learnt that if this was love, it was pain. I learnt that if love was wanting to be with the other person, then its corollary was that separation was suffering; the greater the love, the more intense the suffering. I also learnt that I never wanted to feel those pangs of yearning again, never wanted to find myself hanging my head out of windows and crying for reunion, for relief. Yes, dear Anna, I fear it made a coward of me, or rather a kind of neuter, a person not willing to risk his heart for fear of getting it broken.

The Régine episode, which I fear I have narrated in excessive detail, drove me deeper and deeper into my obsession with books. My parents probably feared that it would develop into a disastrous aspiration to write them or, worse still, teach people about them, but they needn't have worried, for it evolved into another, unexpected form.

One of the writers I most admired, though largely on the strength of a single book, was Scott Fitzgerald. The book in question was *The Great Gatsby*, and I began to collect its many editions, chasing the always elusive firsts, both British and American. (I did not secure one of the latter until many years later when I took a trip to St Paul, Minnesota, Fitzgerald's birthplace, and paid without resentment a truly criminal price for a battered, shamefully thumbed copy.) In a less committed way I also collected books about Fitzgerald himself and his literary contemporaries, filling a long shelf with the works and biographies of Ernest Hemingway, Sherwood Anderson, John Steinbeck, Nathaniel West, Ezra Pound, Ring Lardner, William Faulkner and so on.

As I began to read this literature I found myself increasingly interested in a certain shadowy figure, not a writer but a publisher: Max Perkins, who was the remarkable editor of Fitzgerald, Hemingway and Thomas Wolfe. (Does anyone read Wolfe nowadays?) The more I read, the more fascinated I became by this elusive and eccentric perfectionist, who wore his hat indoors, crushing it behind his ears to push them forwards and mitigate his deafness. My interest in Perkins predated the publication of his biography by Scott Berg in 1978, as well as his exchange of letters with Fitzgerald (*Dear Scott/Dear Max*, 1971), both of which threw him into the literary prominence he deserved. In the absence of these books I was obliged to pursue him like a detective among the biographies of his authors, checking his name in their indexes and chasing him down in the few paragraphs devoted to the publishing process. Biographers generally skimped this material, assuming it would bore their readers, and hurried on to juicier material connected with marriages, mistresses and alcoholic misdemeanours, but to me these niggardly paragraphs were enthralling. I took to copying them out, making a little commonplace book of references to Perkins. Later, I compiled references to other publishers and then to authors' agents (Harold Ober, for example, Fitzgerald's long-suffering agent).

In short, I became obsessed not simply with books and their writers, but with the business people behind them. Publishers were my unlikely hero figures, and I conceived the ambition of becoming one of them. I imagined myself as a kind of rock on which genius would depend for its flowering; discreet, unseen by the public, but quite indispensable. As anyone who has had the slightest acquaintance with the book industry will know, my conception was laughably naïve, but there it was. By the age of seventeen, eighteen at the latest, I had fixed on the profession, or mission as I saw it, that would be my life's work. I would be a publisher in the mould of the great Max Perkins. I would be the British Perkins of my day.

If I was a Minotaur, my room at home was my labyrinth. It was an unremarkable, pleasant room with a window overlooking the street and another, opposite, that overlooked the uneven patch of lawn where the beech had once stood, the tree that had been my sister Rosemary's playground and the engine of her execution. But, like a murderer, I made this room my gaol. No Daedalus was needed to confine me in my labyrinth; I was a willing inmate and eagerly sought its sanctuary whenever I returned to the house. My father's disgust had reached the point where instead of mocking me, he behaved as if I no longer existed. He comprehensively shunned me. At mealtimes, when my company was unavoidable, he devastated me with silence. Have you ever been assaulted by silence, Anna? I hope not for your sake.

In those days my explanation (and excuse) for everything that happened under our roof was Rosemary's death. My spectral sibling haunted our house day and night, keeping my father in the eternal darkness of his grief. It was as though she had never died, or, rather, as though she died afresh every afternoon, allowing his grief no diminution. In his invariable black suit, his black eyebrows drawn across his brow like shutters, his mouth forever frozen in a scowl, my father was the embodiment of grief. As a man cruelly punished, he could not be expected to be any kinder to others than fate had been to him. Or so I thought.

I took refuge in books – not literature, but books themselves. At that age I had not yet acquired many volumes, three or four hundred at the most, but I had already learnt to take pleasure from arranging and sorting them. I played librarian to my own little collection and made elaborate records on a card index for every book I purchased, noting its author, title, date of publication, publisher, price, place of purchase and, in the case of second-hand books, its condition. I gave the books catalogue numbers, which I pencilled into their flyleaves, and I developed my own simple system of classification.

I did not pass judgement on my parents; that came later, under Darling's tutelage. My father's cruelty didn't lead me to condemn him as a cruel man; nor did I condemn my mother for being a bystander. Instead, I adopted strategies for my own protection. Death ruled over life in our house, darkness was forever encroaching, and all I knew was that survival depended on bringing light into my labyrinth. (Perhaps my mother was trying to do the same by keeping a box of rainbows in her bottom drawer.)

Notebook 2

Have you come this far, Anna?

You must be wondering why I've chosen you as the recipient of these confessions. As I told you at the beginning, my intention is to show you I am not who I was; at least, not who I was during those last weeks before the debacle and my removal here.

The man you met when you first joined the company was closer to the person I like to think of as myself. I was calmer then, wasn't I? Not conspicuously manic, and never (noticeably) drunk. I am a drinker – foolish to deny it – but not a drunk. Perhaps that's the kind of deluded distinction that only drunks try to insist on.

I'm confessing, or rather explaining myself, because I'm hoping to get back into your good books, and contrary to what I said at the beginning, I do intend the pun. Despite recent events, I've no intention of abandoning the business and I have a plan for a new and glorious future that could include you, Anna. I'll say no more for the moment.

Back to the booze. I can only say in my defence that since coming here I have been sober – sober, that is, in the sense of not being drunk, certainly not drunk the way I was on that last spectacular, shameful afternoon in the office.

Cynthia's trusty dictionary tells me that 'sober' means 'not addicted to the use of strong drink'. It also means 'free from the influence of intoxicating liquor; not intoxicated; not drunk'. As a drinker, I belong to the category that is lodged in the crack between these two meanings: I am addicted, but never, or only very rarely, drunk. I'm addicted in that I haven't gone a day since university without a drink of some kind, though now my addiction, if that's the word, is restricted to wine, and mostly red wine at that. Since coming here I've rationed myself to the best part of a bottle per day, which spread over lunch and supper is, I think you'll acknowledge, pretty abstemious. No shouting, weeping or smashing. You've seen it all, Anna, but you'd find a different person here, if you came to call. You would find me industrious and clear-headed, at least by my standards.

By the way, Cynthia has a splendid collection of Bordeaux and local wines stored in her *sous sol*, but I regard it as a proof of my good behaviour that I haven't broached a single one of her bottles. I'm buying my own from the local supermarket, excellent stuff at heart-breakingly low prices.

When you began this I expect you thought there was something pathetic about the fact that I was addressing it to someone in your position. Didn't I have a friend, a lover, a trusted relative? Why you? I have my motives, Anna, as you will see, and I trust you won't consider them at all pitiful.

Now we must go back to my chimes at midnight.

In my desk at home I keep a black and white photograph that was taken of Nick Armstrong and myself in Madrid during our first summer vacation as university students. It shows the pair of us seated side by side on a large, baroque sofa. The wall behind bears a long horizontal smudge left by the backs of innumerable, well-oiled heads. I am massively ensconced on the sofa, my feet square on the marble floor, my hands square on my knees, my head thrust forward. Vanity has impelled me to take off my glasses, with the result that I can see nothing but fog and my expression is inscrutable. Nick, by contrast, has fully engaged the camera lens and is a model of elegance; his long legs are carelessly crossed and he holds a glass aloft in an ironic toast.

The photographer working the bar was evidently off his game that night. To my left, on the very margin of the picture, he has inadvertently included the flared corner of a tablecloth, a squashed cigarette butt (mine, no doubt), from which a last gasp of smoke still curls, and a woman's disembodied foot in a white shoe with stiletto heel and narrow ankle strap. Our all but invisible companion, she of the shoe and lissom ankle, had generously allowed us to buy her a drink and was trying to persuade one or other of us to join her on the coin-sized dance floor. The bar boasted a jewelled juke box that played tangos, mambos, sambas and cha-cha-chas, and we could see several couples as they smooched in more or less South American tempo. My forbidding expression was not just the product of myopia, for I had just realised that our new friend and most of the other women in the place were prostitutes.

I've no intention of revolting you, Anna, or humiliating myself by describing my sexual evolution in detail. By the time of our Spanish summer I had ceased to fear the growth of Minotaurian tail and horns, though I was still sure that my bullish appearance rendered me repellent to women. However, I had come to nurse another secret fear, which I had not confided to Nick, and for that matter have never confided to anyone until now. You are the first, Anna, and will be the last.

I now feared metamorphosis of my behaviour rather than my physical being. I feared that lurking inside me was a demonic *alter ego*, a Minotaur of the mind, which would be released if I allowed my libido to have its purple head. I had convinced myself that the brute in me possessed such violent and uncontrollable strength that, once it was unchained, I was bound to ravage whatever I attempted to caress. I sensed the havoc I would wreak from the hammering in my head and thudding of my heart, from the panting, trembling, sweating and swooning, from the uncontainable tumescence that occurred whenever I looked at certain clandestine pictures (Claudia, Gina, Sophia) which I kept beneath my monkish bed. I foresaw sex as a convulsive outburst of mayhem, the *Götterdämmerung* of my virginity, when chaos would finally overpower restraint. Absurd, of course; I had never committed a brutal act in my life, but the very fact that I appeared to be mild-mannered was further proof that my inner self was vicious. After all, everyone had liked and admired Dr Jekyll.

You probably think I'm reporting the ravings of a madman, but then adolescence is a season of madness, isn't it?

At university I imprisoned myself in celibacy and isolation (from women). Like a guilty Victorian, which in many respects was exactly what I was, I devoted my sublimated energies to studying (English Literature, of course) and found it deeply satisfying. I was not a star pupil. My essays were never more than mediocre and I was incapacitated by nervous amnesia in exams, but no tutor ever found fault with my assiduous reading. For all my short-sightedness, which worsened significantly during these three years, requiring me to wear thicker and thicker lenses, I turned myself into a reading machine. I worked my eyes like combine harvesters, driving them up and down acres of ripe print, but my response to the words themselves was far from mechanical. Though I made a poor critic, being too quick to condemn what bored me and far too eager to rejoice in what I admired, I became a passionate enthusiast. In short, I read like a publisher.

(A word on the subject of eyes: they are the most harmless of organs, no more than vile jelly, and nobody was ever struck or raped by an eye; and yet the mere act of looking can violate. Think of Susanna and the Elders. In vowing celibacy, I did not commit myself to blindness; on the contrary, behind my bottle-bottom specs I was ferociously watchful.)

And so it was that I reached that summer in Spain with my explosive virginity intact. I had no secrets from secretive Nick, and as we drove south on our way to Madrid, he announced in his bantering way that he was going to make it his summer's project to liberate me from celibacy. I begged him to do no such thing, and he didn't mention the subject again.

One of the many secrets Nick had kept from me was his ambition to turn himself into an *aficionado* of the bullfight. No sooner had we arrived in Madrid, and installed ourselves in a dusty, shadowy hotel room overlooking a square in which a small fountain wept day and night, than he hurried away to book tickets for that day's bullfight. I don't suppose you've ever seen a bullfight. Anna, and I never want to see another myself, though not for the reasons you might suppose. As squeamish as the next man, I'd read enough Hemingway to steel myself for a gory afternoon, but neither of us was prepared for what we actually witnessed.

It turned out that Nick, still the neophyte, had mistakenly booked us into a *corrida* that was a kind of circus event. The audience assembled, the band played, trumpets sounded and the ceremonial march began, but instead of the expected *toreros* the ring filled with capering clowns, all dressed in traditional costumes: baggy trousers, elongated boots, battered hats and so forth. They performed for a while, doing somersaults and cartwheels and pratfalls, and then the trumpets blew again to announce the entrance of the bull itself, which proved to be a gangly bullock. The terrified creature rushed round the ring, searching for escape. Nick was disgusted with himself for making such a beginner's error, but the crowd was delighted and laughed loudly at the clowns' antics. A great cheer went up when a comedian dressed as Charlie Chaplin waddled up to the animal, twirling his cane, grabbed its tail and allowed himself to be spun round and round. An even greater cheer greeted the appearance of a particularly squat midget who was costumed in a beautiful suit of lights made of gold braid and salmon-pink silk.

This miniature matador performed a Lilliputian version of the bullfight ritual with an air of utter seriousness. He executed a series of flowing passes using a pocket-sized yellow-and-magenta cape and drew a bewildered bullock through a labyrinth of invisible paths. Yet the more conscientiously he aped the graceful posturing of his full-grown colleagues, the louder the audience howled with laughter. I did not laugh. On the contrary, I was horrified, and felt no pity for him. Though I was twice the runt's size, we shared a certain cuboid quality and I felt mocked by him. (What an egomaniac, you are thinking, Anna, and you are right.) I could only see a caricature of myself in this froggy homunculus with his preposterous handkerchief and stumpy flourishes, this pansified gnome, this spangled manikin. I felt betrayed and angered that he should draw the world's attention to those of us who had failed to achieve the physical norm. I saw no dignity in his earnest parody, and as the crowd laughed I longed for the bull to crush and crucify him. The Minotaur rose in me, its blood raging in my head, and demanded a sacrifice.

Taunted by the dwarf, the bull made a gawky charge, but stumbled over something in the sand, which caused it to change course. Taken by surprise, the dwarf leapt back, but not quickly enough, for the tip of the bull's horn got caught in his cape. He was jerked forward and thrown to the ground. The bull rounded with fearsome agility and rushed at its victim, head down. The dwarf was just rising to his feet in an effort to run for the barrier when the bull's horn pierced his inner thigh close to the groin. Lifting its head, the bull carried him aloft, transfixed like a cube of meat on a kebab skewer.

At first the crowd had laughed and then, on its feet, it had gasped, perhaps thinking a death-defying trick was under way. Now it was silent and we could hear the little man's shrieks of pain. The clowns ran into the ring waving their arms and shouting to distract the bull, which trotted swiftly towards the barrier as if to squash its victim against the red planks. As it lowered its head, the dwarf fell free. The bull turned, but was diverted while the little body was dragged to safety. The audience applauded vociferously to show their appreciation of the dwarf's courage.

Nick and I left before watching any more of the programme. I discovered that my throat was hoarse from shouting. I discovered too – forgive me, Anna, but these shameful, sordid details are indispensable – that my trousers were stained with a damp and sticky patch. Mr Hyde had left his mark.

I must return to our photograph.

The owner of the white shoe and slender ankle, which, by the way, was a dancer's ankle, well-exercised, supple and muscular, connecting a dainty foot to an athletic calf, called herself Conchita. If I had forgotten her name I could remind myself by consulting a second photograph that has survived from this era, a professional portrait, also in black and white. It shows a sprightly, shapely young woman in a frilly dress holding a flamenco pose that simultaneously draws attention to her sinewy legs in fishnet stockings and an impudent cleavage, which is the product of crafty lighting and padding. Scrawled across the backcloth are my name and the words, *con amor, Conchita!* I recall that she sealed her flamboyant inscription with a kiss, though for fear of soiling the picture with her lipstick it was all passion and no contact. This photograph is present but invisible in the portrait of Nick and me on the sofa – he so elegant, I so ill-at-ease – because by then I had stowed it in the inside pocket of my jacket. It was next to my heart, as coquettish Conchita pointed out through the medium of Nick's translation.

Our portrait was taken on the evening of the bullfight. I had by then changed my clothes, but my agitation had by no means slackened off, which also accounts for the intensity of my expression. My feelings were made all the more disturbing by the guilt I now felt that my desire to see the dwarf punished had been granted. Conchita had heard through the Gypsy grapevine that he was expected to survive the surgery on his thigh, but had sworn never to fight again. She scorned his cowardice. The bullock had been ignominiously slaughtered and Conchita assured us that its balls were being served as a delicacy in a restaurant round the corner. 'Small but delicious,' she said, kissing her finger tips. 'They would make a brave bull of you,' she told me, or so Nick reported after much ribaldry between the two of them.

What I didn't realise was that during this same mirthful exchange Nick had negotiated terms on my behalf with Conchita. She suddenly stood up, took me by the hand and led me onto the dance floor. I followed submissively, imagining that I was destined to stumble through a reluctant rumba with her, and was therefore surprised when, after half a dozen flirtatious steps, she whisked me off the floor and began to ascend the staircase behind the jukebox. I looked back at Nick for an explanation, but he shrugged. Conchita's grip on my hand was relentless.

At the top of the stairs she opened a door and drew me into what proved to be a bedroom – double bed, basin, ewer, towel. As soon as the door was shut, she kissed me violently. I don't know what Nick had told her (presumably, that I was shy, virginal, mysteriously diffident) but she had evidently got the idea that shock tactics were required if I was to be seduced and she thrust her hand inside my trousers. Pushing her away and tugging at my zip, I tried to open the door. She must have locked it, because I found myself ineffectually and farcically rattling the handle.

I would only be playing the pornographer, dear Anna, if I were to give you a blow-by-blow account of the next few moments, but I cannot spare you the scene that brought matters to their climax (hardly the *mot juste*).

There was a struggle during which I fought to escape and Conchita contrived to keep me in the room while completely stripping herself. She was the first living woman I had ever seen naked. At the sight of her I felt the Minotaur in me stir, and I dreaded the consequences. I feared for her safety; I feared for her very life, but the more I tried to fight her off, the more lasciviously she fastened herself to me. In the midst of our grapple, I was overtaken by a kind of hysterical blackout, from which I recovered to find myself in the tableau vivant you must look at, if only through the *mashrabia* of your latticed fingers.

We are panting and sweating, but we are not performing the beast with two backs; instead, it appears that one beast, a truly beastly Beast, has unmasked his true nature. I am lying on the bed, my trousers in disarray, while Conchita stands beside the bed, a look of horror on her face. Splattered over her brown dancer's body is blood, gouts and splashes of red, murderer's blood. She is drenched in it, but if I've gored her, where is the wound that's spilling all this gore? She looks down at her reddened, slippery skin and screams. Where has my horn pierced her?

The explanation for Conchita's blood-soaked state turned out to be far from gothic. I had not stabbed the poor woman. In the excitement of the moment I had suffered a nosebleed, a spectacular haemorrhage that had painted her red and caused me to faint and fall on the bed. Still naked and daubed with my vital fluid, she gave me a damp towel to hold against my nose, and in an act of charitable decency I did not deserve she also cleaned me and pulled up my zip. Having no language in common, we couldn't discuss what had happened. I repeatedly gesticulated my apologies and shame; she talked incessantly while she washed herself, dressed and bundled up the bloody sheet. She appeared to be more puzzled than angry, and would occasionally pinch my cheek and shake a finger in front of me, tut-tutting furiously. Without knowing how much it was, I offered her all the money I had in my wallet, which she accepted, stashing the wad of notes in her petite, reconstituted cleavage. She looked at herself in the glass over the basin, smoothing her dress and tidying her hair.

Adiós, mi amor, she said and was gone.

Most of my blood had fallen onto her, and I was able to conceal the few drops that had stained my shirt by buttoning up my jacket. By the time I felt well enough to go downstairs Nick had left the dance hall. It was entirely typical of him that when we did meet the next day at breakfast he made no enquiry concerning my adventure, and I never knew whether or not he assumed that Conchita had claimed the dubious prize of my virginity. The subject was no longer of interest to him.

As for me, it may surprise you to hear that I tripped down those stairs to the bar filled with elation. Blood had been spilt, but no one had been hurt; indeed, it might have been tomato ketchup for all the harm that had been caused in its shedding. I could hardly claim that I had 'slept with' Conchita, yet we had undergone some kind of sexual experience and, bizarre though it was, it had not transformed me into a psychopath. My pulse had hammered in my head, but Mr Hyde had not materialised.

However, my relief was short-lived, for I realised that the Minotaur in me had turned out to be a comic figure, not a monster. As a lady-killer I was a clown, a buffoon, no less laughable than a dwarf posing as a matador. I was not a destroyer of women, nor even an object of revulsion; I was simply a joke. Thanks to my father, this was a familiar role. The maze designed to keep me confined was a simple circle made of nothing more complicated than mockery: a ring seated in sun and shade with laughing women, who jeer at my awkwardness. I bleed and they giggle.

There's no limit, Anna, to the torture that a solipsistic young man will inflict on himself once he's been convinced of his worthlessness.

My father stopped speaking to me during my last year at school, and the habit had become quite entrenched by the time I graduated from university. I don't mean that he never spoke to me, rather that he avoided addressing me directly if he could communicate via my mother. On the few occasions when he was obliged to talk to me face to face he would limit himself to the briefest, briskest exchange. There was one question he never failed to ask me when I came home, and he would bark it out as soon as he saw me, before saying hello or greeting me. It was his version of a greeting, for I got no other.

'Difficult journey?' he would say, and without waiting for a reply, since it was not a question so much as a wish, he would ask, 'How much was your train fare?' I would tell him the exact figure and the next morning the money, down to the last penny, would be lying on the silver tray in the hall. So profound was his dislike of me, and yet so sharp his sense of responsibility, that he felt impelled to make an immediate paternal gesture, for then his conscience would allow him to ignore me during the rest of my visit, not an easy feat in a small suburban house.

My father was taciturn at the best of times. (What am I saying? There were no best or worst times in our family, only an even flow of the humdrum.) Outside the house, especially in the company of a client who needed 'buttering up', he occasionally became 'gabby', to use his words, and when alone with my mother he would sometimes turn talkative. I could hear their voices, even laughter, rising through the floor when I was in my bedroom, but my appearance would immediately silence him.

A book could be written on the subject of silence; as you well know, I'm constantly urging an author of mine to do so. Silence is a versatile medium that takes many forms. What you might call social or conversational silence, far from being vapid, can be turned into a powerful tool of aggression. The other person says something but you, the contemptuous silence-monger, don't respond; you deprecate his offering by keeping mum.

(A footnote: in our house *mum* was not the word by any definition. It was a colloquialism I never used and was never encouraged to use. My mother was unthinkable as 'Mummy', 'Ma', 'Mama', 'Mater' or anything but 'Mother', the term I used from infancy onwards. Nor was she a *stumm* mum; the opposite of my father, she was talkative, even garrulous, especially when an opportunity arose to exercise her brand of waspish denunciation. She had a bright, brittle voice made husky by cigarettes.)

My mother would encourage me to talk about my doings at school or university, to talk about Nick, my work, my professors and (at her most arch) *my girlfriends*. Smiling wickedly through her cigarette smoke, she would interrogate me. Because she was an animated listener and responded to my feeble jokes with her bronchial chuckle, I would become expansive. She was easy to entertain, and it was easy to be entertaining in her company. With her I was amusing and anecdotal; a veritable Noël Coward.

Or, rather, I was on one side of my face. On the other, the one directed towards my father, I presented a mask as stony as a statue's. Ridiculous and impossible, of course, but these occasions required me to split myself in two. I presented to my mother a face that was all merriment and brio, but I tried to freeze the face I presented to my father, hoping to match his deadpan mug. Whenever I began to speak he would turn his features into a balaclava blank, eyes focussed on the middle distance, chin elevated in disdain, lips pursed in a *moue* of disapproval. His silence withered any gaiety my mother and I managed to conjure up.

Let me tell you about silence; I know all about it. Silence is Remembrance Day when the nation wonders what to think about for two minutes. Silence is the rule in the dorm, and if you break it you'll be beaten. Silence in chapel, silence during prep, silence when I'm speaking to you, silence in detention, but God help you if your silence looks like dumb insolence. Silence is a right you've lost. Shut up, I can't hear myself think. Ring, telephone, ring: the silence is so loud now you've gone. Silence is golden, but money talks. Nothing golden about the silence of the grave, where the rest is silence. Autism is silence. Shame, shyness, writer's block, no speaka da lingo, stuttering, stroke damage – they're all prisons of silence. Send him to Coventry; give him the cold shoulder; give him the silent treatment. My father, the strong silent man gave me the silent treatment.

When he did speak (and, by the way, he had a deep, melodious voice, which as a sheer instrument was pleasant to hear – such are the jokes the gods play on us) it would be to ask me a question that could not be answered. Thus, when I announced that I had chosen to read English litera-ture at university, my mother was provoked to say, 'Fancy that, Carl! They're going to give him a degree for reading all those lovely novels.'

But my father snapped, 'What's the point of it? I'm not going to support you like a drone for the rest of your life, you know.'

I began to stammer something about publishing and Perkins, hating myself for playing his game and for playing it so ineptly. In any case, I was wasting my breath because he had turned away, his lips locked up, his eyes fixed once more on the motion picture that played on our sitting-room ceiling, invisible to us but so absorbing to him. At such moments my mother neither supported nor betrayed me; she simply evaporated from the room in her most ghostly style.

I could never win. I remember his reaction to my telling them, with not a little pride, that I had been appointed to my first job. (My only job, since I have worked in the same place ever since. Did you know that, Anna?) Naively, I imagined that it would please my father that I had elected to pursue a profession, instead of entertaining airy-fairy ambitions of becoming a writer. I told them the name of the company where I was to be a junior editor, but they were not great readers and had never heard of it.

'It sounds frightfully foreign and exotic,' my mother commented, which I knew was her way of saying the name sounded Jewish, as of course it was.

'Who owns this outfit?' my father demanded.

I had no idea, but mentioned its legendary founder, who was still alive at that time.

'It sounds shaky. If they're asking you to put money up, don't come to me.'

Let me give you one more example, even if there's no point in citing it. You get the point, I'm sure, but these things have a compulsive quality, and like the Ancient Mariner I am doomed to tell my story over and over again.

On a visit home, when I was still foolish enough to think I could impress my father, I broke the news to them at dinner that one of my authors had won a prize. It goes without saying that the writer was unknown to them, along with her book and the prize itself, which was, admittedly, a somewhat obscure award for translators of Urdu.

'How many copies has this masterpiece sold?' my father demanded.

I lied, telling him it had sold in many thousands, that our printers could hardly keep pace with our orders for new impressions. (In truth, I doubt the book sold more than a couple of hundred copies, most of them bought by the author herself to distribute among her numerous family.) I then committed the mistake of making an angry speech in which I used the word *philistine* to describe the attitude of those who estimated a book's quality by its sales figures. My father reddened, but possessed the self-control to pull up the drawbridge on his citadel of silence, leaving me to fulminate in his muddy moat.

Just as nothing comes of nothing, so silence begets silence. By the time I was twenty-five, I had fallen silent in my silent father's company, and yet it took my therapist many sessions before she finally coaxed me into admitting that this was an unnatural state of affairs.

I must get the business of my sexual progress (hardly the word) out of the way; it's not a topic I care to linger over, and I'm sure you've had your fill of it by now. I'm only telling you these things because they seem necessary to understanding what comes later. In any case, I want to move on to more important matters.

You must remember that the events I'm about to describe took place in the late 60s, the age of the mini-skirt and the pill, which no doubt seems positively ancient to you. (How old are you, actually? Thirty? Surely not more than thirty-five?) The ethic of the period, as you probably know from your history books, dictated that sexual satisfaction was not only a right, but a duty. Joy and sex were indivisible and synonymous; I shall say no more, except that it was not an easy time for one dedicated to celibacy. I'm able to write coolly about these things now, but at the time they tormented me: on the one hand, I was fired with a young man's desires and energies, which made celibacy a continual ordeal; on the other, I remained convinced that any attempt at intimacy with a woman would only result in ridicule and rejection.

At this point I ought to add that despite the difficulties I confronted in my private life my publishing career was turning out to be wonderfully enjoyable and rewarding. I loved my work and without the enticements of a domestic hearth to lure me home I spent many contented evenings at my desk, alone in the office. I was given the power to commission new books at a flatteringly young age and rapidly acquired authors whom I admired and who seemed to value my assistance. I was paid more money than my modest needs called for, and my colleagues, some of whom you know well, were as congenial as could be expected. (You'll be amused to know that this was when the girlish Cynthia, then a sylph costumed by Biba and coiffed by Sassoon, wrote her first, and best novel, *Jack and Jill*, which I had the honour to publish. It was a *roman-à-clef* about her love affair with Oliver Breakspear. Have you ever read it? He treated her abominably of course, but she took her revenge in the book and was launched as a celebrity.)

In that far-off era lunch was a respected institution and the occasion of important business. Funded by an expense account that was never questioned (happy days), I became a legendary luncher and there was hardly a restaurant in Soho which I did not sample at least once. In a futile attempt to inhibit my expanding girth I made it a rule to walk every day from our office, stepping out briskly and defying all weathers. My perambulations took me through the maze of streets, Greek Street, Old Compton Street, Berwick Street, St Anne's Court and so on, that formed the heart (a misnomer, if ever there was one) of what in those days was London's busiest red-light district. It was a curious feature of the era of so-called sexual liberation that prostitutes suffered no loss of business. If anything, they flourished, or so it appeared to me as I wandered back from lunch, less brisk now, surreptitiously looking up at windows lit with cosy pink lamps and studying doorways that bore the names of 'models': Kiki, Lulu, Fifi, Monique (French names were fashionable then, though I never saw a 'Régine').

I'm sure you can see where this is leading, dear Anna, and I hope you don't despise me. I knew that my heart was not going to be broken if I climbed one of Old Compton Street's uninviting, lino-lined staircases and I assumed that my money would forestall rejection. Even so, I remained terrified that nothing would protect me from mockery, especially when the moment, unimaginable and disabling, came for me to remove my clothes and expose my bullock's body to a strange woman's gaze. In addition, I was alarmed by the thought of having sex for its own sake with a stranger in her strange room. Would I be murdered – robbed – blighted by disease – exposed to blackmail? The idea of buying another human being, however willing she was to engage in the exchange, seemed appalling. I had no idea what these models charged, but even the most expensive call-girl was a kind of victim, for didn't women's lib (how archaic that term seems now) teach us that using prostitutes was yet another form of patriarchal oppression? And yet, and yet . . .

I struggled with these problems for a long time, faint-heartedness lending strength to my moral sensitivity, and then, to cut a dishonourable story short, I finally succumbed to spontaneity one afternoon in Shepherd Market, without having settled any of the arguments in my mind. The woman ('Juliette') did not laugh at me; she hardly seemed to notice me at all, so mechanical was her manner. No blood was spilt and, needless to say, neither satisfaction nor pleasure was achieved, only a sense of shame. But shamefulness is no match for lust, and this became the first of many commercial visits (though my last to the joyless Juliette). Prostitution is as addictive as opium.

I was far too fastidious and discreet to visit Soho prostitutes, but I had no difficulty in finding addresses in other parts of the West End; as I said, business was booming. The most disturbing aspect of my postprandial liaisons, which seemed so necessary before they took place, and so point-less in their aftermath, was that for all their erotic trappings – underwear, pictures, perfume and so forth – they served a function that was more therapeutic than sexual. I would put my turgid need in the practised hands of long-suffering women, who for a trifling sum would give me a sense of deliverance such as the victim of toothache feels after a fiery molar has been extracted. I never lost my sense of gratitude to this despised race of women, to whom I presented myself in all my hairy, massive, myopic monstrosity without once being insulted or repulsed. They sometimes mocked, but never out of cruelty; they just accepted me as yet another variation on the infinitely variable range of male importunity.

Why am I telling you all this? I'm trying to describe the struggle to achieve adulthood.

Most people become adults without too much difficulty, but for some unfortunates, and I am one of them, adulthood is not a simple function of age; they acquire the physiology, but not the mentality. They find that the door is locked, and they can't reach high enough to turn the handle. In horror, they look down to see their scabby knees exposed below short trousers and behind them, turning their muscles to water, the shadow of an upraised brawny arm. Some people need their parents to die before they can achieve adulthood.

Nick was always a man of his times, but it was never thus for me. Although our paths had run in parallel since boyhood, I lacked Nick's happy capacity to be comfortable in his own history. I had not felt 'at home' at home since the day my parents had despatched me to the Welsh concentration camp. Thereafter, I never belonged in either my school towns or my so-called home; I had been uprooted, and my ability to re-root never developed. In puberty my monstrous physique only reinforced my sense of estrangement: I was in exile from a homeland which had never acknowledged me in the first place. Worst of all, I felt no affinity with England (still less Britain, wherever that is) and its culture. Though I was indelibly marked by the England of my public school I felt no allegiance to it, any more than I did to the professional middle class of my parents and its incorrigible conservatism. Nor had I identified with the bohemianism of the 60s, the England of Swinging London, flower power, pop music and so forth; I doubt I could have named all four Beatles. For that reason I did my best to infiltrate the company's list with authors outside the Anglophone canon: Italians, Japanese, South Americans, Turks and so on, writers with unpronounceable names, among them a couple of Nobel prize winners. Alas, their obscurity in these fair isles was not alleviated by publication under our colours, and they rarely made us a penny profit (believe it or not, in those days the Nobel prize was, if anything, the commercial kiss of death), but at least they gave me a cosmopolitan reputation.

After graduating Nick also came to London and found employment with a small auction house. Before long he had acquired random spots of expertise and could be seen pronouncing authoritatively on the value of cuirasses and amphorae, tazzas and netsuke. He also became a collector in his own right. That, at any rate, was the term he used to account for the fact he stuffed his flat in Trebovir Road with *objets d'art* and curios, though they were seldom on display for longer than a month before being replaced. Nick's domestic style could not have differed more from mine. All my possessions, no matter how trifling, were (are) invested with a kind of monumental permanence once they had been allocated their place, but in Nick's Aladdin's cave everything from the carpet to the chandelier was for sale and I never sat in the same chair twice. His flat was like a caravansary where the furniture and ornaments were all embarked on adventures of their own and had only paused there, as travellers do, to rest and swap tales. I remember going there one evening when a guest took home the dinner service, still unwashed, in the back of her car.

By the way, in those days I rented an attic apartment in Marchmont Street, Bloomsbury, not far from the office. The whole terrace was demolished soon after I moved, and I had the disturbing experience of seeing my old sitting room disembowelled by the wrecker's ball. I even saw my very own lavatory clinging to its post on the cliff-face of the bathroom wall, poised above a five-storey drop.

Let me tell you about the first time I met Natalie. From Marchmont Street I moved to my flat in West Hampstead, of which I was immoderately proud, and after living there for eighteen months I decided to show off the place by giving a party. In a misconceived effort to advance my career, I invited an assortment of writers, agents and friends for lunch on the last Sunday of August. It was one of those gestures that ambitious young men feel obliged to make and usually regret. My plan was to gamble on the weather by holding the event outdoors in my garden, a term quite undeserved by the patch of grass and moribund apple tree that lay beyond my back door.

There was another reason for holding the event outdoors. By then I had accumulated the beginnings of a serious library, perhaps a couple of thousand books, which I had fastidiously arranged in custom-built bookcases lining the walls of my sitting room. As a result, my professional aspirations clashed with my protective instincts, because I didn't want to run the risk of some tipsy guest spilling wine over my shelves or spoiling a precious page with his buttery fingers or, worse still, slipping a coveted volume into his pocket. *Al fresco* was therefore the order of the day, and as an added precaution I locked the sitting-room door.

I had of course invited Nick to my party, and he in turn had invited Natalie. I recall my first sight of her with unusual vividness: I was fussing over plates of food and bottles of wine when they appeared in my kitchen, a pair of figures in white, he in a linen suit and she in some sort of cheesecloth outfit, which was then fashionable. They seemed to shine, suggesting that the sunlight outside had gathered in their white clothes to illuminate my galley of a kitchen. While he introduced her, they stood together, light streaming from their Blakean halos and smiling jubilantly as if they had achieved some great and wonderful thing, which in a way they had, for I had never seen a couple more conspicuously besotted with each other.

In those days I thought Natalie was the prettiest woman in London. Slim, tall, graceful, she had one of those compelling faces that is not simply beautiful, but radiant with intelligence; furthermore, she had a light-hearted vivacity that transmitted itself to everyone around her. In her company the dullest man came to life for a minute or two, galvanised by her good humour. And Nick, the least dull man I knew, was positively incandescent with her vitality.

The party went well: the sun shone, the food was eaten and made nobody ill (I am no cook), my guests looked handsome scattered about my freshly clipped rug of grass, the wine flowed and a sweet cloud of marijuana smoke hung over the festive scene. My idyll was threatened only once, and, as anyone might have predicted, the culprit was the novelist Oliver Breakspear (Cynthia's ex-lover and cruel conqueror of her virginity). The chief ornament of my guest list, Breakspear had a reputation for being the scourge of modern manners and that year was at the very pinnacle of his, admittedly low-altitude, fame. Though hilarious on paper, it has to be said he was a considerable shit in the flesh, but I had always got on with him and I nursed hopes of attracting his next novel to our list. I think he probably saw straight through my little scheme, but was happy to play the game and drink my wine and meet people of my generation. He was much feared at parties for his habit of attacking pretension whenever he heard it, especially if he heard it in the mouth of an attractive young woman; and if she was foolish enough to get into an argument with him, it was his particular pleasure to goad her until she cried. As I said, he was a nice chap.

During lunch Breakspear overheard another guest saying that Natalie was committed to conservation. Too idle to get out of his deckchair and insult her face-to-face, he bawled at the person nearest him something to the effect that, as any sensible man would acknowledge, so-called conservation was bollocks, complete bollocks in which no one believed except the socks-and-sandals brigade, whose brains had long since seeped into their woolly hats. Silence followed this outburst and, wondering how she would respond, everyone turned to look at Natalie, whose hat, so far from being woolly, was a chic straw confection with a large brim and a dashing ribbon.

It is hard to believe it nowadays, when conservation is universally accepted and not even the most curmudgeonly old fart of a novelist would dream of challenging it, but in that primitive era (the late 1970s) the idea of protecting the countryside from chemicals and greedy farmers was dismissed as crackpot nonsense.

'It's a question of loss,' Natalie said. 'We're losing what belongs to all of us without realising it.'

'Bloody nonsense,' snorted Breakspear, without looking up at her. 'I suppose you're one of those loonies that thinks we should turn the countryside into a bog so all the little toads and slugs and bunny rabbits can have a nice life while the rest of us starve to death.'

I saw Nick make a move to step between her and Breakspear, but she restrained him with a hand on his arm.

'Do you like apples?' she asked him.

'What?' he demanded apoplectically, sensing that the goal-posts were being shifted to another part of the pitch.

'Apples,' she repeated innocently. 'If you like them, you'll know how hard it is to find a good one in the supermarkets.'

Breakspear had never been to a supermarket in his life to buy apples, or anything else for that matter.

'I'm not talking about fucking apples,' he said.

'The tree you're sitting under,' she continued relentlessly, 'has delicious apples, but they're small and have little blem-ishes on their skins, like beauty spots, so the supermarkets won't stock them. They're becoming quite rare. You should look after it,' she added, looking at me.

I stared with newborn pride into the branches of my decrepit, shamefully neglected tree, studying its half-formed fruits and searching for their romantic imperfections.

Then, as if reciting a poem, Natalie slowly chanted, 'Ashmead's Kernel, Beauty of Bath, Blenheim Orange, Catshead, Cornish Gilliflower, Dumelow's Seedling, Egremont Russet, Foxwhelp . . .'

As she proceeded with her incantation it gradually dawned on us that she was rehearsing the names of apple varieties. Interrupting herself, she said mournfully, 'all lost or about to be lost', and then took up her apple roll of honour once again.

'Golden Noble, Kentish Fillbasket, Kingston Black, Laxton's Superb, Newton Wonder, Norfolk Beefing, Ribston Pippin, Reverend W. Wilks, Rosemary Russet, Spartan, Winter Queening, Worcester Pearmain . . .'

Obviously, I can't remember what Natalie said all those years ago; I've culled these names from one of Cynthia's books, imaginatively entitled *The Book of Apples*, but I do remember that she rehearsed a list which took many minutes to complete. It was a *tour de force*, not only of memory but of sheer poise, and to do him credit Breakspear acknowledged it with a measured if sardonic handclap.

'Bravo,' he said, lifting his glass to her. 'Bravo, young lady.'

He patted the grass beside him to indicate that she should sit at his feet, his version of a compliment, but she simply nodded to him and returned to Nick, whose face was alight with pride.

It probably sounds ridiculous to you, but during the rest of that afternoon I slowly ascended into a state of paradisal bliss. Like a hot-air balloon my mind floated into the sunny heavens and I tossed my anxieties overboard as if they were so many sandbags of ballast. I lay in a deckchair, eyes closed, my head forty, fifty, sixty, a hundred feet above the rooftops of West Hampstead, above the great steel tangle of railway lines that took the trains northwards from Euston Station. I released myself into a celestial realm where body and soul melted together in contentment, all senses sated, all desires of the spirit fulfilled, where the division between self and others dissolved and everyone in my garden and, for all I knew, the whole of London, was irradiated with the same joyful light that threw no shadows, the light of pure benevolence. The beauty of this radiant state was that it derived from the ordinary material of my life: friends, food and drink, perilous deckchairs, the neighbour's scavenging cat picking over the debris of lunch, a broken glass, the chimney that needed new flashing, the untended papers on my desk visible through the window, the possession of an enviably rare apple tree; all these humble, familiar elements had magically combined to carry me away in transports of ecstasy.

I know what you're thinking, my dear Anna: that I was high on dope. It's true that I was the worse, or rather the better, the infinitely better, for having smoked a potent joint put together by one of my authors. This was an enterprising young man who subsequently disappeared into the mountains of Mexico with a contract in his knapsack to write a book about the elusive and gloriously plumaged quetzal. He never reappeared and he may well be there now, still chasing his legendary bird through the cloud forests, still determined to earn back his advance, though I doubt it. All I can say in his memory, if it has come to an elegy, is that he had a rare skill amounting to genius for rolling a three-skin spliff. I acknowledge that under the narcotic influence of my explorer friend my mind was hardly more substantial than the blue, perfumed smoke that spiralled from his numberless cigarettes, but I assure you that I did know transcendent happiness that afternoon. Its chief source was not dope, nor wine, nor the intoxicating warmth of August's last sunny afternoon; no, I was happy because my friend Nick was happy with his beloved Natalie.

Have you ever experienced such a feeling, Anna? Has another's joy inspired you with joy? Has your heart ever been filled with someone else's rapture? I can only say that it happened to me that afternoon when Nick introduced me to

Natalie, and that thereafter my happiness was doomed to be moon to their sun: it shone with their reflected light.

A last note: as anyone except me could have foreseen, Oliver Breakspear did not join my list. However, I did recruit a new author that day, for I commissioned Natalie to write a book about Victorian fruit. As a general principle conservation makes me queasy (who wants to be imprisoned by the past?) but in Natalie I saw a potential writer. My instinct was right because her text, when it arrived a trifling four years later, was elegant and scholarly. We made a beautiful production out of the book and invested a fortune in the illustrations, but for all its virtues it didn't sell and had to be pulped. Have you ever seen a copy? I keep one in my office as a kind of memento mori.

During this period my life proceeded in an orderly fashion, measured out in books. I commissioned and rejected books; I read them, edited them, read them again in galley and a third time in page proof; I also read them in every other form and stage of development: manuscripts, typescripts, translations, chapter outlines, plot synopses, sample chapters, sketches on the backs of menus, works in progress, revisions, revisions of revisions and final drafts. Well, I don't have to tell you what publishers do, but on top of all that professional reading I read tirelessly for my own amusement, and when I wasn't reading books, I was buying them. My idea of a revitalising weekend was to pick a provincial town, take a room in its best hotel and raid the district's second-hand bookshops, and it wasn't long before my library had expanded to fill every corner of the flat in West Hampstead. Instinctively, I had turned my home into a kind of book bunker, a new labyrinth built on a heroic scale.

Incidentally, people who wear glasses are often described

as having 'weak' eyesight, but this was not true in my case. Without my glasses I could see nothing that was not six inches in front of my nose, but the optic muscles that went to work behind my goldfish bowl specs were indefatigable, and like athletes in peak condition they were equal to any feat of endurance I demanded of them.

Meanwhile, I steadily mounted the company hierarchy and if I did not become the Perkins of my generation (where were my Fitzgeralds, Hemingways and Wolfes?) I was at least respected by my colleagues and valued by my authors. (Am I deluding myself? Surely not. You would know.) I strove for the *gravitas* of middle-age, hoping that my three-piece suits, silk handkerchiefs, opulent ties, polished shoes and cigarette holders would distract attention from the curly pelt and gross torso concealed beneath my Jermyn Street shirts. Those who were curious about my sexual self-sufficiency explained it by seeing a repressed homosexual inside my fussy, foppish persona. I did nothing to dispel this reputation, since it served me as a very necessary smokescreen for my addiction to prostitutes. As with my bibliomania, I tried to regularise rather than suppress my lewd habit, knowing that its energy was far too forceful for will-power.

Publishing is a sociable profession, and though I detested cocktail parties and dinner parties, and turned down every invitation, I maintained my practice of lunching with someone most days of the week. (Power is the name of the game; at parties I feel vulnerable, exposed to mockery, on display, required to perform, whereas the host's chair at a restaurant table is a throne, and the guest, no matter how honoured, is your subject.) Yet, in spite of having a large, mostly professional acquaintanceship, I only had one friend worthy of the name, and that was Nick.

Many years ago I swore that I would remain childless. This vow may sound histrionic, but when I made it, in my twenties, it didn't seem to be much of a sacrifice; it almost represented a relief as I watched my (male) friends and colleagues go through the ordeals of parenthood, which, so far as I could judge, brought them as much heartache as joy, and far more problems than pleasure. I told people that I had no interest in children or childhood, and when a colleague tried to persuade us to start a children's list I decisively rubbished her proposal. The truth was that I dreaded the reproduction of my own monstrosity. Here was another reason to bless Kiki, Lulu, Fifi and their sisters: who ever heard of prostitutes telling a client he was due to be a daddy?

But from this, as from so many curses, I was redeemed by Nick.

He and Natalie married shortly after my summer party and in due course she became pregnant. Though I said nothing to them, this development did not please me, since I knew that their attention to me, which I valued above all else, would dwindle. It was therefore in a dutiful and self-pitying mood that I called on them to pay homage to their newborn babe, a gesture which I intended to make as swift as etiquette would allow. To my acute embarrassment, Nick, the beaming father, thrust a pungent bundle into my arms and I found myself confronting a reddened, rubbery, squinting humanoid face.

'We're going to call him Eddie. What do you think?'

I couldn't reply. I was consumed with feeling and incapable of thought.

Eddie must have been the first baby I'd ever held in my life, and perhaps it's as well that he was the last apart from his sister yet to come, because a sensation of such fervent tenderness overtook me that I was blinded with tears and nearly dropped him. The moment was glorified by the sound of a brass band (it turned out to be the Salvation Army), which struck up in the street below, blowing heartily.

I was overpowered by a sudden torrent of what I can only call fatherliness: I felt a profound and aggressive sense of protectiveness, which was combined with an aching affection for the little creature. I have read somewhere that in early infancy babies will react with every sign of delighted recognition to a card with a smile-shaped line on it. I was in the reverse position: I've no doubt that if Nick and Natalie had handed me a loaf of bread with a baby's face drawn on it, I would have experienced the same eruption of emotion. But the bundle was by no means a loaf, and it grew into a certain Eddie, to whom I have been devoted ever since.

My epiphany was one of those instances when an emotion splits like a cell, producing two of itself. Until then I had been devoted to Nick, and by association his wife, but henceforward my love for him had its twin in my love for Eddie, and, as with cells, it sprang into existence fully-formed, requiring no time to grow and develop.

I cannot resist adding a detail here, one of those poignantly coincidental events that often seem to accompany the arrival of children and suggest to their suggestible parents that the gods who dice with our destinies for their amusement are taking a merciful interest in this newest plaything to enter the world.

In order to disguise my tears, I turned my back on anxious Natalie and stumbled towards the bedroom window as though to give him a closer examination in strong light. Natalie ran to join me, and I thrust the boy in her direction, thinking that she feared I might damage him.

'No,' she said, pushing him back into my arms. 'The music. Don't you recognise it?'

Nick opened the window and the band's trumpet pealed into the room.

'It's "Unto us a child is born" from Handel's *Messiah*,' she said.

'How absurd!' Nick said.

'How miraculous!' said Natalie.

Responding to the spirit of the moment, I threw my wallet down to the band.

'You're a lunatic,' said Nick. 'I'm going to close the window before you chuck the baby away.'

But Natalie kissed me and said, 'Bravo!'

I should add that my gesture was less quixotic than it might appear today, because this was long before credit cards were in use and there was nothing in my wallet but notes. In any case, the Salvation Army pushed it through the letter box, having taken only a modest levy for their collection box. Thus is chivalry rewarded.

Once Eddie was born his parents were kind enough to grant me the status of honorary and strictly secular godfather, and I have never taken a job more seriously. The idea of my becoming a godfather in the formal Christian sense was anathema both to Nick and myself. As a result of our experience at the Welsh reformatory, we shared what might be called a fundamentalist atheism. Christian discipline was the backbone our fanatical headmaster tried to insert into his spineless pupils and his method had a fanatic's brutal simplicity: at five-to-nine he preached brotherly love to us, and at five-past-nine he beat us for our sins. I have heard this tyrant described as a muscular Christian of the old school. If so, his brawny right arm did nothing more evangelistic than whack into our seven-year-old rumps the lifelong conviction that God was a fallacy and religion a trick for keeping the meek in their place.

On the other hand, I've never forgotten a phrase I heard at a christening not long after Eddie was born, when godfatherly duties were on my mind. The ceremony was barbaric – screaming infant, water all over the place, women in ghastly hats (admittedly, this was a country event) – and the liturgy revealed Christianity at its most abject and grovelling. (You're not a Christian, are you, Anna? Surely not.) The assumption is that the new-born babe, being human, is filthy with sin and needs to be washed clean in Christ's blood, not an hygienic thought. The godparents promise on behalf of the poor little brat that he will renounce the devil and all his works, including his carnal desires, and in the meanwhile they agree to clap on the mind-forged manacles at the first opportunity – the Creed, Lord's Prayer, Ten Commandments – and bring him up in a state of perpetual mortification. (You think I'm exaggerating? Check the Prayer Book for yourself.) However, what jumped out of all this mumbo-jumbo and stayed in my memory was the injunction that godparents should make themselves responsible for the 'health' of the infant's 'soul'. I have pondered those words in my heart ever since. (A biblical quote, Anna. Our husky headmaster made us learn Bible verses by heart, and the stuff sticks to the side of the mind like baked pastry.)

I don't know if the idea of a healthy soul can be translated from Christianity into secular terms. I am no philosopher, and certainly no theologian, but my definition of the soul would be the *moral essence* of a person, and, preposterous though it may sound to you, I thought I could contribute to keeping Eddie's moral essence healthy. How? By giving him books, of course. (I never mentioned my spiritual motive to Nick, who would have suspected me of going soft on religion and probably banned me from seeing his precious son.) Long before the poor child could read I filled his nursery with alphabets, picture books and fairy tales; I also supplied the bookcases needed to hold his junior library, and commissioned one of our illustrators to decorate them with classic characters beloved by all boys: Captain Hook, Toad, Robinson Crusoe, Ulysses, Scrooge, Sherlock Holmes and so on. Alas, as he grew older it became obvious that the lad, though delightful in every other way, was not at all interested in reading and would never become the bookworm of my doting fantasy. This had to be broken to me delicately by Natalie, but I didn't despair, since she also told me that insofar as he had a literary appetite it was for comics. I therefore arranged for Hatchards to send *The Beano*, *The Dandy*, *The Eagle* and half a dozen other such titles to Master Eddie on a weekly basis.

The healthiness of the boy's soul and all other godfatherly obligations have since been taken out of my hands. The most I can hope for now is that I did him no harm.

For the sake of completeness I'm going to add a last chapter to the history of my sentimental education.

I became an habitué of a certain Claudine and made it my custom to visit her on Fridays around six o'clock at the end of the week's work, persuading myself that I had 'earned' my moment of indulgence. Claudine received her clients in rooms at the top of a building in Half Moon Street (its name helped to glamorise the glum nature of our proceedings). To reach her eyrie one had to ascend by means of an old-fashioned lift with a folding metal door and a brass handle, which was always kept highly polished. It was part of her protocol to wait at the lift entrance on her floor, ready to greet her client as the machine delivered him. Thus, one's first view of her, glimpsed through the grillwork of the lift doors, was of her feet, invariably shod in chic high heels, and her short, meaty calves. ''Ello, chéri,' she would say in a spurious French accent as one's head glided past the rest of her body, which was stocky and well-rounded, with a low centre of gravity. I often used to think that her sons would make soccer strikers.

At first I was drawn back to Half Moon Street as much for the sake of Claudine's antiquated elevator and smart, airy little apartment, which lent an illusion of dignity to our transactions, as any erogenous quality she possessed herself. Her manner was always formal and businesslike, allowing no sense of familiarity to develop between us, despite the regularity of my visits. In time I came to value this very detachment because I discovered that my sexual nature was by no means rampant or bloodthirsty, it was ignominiously lachrymose. I don't want to dwell on the matter – of what possible interest can it be to you? – except to report that at my moment of release I would often shout out in wordless torment and then sob uncontrollably for a minute or two. Phlegmatic Claudine would permit me these excesses without comment; she would neither comfort nor discourage me, and I was always grateful for her detachment. Once again sex, in the libidinous sense, seemed to be playing only a small part. True, we were naked together on a bed, but in other respects these sessions had the character of a remedial rite.

What was this emotional lava that poured out of me, and why did it take the detonation of orgasm to release it? I can't explain it; I can only tell you that I was racked by anguished weeping that would have been proportional to grief or some other great unhappiness, which I was not aware of suffering. At first I was disturbed by these mysterious eruptions, but as the months went by I valued the tranquillity that came in their aftermath.

One Friday evening a strange little incident took place. As I lay back on the bed recovering from my tearful convulsions, I realised that contrary to her usual practice Claudine had not sprung up to put on her clothes, but was lying beside me, quite still, her head in the crook of my arm. The poor woman, exhausted by being on her back all day, had fallen clean asleep. I had never before shared a bed with a sleeping woman. Suspended from the ceiling was a mirror, in which I could observe the pair of us: I, huge, darkly furred, and beast-like; she, pale, smooth as soap, and pocket-size within the enclosing bulk of my body. We looked mythological, like a debauched god and his nymph. I don't wish to sentimentalise the episode. She soon woke and after looking at me with a fleeting expression of confusion was immediately her usual self. She never referred to our brief interlude of extra-professional intimacy and, out of deference to her need for privacy, nor did I. Despite having literally slept with me, she always addressed me as another anonymous 'Chéri', and I did not object.

I continued to make my way to Half Moon Street on Fridays, relishing the clanking respectability of Claudine's lift, until one evening I rang her bell and got no answer. Curious, even anxious on her behalf, I went up to her floor and found a young man wheeling a filing cabinet into what had been her boudoir. If I was looking for the French whore, he told me, she'd scarpered without paying her rent and no one knew where she'd gone. Behind him I could see a couple of men in overalls lifting down her mirror from the ceiling.

'She charged ten quid. Isn't that right, mate?'

I returned to the lift, without answering.

'That's a lot of money to see a tart's arse.'

I can't believe you've suffered a breakdown, Anna, or even a psychological flat tire. *Breakdown*: what a perfectly apt word.

As I was preparing to leave for work one morning – Eddie must have been six or seven by then – I interrupted my usual routine and sat down in the hall for a moment. I put my head in my hands. My briefcase lay like a patient dog on the rug at my feet (my shoes were newly polished). Outside I could hear the noise of rush-hour traffic. I heard the throbbing rumble of my own bus as it paused at the stop opposite my front door, grumbled in disbelief at my absence, and rattled away. My head remained in my hands, and it might have been a coconut for all the attachment it seemed to have to my body. Tears were dripping through my fingers.

I couldn't find a reason for changing my position, and there I sat for many minutes, bereft of purpose, of meaning, of hope. Finally, I found the will-power to stand up, but could think of nowhere to go. The office seemed pointless. Why publish more books in a world already overloaded with them? Why make money for shareholders? Why choose this author over the other? A telephone sat on a small table in the hall and it occurred to me that I could reach it by stretching out my hand, but I couldn't think of anyone to ring, or anything to say.

I am describing this situation by means of exterior signs, but I recall feeling as if I were imprisoned in a cage and that these things, the phone, doors and so on, lay outside the bars, unapproachably remote, irrevocably abstract. The interior of this cell – the hollow space within the shell of my skull – was incorporeal, a void in which no sensation or emotion registered itself; I was consciously brain-dead. It was as if someone had thrown a sack over my head, and yet I was plunged into a state that was neither dark nor light. My depression, if that is what it was, was not an agony of sadness, nor a bottomless entombment in blackness, but an ashy nothingness, utterly bare of feeling. I was a vacuum, without colour, without heart, without personality.

This is a forlorn exercise because I am trying to use metaphor to describe a nullity, mind-zero; to describe the literally indescribable. Metaphor describes one thing in terms of another, but my mind was an empty hole. I couldn't say I was immured in fog, for example, because fog is only explicable in terms of sight, clarity being the norm and fog a blindfold. I had lost touch with norms and exceptions; I was free-floating in labyrinthine nothingness; I was a nothing imprisoned by nothing, a non-person fixed in a non-event.

Obviously, at some point I rejoined the ordinary continuum of tick and tock. A flock of envelopes may have fluttered through the letter box, or I may have emerged spontaneously from this ghastly state. I can't remember now. The point is that the experience wasn't a linear incident within parentheses of time: once it had begun, it seemed to connect with all sorts of things that had gone before, and once it was over, it continued to pervade my mindscape for many hours, and its ash continues to fall even now.

Finally, I got myself to the office, late for the first time in my entire career, and telephoned Cynthia. It shames me to recall that, although I've often been bitchy about her, she was the one I turned to for help, knowing that I could trust her discretion. (Why are mental ailments shameful, while physical ones are heroic?) Cynthia recommended a woman psychotherapist to me, the improbably named Dr Darling, and I was not so far gone in despair that I didn't recognise an irony when she proposed a weekly appointment at six o'clock on Friday evenings. I took it.

Notebook 3

Everyone has a story, a myth if you like, of his or her life that explains it, and these myths are what patients first present to their therapists. By now you won't be surprised to hear that my story, the one I recounted to Dr Darling, ran as follows. The death of my sister Rosemary, to which I was witness *in utero*, determined the entire narrative of my life. I was born in its shadow and had never managed to creep out of it. My father was crippled by grief and grew to resent me, understandably, for usurping his beloved daughter. Matters were made worse when I began to develop abnormally . . .

I had only got so far, making no mention yet of my recent collapse into the void (coconut in the hands etc.), when Darling interrupted with a question that caught me by surprise.

'You used the word "understandably"; why is it understandable that he should resent you?'

Not that it matters, but Dr Darling held her consultations in a rather grand, redbrick mansion in Wimpole Street, not a Molotov cocktail's throw from fabled Harley Street. However, her room was small and ignominiously located on a mezzanine floor compressed between the surgery of a fashionable gynaecologist and a private apartment. She would sit with her back to the narrow window that illuminated her room, and her wispy hair in its dishevelled bun would be transformed into a halo on sunny days. Rather than reposing on the couch beloved of cartoonists and Freudian analysts, I was asked to sit in an armchair during our sessions.

As I trudged up her Wimpole Street stairs on Friday evenings, apprehensive yet excited, I couldn't help noticing, though I'm hardly the first to point it out, the similarities that lay between visiting a therapist and a prostitute. The Doctor's tubular legs, which she lagged with corrugated navy woollen tights (literal blue stockings), were no substitute for Claudine's peachy calves; nonetheless, here I was visiting a professional woman who did business with her 'client' alone and privately in a special room, and was paid money for her singular services, which were intimate and involved a kind of nakedness.

'Why "understandable"?' she repeated.

I don't propose to reproduce every ping and pong of our sessions, which had the quality of interminable rallies during which neither player, if that's what we were, succeeded in securing a point. Not that I was interested in competing with her, but I simply couldn't accept the thesis that lay at the bottom, I gradually realised, of most of her questions. Her thesis was that my 'internal conflicts', cause of my 'depressive episode', were produced by my belief that my father had a right to dislike me. Indeed, for many sessions we struggled over the very notion of admitting my parents as a legitimate topic to our discussions. I demanded that we concentrate on my breakdown in the hall. Instead of answering her questions about my feelings for 'Father' and 'Mother', as she sternly called them, I would construct more and more baroque accounts of the nothingness into which I had been plunged. I attempted to argue that what I had undergone was a philosophical rather than a psychological experience. I had been overpowered in an unusually dramatic way by what threatens all of us – all of us, that is, who have not been bewitched by the fairy stories of religion – which is the realisation that existence is a zero, a joke, a dream, a swirling of so many meaningless particles of matter. Not having much actual philosophy to draw on, I resorted to literary authorities, citing Samuel Beckett, King Lear, Thomas Hardy and, in a wild and ignorant stab, Schopenhauer. I might just as well have cited A. A. Milne or Barbara Cartland for all the interest

Dr Darling took, because she obstinately persisted in returning to her theme.

You may think it strange, dear Anna, in view of what I have already said about my father and his hatred, a word not yet invoked, that I went to these lengths to evade discussing him. You must remember that I was still a young man – or perhaps a late developer – at any rate someone in whom the habit of introspection, contrary to the impression you may have got from this memoir, was largely unpractised. If I ever thought about my father in those days it was to duck, so to speak, and quickly think of something else.

'So, why *understandable?*'

Darling was relentless, and I clung just as tenaciously to my myth: tragic demise of infant sister, father's unbearable grief, father's spurning of unlooked for, unwanted son. It was surely obvious to anyone who heard the story that his repudiation was a symptom of grief. In the famous phrase, it was 'nothing personal'.

'So you can't even claim his rejection as your own?'

I regarded her questions as preposterous, provocative for their own sake, impertinent and so forth, but one thing nagged me, and that was the ease with which she could return me to childhood.

My father would angrily rebuff any enquiry concerning his past, and I never heard him tell a story about his early years, nor saw a photograph taken of him as a child or teenager. I was my father's son until Darling insisted on the door being unlocked, whereupon my childhood became a vivid and proximate dimension that was always accessible. Everyone has had the sensation of being returned momentarily to childhood by the odour of tar or the cry of a gull across the beach, but I found that my childhood self had joined me as a constant companion, a kind of junior doppelganger in short trousers, a small boy who holds my hand in a clinging, sticky grip. Or am I holding his hand?

Darling never abandoned the chase.

'If Father were sitting here with us, what do you think he would say to you?'

'To me, or about me?'

'To you, or about you if you could hear what he said.'

'He would say he had produced a monster in place of his beloved daughter. He would say he despaired of me.'

'A monster?'

'Look at me.'

'I see a man.'

'He saw a freak.'

'What do you see?'

'I don't look in mirrors.'

'What did Mother see?'

'I have no idea.'

You probably think that I've invented my therapist's name for cheap comic effect, but ludicrous as it sounds Darling really was her name.

For the first half dozen of our sessions I persisted stubbornly with the idea that my depression was the result of what I believe are called exogenous causes in the trade, causes that originate outside rather than inside the patient's mind. With diminishing conviction I tried to argue that my despair was no more than a rational response to the existential here and now (there and then). I told Darling that I had a buoyant temperament and for the most part conducted my life, especially my professional life, in accordance with my natural, bustling optimism. However, if I ever paused in my busy round to think about the state of the world (incorrigible cruelty, corruption and injustice – factors that could surely be counted as exogenous) I was brought very quickly to the brink of melancholy's precipice. On that terrible morning (coconut head) I had simply tripped over the edge and gone into free fall.

My rationalisations never drew anything from dogged

Doctor Darling except a new question about my parents.

'You must appreciate,' I said in exasperation, 'that my father never forgave me for being present, so to speak, when Rosemary was killed. I was like a secret witness, a spy, hiding inside my mother. Perhaps if my mother had not been pregnant, Rosemary might not have died. Who knows? But his grief was so acute that I was implicated simply by existing. In his eyes I was as guilty as they were.'

'Do you think you killed her?'

'For Christ's sake!'

That is when I came closest to walking out on Dr Darling. I sprang to my feet and made for the door. She didn't stir, but continued to look at me with an expression that was insistent without being provocative.

I returned to my chair and as I collected myself a very paradoxical thought popped into my mind. I realised that despite her probing and interrogating Darling was on my side; I could trust her to sympathise with my version of events – if I gave her one. It was a revolutionary notion.

In the same mental breath I also realised that if I didn't confide in my therapist she would not be able to perform her mystery. This may seem elementary – after all, what is the point of using the so-called talking cure if you are not willing to talk? – but I had only sought help for my 'breakdown', which I saw as an isolated, discrete catastrophe. You may not believe it, Anna, because it sounds so naïve (or self-deceiving), but when I consulted Dr Darling I had not prepared myself for discussing my father, my minotaurine development and all the rest of it. At some unconscious level I may have wanted to spill these beans, but by definition I cannot comment on that.

There was another inhibition, which was that I had next to no experience of confiding. I had never discussed my bizarre teenage anxieties with Nick and had only whispered a very bowdlerised version of them into Régine's exquisite, ivory ear. Otherwise, I had remained dumb on the subject throughout my entire life. Shame is a great silencer.

Parents beware! If you send your little treasure away from home to serve time in a prep-school chain gang you can't expect him to be eager to chat to you about his experiences when he returns in the holidays. He'll tell you what you want to hear and what you need to hear, but he'll divulge the least possible information about himself and won't say a word about his feelings. If he has been truly miserable, and not just ordinarily unhappy, he'll be further silenced by shame. Yes, fond parent, you never thought of that, did you? Boys, and girls for that matter, are ashamed of their unhappiness. Homesickness is not only painful, it's as humiliating as wetting the bed, and can't be confided in anyone, least of all in the people who signed away your freedom in the first place. (The sacrifices we make for our children!)

'Did you kill your sister?'

'Of course not.'

'Did you grow up with her death on your conscience?'

'Yes, I suppose I did. Because of my father's suffering I felt guilty that I was alive while Rosemary was dead.'

'Who made you feel that way?'

'The circumstances.'

'Do you think your parents played any part in making you feel guilty?'

It was another outrageous question.

'No.'

I had always seen our family situation as something fixed and irrevocable. We were all the victims of Rosemary's accident; four people had fallen out of the beech tree that disastrous afternoon, and our subsequent fate as survivors was inescapable. We were locked in our history. Melancholy was bound to pervade our house; it was the inevitable consequence of Rosemary's death. I was the victim of my father's grief, but my suffering was nothing compared with his, for he was the victim of the worst kind of loss a man could endure.

The idea that my parents might have manipulated our tragedy to ease their own feelings seemed so abhorrent that I could not ingest it at first. I couldn't accept that they might have done something to me that was additional to the dreadful thing that had already been done to all of us. Am I making sense, Anna?

'Do you think your parents were trying to transfer some of their guilt onto you?'

'They had nothing to be guilty about. It was an accident.'

'It's sometimes said that grief is another name for guilt. You said that Father turned his grief into a one-man cult – was it his way of avoiding his guilt?'

I couldn't answer her. It had never occurred to me that my father might feel guilty about Rosemary. He had always seemed to me as innocent as Job, his grief pure suffering.

'How did his grief affect you?'

By way of answering I launched into a precipitate account of the occasion when I joined my father in his Sunday vigil at Rosemary's grave. It seemed imperative, if the exact quality of the experience was to be conveyed, to describe in detail the glittering brilliance of my birthday bicycle, its silvery spokes, shimmering chrome, white-walled tyres and so forth. I wanted Darling to understand exactly how beautiful a machine my bicycle had been, and I found myself growing angry with her impassive reaction to its lustre. For once her professional detachment seemed utterly inappropriate, even boorish. Leaning forward and hectoring her, I began to tell her about my journey up the hill to the churchyard. To my amazement, she checked me.

'We must continue this line of thought next week,' she said, looking meaningfully at her clock, an officious timepiece that did its tut-tutting duty on the mantelpiece above my head.

You've heard about the psychiatrist's hour, haven't you, Anna? It's precisely fifty minutes long and not a minute more; not an extra merciful minute to complete the story that explains your entire life. Yes, before you know it, you're stumbling along Wimpole Street, tears streaming down your face, scarcely able to remember your own name. Claudine was never this cruel.

The work of psychotherapy does not stop when the fifty-minute whistle blows. In fact, it's extraordinary that the product of less than an hour can expand like a gas to perfume or taint every waking hour, at any rate every thinking hour (by no means the same thing), of the next six days.

It was only during the week following Darling's brutal abortion of my bicycle story that I finally invoked the term 'hatred' to describe my father's treatment of my childhood self.

'The man hated me.'

I remember muttering these words to myself over and over again, as if they had magical power, while I made my way to the office in the mornings. 'My father loathed me,' I used to say between meetings or while signing my post. 'The bastard couldn't stand the sight of me,' I chanted on my way home.

You may find it surprising, but this discovery, which fell upon me like a revelation but took some time to make its full impact, filled me with a kind of liberating anger. It was a relief finally to see the thing clearly for what it was. I was no longer interested in explanations, since they would only obscure the fundamental fact, which in its way explained everything else. He had hated me, hence his silences, mockery and contempt; hence his unfailing, unfeeling duti-fulness. Now that I'd put the real name to these many aliases, I had no further use for them. What could therapy do in the face of such a perversion? Now we knew the truth, Darling and I, what was the point of trying to take our family dynamic to pieces? Fuck him! Fuck her! Fuck them all!

With this edifying sentiment to galvanise me, I was in high

spirits when I next visited Darling, and took the stairs to her little den two at a time.

'My father called me "Ape-boy".'

Anger had released in me an intoxicating confidence. Because my father was to blame for everything, I felt free to tackle subjects with Darling that had previously seemed utterly unapproachable, and none had been more sealed off than my bull-calf past. Anger had also inspired in me the gift of self-analysis: I had come to understand that the Minotaur in me, which still rattled its horns somewhere in a dark stall, was not my savage, secret self, nor even an intrinsic part of my personality. Rather, it was an intruder forced on me from outside. My father, and this was the core of my devastating insight, had stabled this monster in my mind, which I had turned into a labyrinthian bull pen. The brute belonged to him, my hating, hateful father. In some unconscious way I had assumed the blame for Rosemary's death. As sister-killer I had called myself Minotaur, whereas the demon's true name was Guilt, my father's guilt. It had never occurred to me that his grief might be a bulwark to protect himself against guilt, nor that his hatred of me was a way of disposing of it. This understanding, which had crept up on me by increments and in many confused guises, doubled my anger when it finally dawned.

I still could not bring myself to confide in Darling my teenage terror of growing horns that would pierce and dis-embowel (horny horn of adolescence), but I was willing to make a circumlocutory start by telling her about my father's teasing, the most obvious manifestation of his hatred.

As usual, Darling's response was unexpected, at least by me, though by then I suppose I should have predicted it.

'And Mother,' she enquired, 'did she protect you from Father's hatred?'

I remember being amazed that Darling seemed to accept

the concept of his hate without demur.

'My mother protected my father.'

'But you weren't attacking him.'

'I don't mean that. She protected him from everything – life, the world outside our house – everything except his grief. I came second to my father in her eyes. I always understood that, and so I didn't resent it.'

'Does she hate you too?'

'No! No.'

'Does she love you?'

'I don't know. I suppose so. I've never asked myself. She's not a warm person. Some people aren't. She did her duty.'

'Does your father love you?'

'He hates me. Haven't you been listening?'

'The two are not incompatible.'

'My father is a simple man. He used to hate me, but now I've left home I dare say he's put me out of his mind. I wish I could return the compliment.'

I stare out of the window. Dr Darling stares at her hands folded in her lap. I look at the clock on the mantelpiece above me. Ten minutes gone. Dr Darling continues to stare at her hands folded in her lap. I stare at Dr Darling as she stares at her hands folded in her lap. My stare is ferocious, eye-bulging; hers is neutral, a way of not using her eyes without actually closing them. I stare at the window, not through it this time, but at the glass itself, studying the finger marks on the inside, bird droppings on the outside, studying the very texture of the glass, its scratches and flaws. Dr Darling stares at her hands folded in her lap. I would like to smash the glass.

Thus do we engage in the talking cure.

Dr Darling was not a strict Freudian, but she did uphold the psychoanalyst's principle of keeping silent at the start of a session until the patient had spoken. On this point she was inflexible. Are you familiar with these quaint Freudian rites,

Anna? It is the patient who must speak first, saying whatever comes into his head, whatever he needs to express, whatever he wants to say if only to break the silence. Until he does so, the analyst keeps his/her mouth zipped. Darling once explained the theory behind this ridiculous rule, but I've forgotten it. In my turn, I explained the special horror that silence held for me, describing the sheer malevolence that my father managed to inject into the void of our family meals, but Darling did not relent. No compromise was possible, she told me, and she was as good as her wordless word.

As a patient you always have the option of keeping silent yourself in a perverse attempt to triumph in this clash of wills, but it's an expensive and futile gesture. I tried it on a couple of occasions, but never lasted longer than five minutes. The pressure to speak is overwhelming and the silence terrified me. I feared Darling's disapproval; I feared the clammy dread of something I could never name; I feared another headlong dive into nothingness, of which silence was an echo.

I surrendered by telling her about the tension that used to prevail in our house like a perpetual winter.

My parents didn't argue, but they were both constantly on edge, in my mother's case literally so, for rather than sitting down she would perch on the arm of a chair or the back of the sofa, seemingly prepared for immediate flight. My father was always wound up, taut with incipient rage. He never lost his temper with my mother and only rarely with me, though I lived in constant fear of it. His fury was mostly directed at the television and the radio, especially programmes about current affairs. He couldn't listen to the news over breakfast without yelling abuse at the journalists and arguing with the contributors: 'Let the hypocritical little bastard answer the question for once!' Even newsreaders were attacked, as if they were somehow responsible for the announcements they were making. 'Bloody fool!' he would snarl when a bland voice reported an increase in the price of fuel or the possibility of rain. This may sound comical, but it was far from funny to experience.

'Did you feel responsible in some way for the strained atmosphere in your house?' Darling asked me.

'I think they tried to make me feel responsible for everything. I was their scapegoat. They loaded me with their guilt, but instead of sending me into the wilderness they kept me at home like the monster in its maze. I was Caliban to my father's Prospero.'

'Caliban accused Prospero of stealing his island from him. What did Father steal from you?'

'My childhood.'

Sometimes, as a means of getting the session under way, I would tell Darling about my work. For example, one Friday I gave lunch to an author who had approached me with the idea of writing a book about paradise. (Freddy Hamilton. Does his name ring a bell? Before your time, I think. Pleasant enough chap. I wonder what became of him?) I took him for lunch at a then fashionable restaurant called *Il Primo Giardino*, but the reference was lost on him. I told Darling that he could hardly eat his food for excitement as he described the paradise that Captain Cook's sailors discovered when they ran up the beaches into the welcoming arms of the women on Tahiti.

'What's your idea of paradise?' Darling intervened in a dry tone.

By then I knew that all therapeutic paths, even ones that began in paradise, led back, however tortuously, to the labyrinth of childhood where my junior self sat in a glum cell waiting to be interrogated. I was already growing bored with this inevitable itinerary and, feeling troublesome that day, I decided to strike out on a route of my own. After all, who was paying for this conversation?

In the teeth of Darling's manifest impatience I launched

into an account of the little second-hand bookshop that used to be on Coptic Street, round the corner from our office. Do you remember it? God knows how the owner – I believe his name was Milton – made any money out of it. I never saw a customer in there apart from myself, and I never bought anything from him. But now and again, especially during difficult afternoons, I used to slip out of the office and visit his shop. He was either too poor or too mean to light the place properly and in winter you could hardly see the books on the shelves. His stock, incidentally, was very eccentric: there was a dubious over-representation of books devoted to Nazism, but his heart seemed to be in his numberless collection of miniature books, little oyster-sized volumes of Restoration poetry, Shakespeare plays, Victorian belle-lettres and so forth, which he displayed in a locked glass-fronted cabinet. At the back of his maze of bookcases, he used to occupy a cubby hole where he kept a kettle continually simmering on a gas ring. He was also addicted to Turkish cigarettes, and the combination of steam and smoke that filled his 40-watt gloaming would render him all but invisible. The smell of the place, an aromatic mustiness, was distinctive, but hardly conducive to business. All the same, I confess I felt at home in his shop.

Milton would never greet me when I entered, but would allow me to potter about for a couple of minutes, inspecting his changeless stock, before offering me a cup of what he called his 'builder's brew-up'. As often as not he would be cataloguing, or just fondling, some item of his fairy library, scrutinising its tiny print through his magnifying glass and sighing with pleasure. I would sit opposite him with my mug of tea and pretend to browse the books piled on his desk, though in fact I would often close my eyes for a minute or two. He never seemed to notice or care.

This was my idea of paradise, I told Darling: a moment of quietude in the company of books, in the embrace of books. If paradise is to be found this side of the grave, and let's face it there is no other, it consists in moments of contentment like that, fleeting intervals of calm and freedom from anxiety, when the tide is poised, neither ebbing or flowing, when the clock rests between tick and tock, when . . .

'Do you think your enjoyment of this man's shop is dependent on his books or his lack of disapproval?'

So predictable! Now she was ushering me into the room where I would find my father and his rubber cosh. The truth was that though the unmasking of 'Father' as the villain of my childhood melodrama had been profoundly illuminating, I didn't want to pursue the matter any further. I had acknowledged his hatred for what it was, and that seemed sufficient. I had no desire to probe the exact workings of our relationship. Despite my anger I was still very apprehensive when his name came up.

'Well, Milton is hardly the father I wish I'd had, if that's what you're getting at,' I told her sarcastically, and pressed on with my evocation of our paradisiacal moments.

I did compensate him in a small way for my profitless visits, because I always brought with me a brand of foreign cigarettes, oval Kyprinos from Cyprus, or perfumed Fatimas from Egypt with a picture of a harem girl on their box, or Russian Imperials filled with grey tobacco and stamped on their cardboard tubes with the golden, two-eagled crest of the doomed Romanov family. He loved these exotica, and would close his eyes in ecstasy as he blew plumes of expensive smoke round his fetid den. If I was feeling generous I would leave him the rest of the packet (provided it was more than half-empty; I'm not that generous).

Darling was shifting restlessly in her chair, but I proceeded to my well-practised monologue on the comparative qualities of Turkish and Virginian tobaccos. (I was, of course, smoking at the time myself. Darling did not smoke. I'll say no more.) She interrupted me, something she rarely did.

'Can you define the satisfaction cigarettes give you?' she asked.

I began to tell her about the fetishistic delights to be had from the paraphernalia of smoking – my Dunhill lighter, crocodile skin cigarette case, meerschaum holder – but she brushed these aside, saying, 'Describe the feeling you get when you actually put the cigarette in your mouth.'

'Well, I don't know. It's something and nothing, isn't it? All this business with lighters and so forth; all this expense . . . what does it amount to? A little cloud in the air for a couple of seconds. It's a drug, no doubt, but I think I'm addicted to that little moment of – what? – *transcendence* that it brings. Yes, transcendence.'

I was rather pleased with my reply, but Darling's next question took me by surprise.

'What would you say to the suggestion that a cigarette is a kind of breast and smoke a kind of milk?'

We were back to Mother again. Two months earlier I might have laughed, or asked for my money back, but on that occasion, extraordinary as it may sound, I didn't protest. I didn't speak at all; instead, I started to cry.

Once I had begun, my face in my hands, I couldn't control the torrent of feeling that flooded out of me. I howled like an infant.

I don't believe this was a reaction to thinking about my mother. I don't recall that I had any thoughts. I was reduced to a conduit for emotion that gushed out of me, and the power driving it was anguish. I was overwhelmed with the same unspecified distress that used to erupt when I died between Claudine's goal-scoring legs. And like Claudine, Dr Darling retained her professional cool. She neither soothed nor spurred me on, but sat quietly until my cataclysm was over.

'Why are you crying?' she asked when I had recovered some composure.

'Aren't you supposed to tell me that?'

'Was there a serpent in your paradise?'

'I'm ashamed.'

'Of what?'

'Being here. Saying all these things to you. Whining.'

These words sprang out of my mouth as spontaneously as the tears which seconds before had spouted from my eyes.

'Why do you call it whining?'

'I feel I have no right to my feelings.'

'What do you mean?'

'I have a horror of self-pity.'

'There is a difference between self-pity and the expression of pain. You have the right to be free of pain.'

'I want to be free of all this – my father, talking to you in this room, forever digging up the corpse of my childhood. I long to liberate myself from . . . from me. More than anything I dread that I'll be imprisoned for the rest of my life by my father's hatred. I've been thinking – maybe the money I spend on you would be better invested in taking out a contract on dear old Dad. What do you say? Wouldn't a knife in his guts be a quicker and more effective cure of my problems?'

'I doubt you'd find an assassin who'd work as cheaply as I do,' she said dryly, and then added, 'Would you like to murder Father?'

'Yes, and I can't wait to jump into bed with Mother.'

'Why have you resorted to flippancy?'

'I don't know where else to go. Why can't you help me?'

I'm trying to give you an idea of these sessions with Darling, their occasional sterility, the tyranny of the ticking on her mantelpiece, their contested silences, my emotional outbursts that came and went like tropical rainstorms, Darling's undeviating focus on an agenda that was always obscure to me, my garrulous digressions and those questions of hers that seemed to take a tin opener to my head.

I could never reconcile myself to what struck me as the fundamental inequality of our positions. There was I, the client, exposing the most vulnerable parts of my life and personality, and there was Dr Darling, the therapist, who confided nothing about herself and remained a stranger, an enigma, a blank screen. The principle upon which most intimate relationships are founded, that's to say *exchange* (you show me yours and I'll show you mine), was not only missing, but positively forbidden. Any enquiries on my part concerning her ordinary human trappings, home, husband, children, dog or cat, taste in music, political leanings, and so forth, were glacially rebuffed.

Nor can I say that I was conscious at any stage of making progress. No doubt the fault was mine ('Why?' I can hear her demanding; 'Why do you blame yourself?') but I never knew where we were going, or what might constitute improvement; I never knew what the project was about, what its aims were, or how its method worked. Darling may have explained these things to me, or it may have been part of her technique to keep me in ignorance and let her purpose gradually reveal itself. Either way, I can only report that I remained eternally mystified. Once in a while I sensed that Darling was guiding me towards an insight into the cartography of my unconscious, a hinterland that was as foggy and treacherous as the Grimpen Mire. A flare would go up, the landscape would be hectically lit for an instant, but then the darkness would return, leaving me none the wiser.

As the sessions proceeded I began to fear that the little enlightenment I had achieved was only illuminating the walls of my labyrinth, in which I was still held fast. However, I was certain of one thing, which was that the winter of my breakdown was slowly giving way to spring. The nothingness that had invaded my mind was being replaced with somethingness: the horror was receding. My depression was slowly lifting, and the fact that I didn't know why or how in no way diminished my gratitude.

Have I mentioned Dr Darling's habit of raising a little Gothic chapel by putting the tips of her fingers together? It was a manual tic that indicated unusually speculative thinking and was often accompanied by a lifting of her concertina chin and a compensatory squeezing of her small eyes. I came to think of that chapel as a refuge in which certain birds, having flapped out of the rookery of my mind, wild as Furies, finally came to perch in orderly lines, tamed, caged and ready to be taken home. However, there were a few birds I kept imprisoned in my head, and one of them was the discovery of my mother's box of lingerie.

On the subject of my father I spoke with swashbuckling eloquence, and merrily blamed him for every misfortune that had befallen me since I was a child, up to and including the last cold I had caught. The catalogue of his neglect and cruelty seemed endless, and at every session I would have a fresh page to roll out for Darling's inspection, but she always countered with a question concerning my other parent. Although I would stand on my right as patient and paying customer to talk about the topic of my choice, I would finally be forced to turn to the complex, never resolved topic of Mother.

Why didn't I tell her about the hidden lingerie? I don't know. I felt guilty, I suppose, and I also felt it would be a betrayal to reveal this secret to Darling; it was my mother's secret, not mine.

What comes to mind when the you think of your mother, Anna? What would you say if you had to give an account of your relationship with her? In my case, I had no myth to offer, no theory, only a sort of oceanic void which defied description because of its very emptiness. Whenever Darling asked me about Mother I was reduced to silence while my mind was invaded by a white mist.

One Friday I missed a meeting with Dr Darling. The following week I explained that my lapse had been the result of unavoidable business at the office and I paid her for the two sessions. We both knew I was lying.

At the session after that, feeling more nervous than I had at any other stage in our brief, illuminating relationship, I told her that I felt my need for therapy had come to an end; this would be my last visit. Darling was not pleased by my announcement and earnestly attempted to dissuade me. There were, she said, many unresolved conflicts in my mind. My new-found attitude to my father was dangerous and no more than a step along the road to self-realisation (whatever that was), which in my case was likely to be long and rugged. My feelings for Mother required a great deal of work. In short, we had hardly begun a process which, if abandoned, would prove still more destructive than the condition we had been trying to improve in the first place.

Not for a moment did I doubt Darling's sincerity, or suspect her of trying to milk me for fees. She was a woman of impeccable good faith, as anyone could see from the tormented way in which she raised chapel after chapel with her fervent fingers, constructing a whole heavenly city, while she urged, almost begged me to change my mind and continue my treatment. But I was not listening to her; I knew that my need for her ministrations had come to an end, at least for the time being.

The crisis of six months ago had passed, and Darling had in effect nursed me through it, for which I was exceedingly grateful, as I repeatedly told her. Moreover – and surely this was a healthy sign? – I had become heartily bored with the subject of myself and couldn't bring any fresh zest to denouncing my father's wickedness. I felt better, and that is all the depressive seeks. The cloud had lifted and the world had filled with colour, if not meaning. There was a spring in my step, a flower in my buttonhole.

Finally, Darling conceded defeat; her last chapel lost its

steeple and toppled into her empty hands. She made no secret of her foreboding in relation to my future, the first truly unprofessional note she had struck, but agreed to let me go. I paid her for the last time and bade her farewell, feeling guilty as I joyfully skipped down the steps from her little mezzanine cave. The air in Wimpole Street smelt of liberty.

Notebook 4

As you can see, Anna, I've had to buy more notebooks. I won't depress you by saying how many more, but take comfort – we're more than half way through our journey.

During my winter of discontent I had neglected my friendship with Nick as well as my avuncular duties, such as they were, in respect of young Eddie. To celebrate the blooming of my mental spring, which in its contrary way coincided with nature's autumn, I took up my old habit of visiting Nick and his family as often as I could.

For some eccentric reason, they had chosen to live south of the river, in Camberwell, a place as foreign to me as the face of the moon and scarcely any easier to reach. Nonetheless, I made my faithful pilgrimage every fortnight or so, usually for Sunday lunch. At the time I'm talking of, Eddie was about six or seven and he seemed to me a paragon of boyhood, merry, vivacious, always a little muddy, oily or inky, and always inculpated in what Natalie called 'scrapes'; in short, an exhilarating presence. I used to think of him as the spirit of the household, and though I was no judge of domestic atmospheres, their household always seemed happy to me as I came through the front door, sniffing the odours of Natalie's excellent cooking. (With a pang of shame it occurs to me only now that I always presumed on my welcome. Was I resented?)

Nick and Natalie had a plan, a life strategy, which they were successfully putting into action, and nothing is more satisfying than that. They were moving forward (no matter where); they had healthy children, a home and a garden; they had rewarding work and every morning they woke knowing what they were required to do during the coming day. I didn't want what they had for myself, but I rejoiced in it for their sake. (I forgot to mention that a daughter was born two years after Eddie, a charming elf of a girl, with black plaits and a habit of performing somersaults in place of speaking. I was fond of her – Nina was her name – but she did not command my love as Eddie did.)

Nick continued to travel, buying antiques and curios for what had by now become his own business, and every room in their house was furnished with foreign movables. Natalie managed to exercise some control over this continuous influx of the world's bric-a-brac, and did not allow their house to acquire the transient feel that had dominated Nick's old flat. Many of his friends, including myself, urged him to open a shop, if only to create a space in which to store his ever-expanding quantity of so-called 'stock', but he always refused, preferring to operate out of a warehouse mysteriously located somewhere in Brixton. It suited his elusive temperament to remain a dealer, a trader, a fixer, the bandit who robbed you with a smile and a mocking bow. He had become the archetypal man who knew a man, who carried a roll of cash the size of his fist and never wrote a cheque, who could compute the value of your dining table in half a dozen currencies at once, who could sell it for you in half a dozen languages; a man of enigmatic comings and goings, wheeling and dealing, a man whose last meal had always been eaten in another country.

Only one thing did not accumulate in their house, and that was books. Thinking that she would have to accommodate a great quantity of them, Natalie arranged to have an entire wall of their sitting room furnished with shelving made of varnished ash, a wood so blond and dazzling the shelves seemed to be airborne, but Nick never traded in books, ancient or modern; indeed, he seemed to have no more interest in literature than his son. As if to fill this unexpected void, Natalie began to write herself. Despite the commercial failure of her work on apples, I encouraged her to persist with her conservation campaign, and in due course she made herself the scourge of agribusiness. (One of her titles gave me special pleasure, perhaps because I had invented it myself: *Their Land – Our Landscape*. It proved to be her best-seller, though I use the term relatively.)

Do you sketch, Anna? There is probably no limit to your talents.

In spite of never showing the slightest artistic aptitude at school, I decided to take drawing lessons as another way of rejoicing over my resurrection from the therapeutic grave. I fondly pictured myself doing a little Sunday painting when I had acquired the necessary skills; the Whistler of West Hampstead. (I had also convinced myself that my function was not sufficiently creative, a quite mistaken idea that most publishers punish themselves with at some point in their careers.) Accordingly, I enrolled in an evening class to be taught by an ARA, whom Natalie recommended.

My *maître* proved to be a florid troll of a man, whose purple complexion was garishly set off, in the manner of Chagall, by a goatee beard of purest cotton wool. He was suffering from an abominable cold, but between explosive sneezes in which rainbows would have arced on a sunny day, he encouraged me to make a likeness of a jug, a bowl and a wine bottle (the relic of a rather nasty Beaune). I laboured with ham-fisted diligence for an hour, my nose an inch from the paper, and produced a composition so shameful I was about to destroy it when, in the nick of time, the maestro intervened. After tugging his beard and cocking his head this way and that, he announced in catarrhal tones that I possessed an 'instinctive feeling for chiaroscuro'. Though his tribute was laughably disingenuous – this was a trial class designed to recruit pupils – it filled me with pride and a sense of my own boundless potential. The next day I went to Cowling and Wilcox in Broadwick Street and purchased a pad of exceedingly costly cartridge paper, together with a set of pencils whose geology ranged from crumbly charcoal to something more adamantine than a knitting needle.

The following week, in a mood of elated fecundity, my new materials under my arm, I bounded up the stairs to the *étalier* for my next lesson, only to discover a notice stuck on the door informing all students with great regret that their teacher had 'passed away'. His place would be taken by another teacher, but as a mark of respect that day's class had been cancelled. I confess my immediate reaction was a pang of annoyance that the tiresome fellow should have put me to the inconvenience of a wasted evening.

As I studied this announcement, I was joined in the dingy corridor by another pupil, a woman who stooped to read the notice. She was shrouded in a voluminous mackintosh, her head wrapped in a scarf, but I remembered her from the previous week. Looking up from my warped wine bottle, I had noticed a chignon in front of me – is that the word to describe hair that has been drawn into a neat coil at the nape of the neck? – as my fellow student concentrated on a sensitive rendering of a pumpkin. When, several months later, I mentioned my memory to the artist herself she insisted that the subject had been a bunch of grapes, but she didn't quarrel with my impression of sleek chestnut hair (hair the shade of a conker at the moist moment of being parted from its spiny womb).

We exchanged a few rueful words and separated, but then found ourselves side by side on the street, hailing the same taxi. I gallantly offered it to her, but she asked me where I was going and, to cut a tiresome story short, it emerged that we lived within a couple of streets of each other and so we shared the cab. We reached her house first and to my surprise she invited me inside for a drink. I accepted and as we stood on the pavement, pedantically paying an exact half-share each for the taxi fare, we introduced ourselves and I learnt that her name was Suzette M.

As we took off our coats in the bright light of the hallway (it was an early October evening – to be precise, it was the evening of the 15th of October, a Monday) I steeled myself to undergo that visual body search which occurs in an all-seeing flash whenever people meet for the first time. I had long been accustomed to seeing an expression of undisguisable horror flicker in women's eyes as they discovered the squat gigantism of my dimensions, but Suzette's expression remained enigmatic. By the same token, I had the opportunity to examine my fellow student and take full account of her most salient feature: her size. I could hardly have missed the fact that she was tall – six feet, perhaps even an inch more – but I had not appreciated that she was also gloriously Amazonian. By this I mean that she was upstanding, broad-shouldered, bosomy and narrow-waisted. In fact, her shape was the stuff of Victorian erotic dreams: she was statuesque in height and shape, her hair was thick and richly coloured, and yet she had small hands and feet, a 'porcelain' complexion and delicate features. A magnificent woman.

She took me into her sitting room and we went through the ritual of offering and choosing drinks, whisky in a bucket-sized tumbler for her, an irreproachable Chablis for me.

I remember saying to her, 'This is a most hospitable room,' and then hastily adding, 'Forgive me. I hate it when visitors pass judgements on my possessions, but your flat feels so congenial I can't help saying it. It must be the high ceiling, and of course the way you've done it.'

What I was really saying, and I think she understood this immediately, was, 'Well congratulations, you clever giantess; you've created a stage set that flatters your height.'

Beware of compliments. Like the language of love, they should be read as mirror writing, don't you agree, Anna?

'*I don't want to hurt you*' usually means '*don't hurt me, I beg you*'. My compliment to Suzette was also an inverted plea to treat me kindly in her 'hospitable' room. I was saying, 'Don't judge me. Be as congenial as your room, in which you look so comfortable, for all your towering altitude.'

She simply replied, 'Make yourself at home.'

I wonder what your home is like, Anna. Do you live in a house or a cottage? A shack or a chateau? Suzette had chosen for herself a flat that was all verticals, if that's not a paradox, a space in which her own notable verticality did not appear so conspicuous. Like many flats in this part of London, hers had been crudely hacked out of what had once been a very large house, and it possessed only one room which retained its original proportions and that was the very drawing room where we now stood, sipping (in my case, hurling back) our drinks. Its ceiling was lofty, its sash windows required the use of a long pole to open their upper lights, and its soaring walls were hung with a paper dominated by perpendicular stripes. I know that many people, especially men, might have felt humiliated, not to say flattened, by the cathedral-like quality of this room, but I was always wonderfully soothed by it. To see Suzette standing in front of her Brobdingnagian fireplace, leaning her heroic elbow on a mantelpiece that could have been an eyrie for eagles was, for me at least, to feel reassured that a goddess was rightly ensconced in her Parthenon.

She offered me a second glass of wine, and then made it clear that the time had come for me to leave. I took my cue, but as I put on my coat I was overwhelmed by reluctance to leave. Gradually progressing towards the door, I was impeded at every step by admiration for the pictures in her hallway, the shape of her umbrella stand, the appropriate-ness of her William Morris wallpaper ('Honeysuckle') and, finally, even the beauty of her doorknob (a handsome brass globe with interesting striations pressed into it).

'Look,' she said, as I grew fascinated with the weft of the

coir doormat outside her front door, 'come for supper one evening this week. Choose your day.'

'Tomorrow,' I answered instantly and she closed the door on me.

Suzette was not to know it, but my reply involved the cancellation of a dinner with an American publisher that had been the result of negotiations between our respective secretaries as complex and prolonged as bringing together heads of state. When I broke the news the following morning to the excellent Mrs B. that I would be defaulting on her arrangements the woman resigned on the spot.

I was sorry to see her go, but on this occasion fate was in a generous mood, because her successor turned out to be none other than your good self, Anna. Do you recall your interview? You asked me what the chances were of your becoming an editor. I was discouraging, but you took the job all the same. A red-letter day all round. Do you still have ambitions to edit? If so, I may be able to fulfil them, after all.

As invited, I returned to Suzette's house the next evening.

From the moment I entered her house to the moment she closed the door on me at midnight I did not stop talking. I was driven by the most urgent compulsion to explain myself to my new friend; I offered her, forced on her, an account of my life and background that would have astounded an eavesdropping Darling with its detail and ready intimacy. Naturally, I didn't confide Minotaurine matters in her, nor did the names of Claudine and her scarlet sisterhood feature in my self-portrait, but otherwise I ranged freely over all the aspects of my tinpot saga with which you are far too familiar by now, my long-suffering Anna.

These things are not easy to gauge, but my impression was that Suzette's interest did not flag throughout my marathon narrative; indeed, the miracle was that she appeared eager to hear more. However, *appeared* is the word, for it has to be admitted that on her side Suzette remained resolutely silent – Sphinxian. In this respect, as in almost every other, she could not have provided a greater contrast with Régine, of beloved memory, whose autobiographical outpourings had been unstoppable.

I know what you're thinking, that I never gave the poor woman a chance to get a word in edgeways. As I walked home at the end of the evening I reached the same dreadful conclusion: I had been a bore all evening, an egotistical, loud-mouthed, thick-skinned bore. I cursed myself for my uncontrollable garrulousness. No one is more tiresome than the moron who lacks the grace and simple human curiosity to shut his mouth for a minute and take an interest in the person opposite. My talking had been as aggressive as my father's silence. More so. Surely Suzette must have slammed her door with relief and sworn never to see me again. I had successfully repelled the one woman in whom I had detected both fellow-feeling and sexual rapport. Or was that too a deluded projection of my incorrigible ego?

I reached my own front door, but was too agitated to go inside. I continued to walk the empty streets, torturing myself with my stupidity. I even walked past Suzette's house, now dark and silent, and imagined her lying in her empress's bed, execrating my name, my insufferable, self-pitying confessionalism.

A telephone kiosk came into sight. Without thinking I went inside and began to dial Suzette's number. I would apologise; I would explain; I would promise. No, no. I would remain silent, show her that I was just as capable of listening as talking; I would . . .

I put the phone down before the number rang.

Autumn is the busiest season in the publishing year, and as was my custom I had arranged to spend the next ten days in Paris and then at the Book Fair in Frankfurt, a prospect I usually relished, but which now hung over me like an exile. My last words on Suzette's doorstep had been to say I would telephone her on my return. She had smiled without replying. What was I to make of that?

Suzette was seldom out of my mind while I was in Frankfurt, for she had dyed and perfumed the whole sea of my consciousness, but when I returned I was too nervous to get in touch with her immediately.

As it happened, my first social obligation was to Eddie, to whom I had promised a treat by way of compensation for my recent neglect, and this allowed me to postpone the dreaded moment of finding out if the captivating giantess would give me a second chance.

Eddie had grown into a most convivial child. He always addressed me by name when I arrived, rushing past on some urgent mission, but shouting back his greeting. He was immensely fond of catch phrases and street slang, which I suppose he picked up from the television. 'How're they hanging?' he said by way of hello when I turned up one day, though he clearly had no idea what was meant by this intimate enquiry. On another occasion he addressed me as 'Dude', and forced me to learn a complex sequence of palm-slapping, hand-shaking and finger-hooking, which I had to repeat, without error, whenever we met.

My chief memory of him from that period is that he was always in uniform and armed to the teeth with an arsenal of swords and submachine guns. His customary mode of moving about the house was first to clear his way with the use of a hand grenade. Drawing the pin with his teeth and lobbing it into the next room, he would hold his hands over his ears while making tremendous exploding noises and then rush in, revolver clasped in the approved manner with two hands at the end of stiff arms. He would spray the room with bullets to mop up any survivors, usually his sister at work with her paints or their dog asleep in its basket, both indifferent to their fate as victims of his massacre.

The lad's chosen treat was to be taken to Hamleys, where I let him loose on the place, saying he could have whatever he wanted for twenty pounds; I forget the precise sum, but I remember it shocked him with its munificence. To my horror, he chose a futuristic weapon of mass destruction which he could hardly lift. It was powered by a whole magazine of batteries that caused various plastic parts to light up and throb in lurid colours while releasing an ear-splitting noise. I was concerned that this psychopath's tool might not be welcomed at home, so I rang Natalie.

'Could it actually kill anyone?' she asked me.

'No.'

'Does it even fire anything?'

'No.'

'Then let him have it. And make sure he thanks you, the little bugger.'

I realised I knew nothing about the upbringing of children.

Eddie did thank me, most profusely. Later that evening, exhausted by fantasies of inter-planetary slaughter, he went to bed early, cuddling his weapon on his pillow. I was the urchin's slave.

I won't detain you with the pitiful methods I employed to pump up my courage in order to telephone Suzette. Enough to say that I was half-drunk and the clock was striking nine when I finally performed the feat of dialling her number in full and allowing it to ring.

'I'd love to come,' she said when I stammered out my invitation to supper at *Aphrodite*, a reliable Greek restaurant within walking distance of her house. It took me a moment to realise that my exclamations of delight were being poured into the phone's deaf ear. Suzette had disconnected at her end without saying goodbye.

As I sat alone at our table waiting for her to join me and rousing my courage with a glass of *ouzo*, I took the most solemn vow of silence I could articulate. Nothing short of Trappism was to be my rule for the evening. Apart from speaking to the waiter, I would only open my mouth to ask Suzette questions about herself. Utterly tabooed were my childhood, my work, my books, and any other topic that might bear even the remotest, most accidental connection to me.

Within five minutes of her arrival I had broken my vow, but my moral collapse was not altogether dishonourable. In my eagerness to tell her about myself I had failed to notice during our previous two meetings what was most obvious about Suzette, that self-effacement was her life's mission. Whether because of her size, or for some other reason as yet obscure to me, she was very shy and therefore anxious to make herself socially unobtrusive. Unable (and unwilling – admirable woman) to disguise her tree-like height, she had adopted the compensatory strategy of hiding her personality. She made it her practice to direct all conversation away from herself by continually grilling the other person, a technique that was all too effective in my case.

During our meal I fought manfully to rein in my own talkativeness while trying to extract from Suzette the story of her life. I failed on both counts.

When I had paid the bill and we were dithering on the street outside the restaurant Suzette invited me once again for a drink. This time, however, she added, 'We could listen to some music.'

I accepted, of course. It was a beautiful October night, sharp and invigorating, and as we walked towards her house I suspected that she might at last have signalled an important fact about herself. Listening to music with someone else is a wordless, but companionable activity, and perhaps a music-filled silence was the environment in which she felt most comfortable.

From one of the few comments she let slip during our meal, I inferred that she did occasional work for a firm of publishers famous in those days for its multi-volume *Companion to Music*. My impression was reinforced by the extensive library of composers' biographies and other musicological books that occupied a large bookcase in her sitting room. She also possessed a truly formidable collection of records stored in custom-built stacks standing on either side of her baronial fireplace. (This was in the medieval days of the vinyl LP.) I had been in record shops that carried less stock than she owned.

Suzette made an awesome sight as she reached up to the highest shelf, inaccessible to me without a ladder, in order to extract from its alphabetical place (soul mate!) the record she wanted us to hear. It was a pleasure to see the fastidious care she took when slipping the shimmering disc out of its paper membrane, making contact only with the tip of her middle finger and the edge of her thumb.

'Ravel's *Miroirs*. Do you know them?'

'I've never heard of them.'

She worked her record player as if it were an instrument itself, lowering the needle, closing the lid and adjusting its knobs with all the attentiveness of a virtuoso. When the music began to flow from her speakers, a pair of mighty edifices that stood like tower blocks in her bay window, she sighed and lowered herself onto a sofa where she reclined at full length, her eyes closed. She appeared to be freed, if only for the duration of the record, from her great bulk. She became as airy and insubstantial as the music, so relaxed on her barge-like couch that she might have been levitating.

'That's called *Oiseaux tristes*. Beautiful isn't it?'

'Mmm. Quite beautiful.'

Anna, I lied. For the rest of that evening she played piano music by Debussy, Chopin, Fauré and Mozart, music that was, admittedly, light, melodic and tender, but not really to my taste. The fact is I am a jazz man. My own collection of records, which was also considerable (and alphabetically arranged, naturally), was mostly devoted to jazz music played during the 1950s by such gods as Gerry Mulligan, the young Miles Davis, Charlie Mingus, Chet Baker, Zoot Sims and so on. (What is your taste in music, Anna? I imagine you might have a penchant for the tango. Just a guess.) I lied and would have lied as shamelessly if she had played Schönberg at his most abstract and atonal because I didn't want to spoil the rapturous contentment that Suzette was drawing from the moment. She basked in the music, and I (covertly) basked in the spectacle of her pleasure.

For the first time in the short history of our relationship I was liberated from the need to talk; our laconic exchanges between records seemed sufficient. The music, the port (yes port – the woman could do no wrong), the warmth of her house, the comfort of her furniture and, above all, the wonderfully reassuring sense of tranquility that radiated from Suzette's silent, motionless monumentality, combined to produce one of those paradisiacal interludes I had been trying to describe to Darling.

As midnight approached and I was thinking of going home, I asked Suzette if she played an instrument herself. The piano perhaps.

'Oh, no,' she said in a lazy, unguarded voice, 'I'm a singer. I was trained at the Royal College. Opera and all that.'

To hear the word 'opera' mentioned in her presence was automatically to think of Wagner. Her enormous proportions, her magnificent shoulders and bust, her fine, strong features, her streaming chestnut hair (when released from its bun): here was Brunhilde in the very flesh, massive, powerful and glass-shattering. As I was about to ask the obvious – had she ever performed a Wagnerian role? – instinct put a leash on my tongue and I confined myself to saying, 'I would love to hear you.'

She did not respond, but closed her eyes again, the picture of secrecy.

As I walked home I recalled seeing a wartime cartoon from *Punch* in which a husband had put the words 'PS I have grown a beard' at the bottom of a letter to his wife. The drawing showed the wife reading the letter with a dreamy, wondering look on her face, surrounded by little portraits of her husband embellished with various kinds of beards: Van Dyke, biblical, naval, spade-shaped, goatee, imperial and so on. What manner of singer was Suzette? She seemed to imply that she had not followed up her operatic training, but if not a Wagnerian, as her physique promised, then what was she? Her speaking voice was soft and melodious, but that indicated nothing in itself. Perhaps she specialised in Victorian ballads or, worse still, madrigals. Had she recorded anything? Was she a closet folk singer, or perhaps a lachrymose country diva in rhinestones and cowgirl boots? With one so uninformative anything was possible.

I had been a guest in Suzette's house on two occasions and it was obvious that the time had come for me to invite her to my flat, but the idea filled me with anxiety. I had not entertained people at home since my summer party all those years ago when Natalie had triumphantly routed Breakspear. (You'll be interested to know that the old devil fell from public favour and couldn't find a publisher anywhere for his last novel, which was a limp parody of porn fiction, a common resort, in my experience, of the flagging imagination. But he had the last laugh. He married a very rich woman – ironically, the widow of a printer – and after his wedding day never did another stroke of work, literary or otherwise. I saw him occasionally at The Garrick, where he went out of his way to patronise the poorer members, especially those who wrote for their crust. For some reason he decided that I was acceptable, and we struck up an edgy friendship.)

It was not so much that I feared Suzette's aesthetic judgement on my belongings and taste, though I was nervous on that score; what I truly feared were the adverse conclusions she might draw about me when she confronted the labyrinth of my library. As a result I had been putting off the one thing I longed to do.

Ridiculous! I thought of little other than seeing Suzette again, and yet I could not bring myself to invite her to my home. Why didn't I take her to the cinema, another restaurant, an art gallery? Ah, why indeed?

In those days I was still attempting to impose an alphabetical and categorial structure on my collection of books, but under the twin pressures of space (absence of) and quantity (excess of) the system had broken down. I wanted Suzette to think of me as an organised, methodical person on the grounds that if my possessions were laid out elegantly, she might overlook the gross lack of proportion in my person. However, the fact was that *slew* rather than *collection* was by now the word to apply to my books. My avarice for them (new, old, antiquarian, first editions, paperbacks – I didn't care) was out of control, and it was beyond my ingenuity to shelve, far less systematise the daily rockfall of books that tumbled into my flat. Suzette's drawing room had been a model of refined orderliness, with every object, volume and record neatly placed, whereas my sitting room (a laughable misnomer – where to sit?) was clogged with books, books double-ranked on every shelf of double-banked bookcases, books in boxes, trunks and tea chests, unopened parcels of books, books bound together with string-like bales, books heaped in columns, towers, pyramids and citadels, all tumbling into rubble as if they had been shelled by more books.

In order to survive among this wreckage I had carved out a network of passages that connected the door to my desk and my armchair with its reading lamp and the record player. The windows had long since been blanked out by piles of books standing on their sills. I would plead in my defence that the state of my room (not only lightless, but airless and musty with a faint hint of decaying mouse) was by no means the result of slovenliness, but, on the contrary, an over-zealous desire for order. Nothing less than the perfect system would satisfy me, and in the meanwhile there was no point, to my mind, in settling for half measures. This pandemonium of books had developed gradually, without my noticing it. At the time of its arrival each new book had been given what seemed a rational position, and it was only when I came to inspect my book midden with Suzette's eyes that I realised it was the habitation of a lunatic.

One Saturday morning I found myself standing amidst the ruin of my bibliomaniac's folly, paralysed with inability to rationalise the placing of so much as a single title, when my doorbell rang. I answered it and discovered Suzette on the doorstep, a majestic sight in tightly belted gabardine and Wellingtons.

'I was going to suggest a walk, but it's raining too hard.'

'Raining?' I said, peering out.

'You know, wet stuff falling out of the sky.'

'I'll get my raincoat.'

'Bruno, I want to come in. I'm getting soaked. What are you hiding in here? Bodies? Women?'

I laughed feebly and led her to my galley of a kitchen, but instead of following me she looked into the sitting room, whose door I had left open.

'Is this how you heat your house? Do you shovel them into a furnace?'

'I'm cataloguing them.'

'Interesting method. I don't want to interrupt you. May I watch?'

'If you want to see a nervous breakdown in slow motion.'

I made her a cup of coffee, installed her in my armchair, itself raised on a dais of books, and cleared a space round her by carrying out to the hall a tottering armful of paperback verse (Penguins with beautiful coloured covers published in the days when their pages were sewn not glued). Suzette sat like a queen on her throne.

'Do you ever go slumming and listen to jazz?' I asked her.
'Try me.'

Have you ever known a very large person, Anna? Or rather
have you ever been at close domestic quarters with a
Goliath? I recognised in Suzette many of the stratagems I had
myself adopted in order to detract attention from my width.
She didn't drop her head as some tall women do, or round
her shoulders; on the contrary, her posture was conspicuously upright, for I believe it was not her height so much as
her general immensity that embarrassed her. She had trained
herself to be dainty and economical in her movements, but
her chief defence was a capacity for stillness, which she had
developed on the principle, I suppose, that what does not
move will be least conspicuous. If so, this was a miscalcula-
tion, though, in my eyes at least, a far from calamitous one.
Her stillness was remarkable: she could maintain it for long
periods, but so far from making her invisible it lent her size
a monumental quality, as if she were a building designed to
inspire awe, like a cathedral.

I put a record on my turntable made in 1975 by Art Tatum,
the pianist, with the sublime Ben Webster. Does Webster's
name mean anything to you, Anna? He was a sax player with
the most ravishing tone in jazz. This record, which I must
have listened to a thousand times, opens with a tune called
'Gone with the Wind'. Tatum doodles on the piano in his
light-hearted rococo way for several minutes and then, taking
me by surprise on every one of those thousand playings,
Webster makes his entry blowing a melodic phrase so melancholy and yet so heartening I always wanted to start the
record again just to experience that little shock of feeling.

Suzette listened to the entire side (four longish tracks)
saying not a word, her chin resting on her fist, concentration
expressed in the absolute fixity of her position. Meanwhile,
on my hands and knees, I busied myself with books, trying
to excavate the landslip that had gathered round my desk
and throwing stealthy glances at Suzette, stupendous Suzette.

Suddenly the vocabulary of size seemed misleading and inappropriate: she was indeed 'huge', even 'monolithic', but there was nothing lumpy or blockish about her, nothing shapeless or lumbering. No, Suzette had a glorious figure; she defined the word 'statuesque'. True, its scale was daunting, but that, I realised as I stared at her from my lowly location, had become irrelevant to my perception of her, now engulfed by quite another sensation. I was over-whelmed by the *warmth* she radiated, which I sensed as a literal calorific value, a dreamy, voluptuous glow. She was wearing a tight-fitting sweater that left her superb neck exposed and her marble arms bare from above the elbow; it was made of lambswool dyed a beautiful rose-pink that seemed to draw its blushing colour from heat generated by her body, and her warmth, which I could almost feel on my face, filled me with sensual longing.

You may be surprised to hear, Anna, that this was the first time I had felt a pang of desire for her, one of those truly stabbing pangs that leaves the mouth dry and the blood pounding in the temples. I looked at her sweater, at her creamy skin just flushing a little round her softly pulsing throat; I looked at the twin blades of her collarbones disap-pearing beneath the neckline of her sweater; I looked at the rounded mountains of her breasts, and I knew I wanted to kiss her.

The record came to an end and the arthritic arm of my player creaked as it lifted the needle and returned to its rest.

'His nickname was "The Brute". I don't know why,' I said, turning the record over.

'May I see the cover?' she said and stood up.

You might think that this was my opportunity to make an amorous advance. After all, the signals could not have been more encouraging: Suzette had twice invited me to her house and she had initiated our present meeting by ringing my doorbell. We were standing close to each other, I could smell her perfume, and, furthermore, I had taken her arm, holding her bare skin between elbow and sleeve, in order to guide her through the short, but convoluted maze from armchair to record player. However, I released her electrifying flesh and placed myself so that the machine, now giving life to Webster's inimitable version of 'Night and Day', stood between us.

The truth was I didn't know what to do next. You must remember that apart from Régine, whom I had never kissed below the neckline, I had never been on physically intimate terms with a woman I had not first paid. The likes of Claudine never wasted their precious time on the niceties of pretend seduction; once the money had changed hands, they were naked before you could fold your trousers over the back of a chair. In Claudine's defence I must say that it was one of her many agreeable qualities that while stepping out of her underwear she always made time to say something like, 'Everythin' all right with you today, chéri?' Hardly a lover's sweet nothing, but a human touch nonetheless, and a rarity in her trade.

When Ben Webster finally put down his instrument at the end of Rodgers and Hart's 'Where or When' I observed that it had stopped raining and suggested we took a breath of fresh air. Would Suzette like to have a drink at the pub that stood on the corner of our two adjacent streets? She agreed immediately and we sauntered along the pavement. Mysteriously, a new intimacy seemed to have sprung up between us: we walked in step, she shortening her pace, I lengthening mine, so we harmonised.

Suzette began to talk about Art Tatum and the dizzying complexity of his pianistic technique when a small boy of about Eddie's age cycled past us, lifting his skinny buttocks out of the saddle to attain extra speed. 'Watch it!' he shouted and artfully steered his wheels through a puddle, throwing up a sheet of grimy water. We cursed him, but he looked back and shouted over his shoulder, 'Who do you think you are – Little and Large?'

Do you understand his reference, Anna? The evil tyke was likening us to a comedy duo, one obese and allegedly hilarious, the other emaciated and pathetically bespectacled, who used to perform on television in those days. Their career appears to have come to a merciful halt in recent years. But that was hardly the point. I would have been no less horrified by his jibe if he had likened us to Laurel and Hardy. The real point was that this brat was voicing what everyone else who observed our ludicrous incongruity was presumably thinking. Together, we made a postcard pair fresh from the ribald mind of Donald McGill: a dwarf coupled with a giantess. A baboon courting an elephant. He had hit the target. Bull's-eye!

We stared in silence at the boy's diminishing figure, water soaking into our clothes.

'I'd better get you indoors,' I told her.

'I'll be fine,' she said curtly, and without another glance she parted from me, striding away in the direction of her house.

That Sunday, after an absence of several weeks, I returned to Nick's house for lunch. (Suffering from a terrible hangover, I had telephoned Natalie early in the morning and invited myself.)

I hope by now I've conveyed the importance of Nick's household: it was my second home, my home away from home, concepts that were given extra weight by the fact that 'home' was a word I had never applied either to my own or my parents' address. I usually referred to the place where I lived as 'my flat', and sometimes, a little pompously, as 'the flat', but never as 'my home'.

As I told you, Nick and I were both sent away to school at the pitiable age of seven, and as a result of this premature uprooting, neither of us was able to reroot himself again. In my case, I was cursed with a sense of exile and dispossession that I tried to appease by acquiring and enclosing myself with books; I only felt at home when surrounded by book-shelves, and in due course I turned what passed for my home into a library. I never grew roots again, but lived like a bookworm, forever boring my way deeper and deeper into my paper habitat.

In Nick's case, rootlessness took another form: he developed itchy feet and became compulsively itinerant; he never developed the possessive instinct, preferring instead to be a trader and have things pass through his hands. But then, with typical perversity, he married, became a father, and found that even though he had preserved his nomadic spirit roots were growing round him. When he and Natalie bought their property in remotest Camberwell in order to give their children a bedroom each, she turned their garden into a kind of Edenic orchard, a paradise from which the serpent alone had been expelled, while he filled the house with stock he happened to have at the time – pictures, furniture, lamps, carpets, bric-a-brac from every continent – stuff he probably intended to sell, but never did. Eddie and Nina proceeded to scatter their toys throughout and, *voila!* without planning it the four of them had created a home.

The bosom of my family, to which I had returned every school holiday, had been a steely, chilly organ, more breast-plate than breast, whereas the Camberwell bosom was always warm and welcoming. I cannot say that I confided my troubles, such as they were, in Nick and Natalie – I said nothing about Suzette, for example, during that Sunday – but their company alone was consoling, and my impression (not a delusion, surely?) was that when we got together as a threesome they were able to set aside any difficulties they had between them. We made a convivial trio, and whenever we sat down to lunch with Eddie and Nina we became a hilarious quintet. This was my surrogate home, and I claim the right to sentimentalise it: home, sweet (substitute) home.

Therapy comes from a Greek word that means healing. When I had cockily quitted Dr Darling's professional embrace, I had assumed I was more or less healed, and since then I had decided that any therapeutic mopping up that was still required could be effected by an old-fashioned combination of work, alcohol and, perhaps, the company of a woman – Suzette. However, not many days after my Sunday lunch in Camberwell, I discovered that my methods were not succeeding.

Back from the office one evening and looking forward to pulling the cork out of a Bordeaux that had cost me a king's ransom, I was suddenly immobilised, just as I had been six months before. I was turned into a pillar of salt. I won't bore you with a longer description, except to say that I felt myself cast adrift once more, paralysed by some nameless but irresistible negative force.

I must have remained thus, a statue of myself, for many minutes until it crossed the empty waters of my mind that I should telephone Dr Darling; but then another thought, like the Mariner's albatross, flew out of the gale, and I telephoned Suzette instead. In a trembling voice I explained what had happened and asked her to come round. To my astonishment she refused.

'It's not me you ought to see, it's your parents,' she said, astonishing me still more. 'Go and visit them before it's too late.'

I protested that they were young, healthy and satisfactorily far away. There was plenty of time to visit them, if indeed that was a good idea.

'My father is dead, and my mother is gaga,' she said. 'I never spoke to my father and then when I did have something to say to him he died before I could say it.'

'I have nothing to say to my father.'

'Speak to your mother.'

'She's impossible, and anyway whatever I said to her would go straight back to him, with additions.'

'Is that so bad? In any case, the point of seeing them is not so much to talk as to get the measure of them. Don't give away your childhood to them.'

I did as Suzette suggested and telephoned my mother to propose a visit. It won't surprise you to hear that my journeys to Liverpool had become rare events; indeed, I realised with a pang of something closely related to guilt (what had I been paying Darling for?) that I had not seen my parents for nearly three years. My father never wrote to me, nor I to him, and he made it an absolute rule not to use the telephone for anything but professional purposes. My mother and I would occasionally communicate by phone, but only when necessary and not to *chat*.

'We're always thrilled to see you, as you know,' she replied, arch as ever, 'but do you mind my asking if this visit has a purpose? Are you going to announce' – she hesitated as she hunted for a suitable euphemism – '*news*? Will we have something to celebrate?'

'No, nothing like that. I must go. See you next week.'

What did I want from my visit? Suzette had said, 'Don't give away your childhood to them,' an injunction that had continued to reverberate in my mind, chiming with another piece of wisdom she had offered: 'There is more to childhood than parents.' What, I wondered, had happened to Suzette as a little girl (in itself a remarkable concept) to cause her to hold these bitter insights, but in her mysterious way she had offered nothing further by way of autobiography.

Without admitting it to myself, I wanted to defy my parents and demonstrate that I was no longer cowed by them; I wanted to flex the muscles of independence I thought Darling had given me. Taking my cue from Suzette, I also wanted to refute the idea, so easily implanted by psychotherapy, that the adult is determined by the child and the influence of parents is irremovable. My new sense of my childhood was that it extended beyond the boundaries of my parents' power, and I hoped to reclaim some of that juvenile territory where my parents' flag had never flown.

As you can tell, my ambitions for the visit were far from coherent.

It did not get off to a good start. Traffic caused me to arrive later than I had planned, in other words after my father had returned from his office. I had hoped to enjoy an hour or so with my mother alone in order to acclimatise myself to the alien atmosphere of my parents' house. In the event, my father was standing on the doorstep as I parked in their driveway. Arms akimbo, he stared at my manoeuvring.

It had never been his style to waste time, as he would have put it, with 'hello' or 'how are you?' On this occasion – and remember, we had not seen each other for more than three years – his greeting was, 'Doesn't that firm of yours pay you?'

I knew him well enough to understand the point of his question; he was referring to the quality of my car. I am car-blind. Apart from its colour (racing green) and its make (Rover, but don't ask me what sort), I can tell you nothing about my current car, never mind the one I was driving all those years ago. My father, on the other hand, knew everything about his car as well as every other vehicle on the street, its vintage, capabilities, mechanical weaknesses, design pretensions. Furthermore, he had devised a finely calibrated hierarchy of cars scaled to people's professional rank: thus, the appropriate car for a senior partner was such and such, a junior partner such and such, and so on down to the caretaker. It was all gibberish to me, but he spent many happy hours refining his taxonomy. Whatever it was, my car was of course quite unsuitable in his eyes for my salary and seniority; hence his question, which was also designed to wrong-foot me in our very first exchange.

In the past, I would have put my head down, red-faced and angry, and pushed my way into the house without responding to his goad. However, on this occasion, I said to him, 'Hello. The garden's looking good.'

Actually, I can't remember what I said; it wasn't witty, but the point was I managed to produce something composed and bland, indicating that I had not been disconcerted by his attack. He looked surprised, but our courtesies were cut short by a pounding noise in the hall followed by the appearance, at high speed, of a dog, a long-nosed, long-bodied, short-legged creature wearing the winter coat of a yak, which greeted me as if I were the most welcome visitor in the entire history of doorstep welcomes. It capered round my legs, wagging its hairy tail and showing its teeth in what could only be interpreted as an ingratiating grin.

'Your mother bought it,' my father said curtly, 'and it's a bloody nuisance.'

He pushed open the front door and said, 'Get inside!' an instruction I assumed was directed at the dog rather than me. The creature apparently made the same assumption, because it immediately transferred its ecstatic attentions to my father's legs before rushing into the house.

I found my mother in the sitting room, coolly reading a magazine (*Country Life*, I noticed, with some surprise) and she tilted her head to allow me to kiss her cheek. The dog, meanwhile, had made his precipitate entrance and after chasing round the room a couple of times, seeming to use the walls as a velodrome, it took to shaking a cushion by the scruff of its neck.

'That's Arthur,' she said. 'He's a Dandie Dinmont. A rare breed. I gave him to your father for his birthday. He was sixty last month, in case you didn't realise.'

As she knew full well, I had remembered his birthday, but not its significance. (The date was inscribed in my office diary and my secretary, your redoubtable predecessor, had bought a suitably neutral card.)

My father joined us.

'Drink?'

He brought whiskies for himself and me and gave my mother her customary gin and French. When he sat down, Arthur, the dog, immediately jumped onto his knee and by dint of acrobatic wriggling succeeded in sitting upright beside him in the crook of his arm, its nose pointed upwards, turning itself into an unwitting caricature of my father's rigid posture. Seconds later it had fallen asleep and was snoring rhythmically. I have to tell you, Anna, it was with a twinge of jealousy – yes, jealousy – that I saw my father give this hairy mutt a smug little pat.

I had only been in the house two minutes and already there was an enormous quantity of new information to absorb. First, my father could not hitherto have been classified as a dog lover. He had never been more than distantly tolerant of the numbskull Labrador of my childhood, making it clear that the evil-smelling brute was my mother's responsibility. To all other dogs he was openly hostile, and for their owners he had nothing but contempt, yet here he was nursing a dog on his lap and – I caught him when he thought he was unobserved – tickling its tummy.

It may sound trivial, but consider this: prior to that trifling pat I had never seen my father make a gesture of physical affection to man or beast. Needless to say, he had never touched me, not even to shake my hand in the stilted English style, still less tickle my tummy, but nor had I ever known him to touch my mother. (By the same token, it must be said that I had never seen her attempt to touch him.) His aloofness was not the product of emotional neutrality; for he was a man of turbulent emotions, which were made all the more so for being locked under subterranean pressure. His dependence on my mother was obvious to anyone who saw them together, but he had reserved his most passionate feelings for two other objects: his deceased daughter and his work.

I never did get round to telling you what his profession was, did I? He was, of all things, a loss adjuster. Do you know what that is? His task, which he had converted into a positive calling, was to re-evaluate claims made against insurance companies. He who had lost so much became a professional assessor of other people's losses.

To be frank with you I have only the sketchiest idea of what his function entailed, though I do know it required a strong nerve, an icy heart and an incorruptible soul. It was not a job for a man who courted popularity. As I understood it, my father was respected by his peers and feared by his junior colleagues. He had worked in Liverpool all his life and had risen to be a partner in a company specialising in the insurance of large buildings: office blocks, warehouses, hotels, theatres, libraries, department stores and so on. There were very few of Liverpool's major edifices that he did not seem to know intimately, having acquired a professional familiarity with their passages, cellars and attics, their plumbing and electricity ducts, their manholes and service lifts, and all their forgotten corners where fire liked to hatch itself, where damp and rot could sap their strength, where the wind could find a handhold and rip off slates and hurl chimneys through their roofs. I remember, on one of the very rare occasions when he took me to the cinema – to see John Wayne's *The Alamo*, I believe, in the wonderfully named Palais de Luxe – he looked round the place with satisfaction, saying to me, in his embarrassingly loud voice, 'You couldn't burn this place down if you filled it with petrol. Those fire doors would have stopped the Great Fire of London.'

Later – in fact, around the time that I began my career in publishing – he capitalised on his unusual temperament by starting his own firm of loss adjusters, which prospered in equal measure to his reputation for objectivity (cold-bloodedness). In the world of dark suits, white shirts, regimental ties and polished shoes, the hierarchical world of bosses, assistants and secretaries, and the weekly grind of nine to five with a strict thirty minutes for lunch (no feasting in Soho for him, no sauntering strolls back to the office past the second-hand bookshops in the Charing Cross Road, and no deviations up linoleum-lined stairways) – in that world my father was king. Very few men possessed his discipline and will-power; very few men were so indifferent to pleasure. For what were my father's pleasures but to work, to see other men fail, and to tell my mother about his triumphs and their defeats?

(A charming friend of mine once put me in my place when we were discussing will-power, of which I claimed to have only minimal resources. 'Nonsense,' she said, 'everyone has it, but not everyone chooses to use it.' By drawing this austere distinction, my stern friend was making will-power a moral issue: you use it or not, by choice. She was right: for my father, work was a moral duty to be fulfilled for its own sake. Will-power did not come into it.)

Nothing of significance had changed in my parents' house since my childhood, which usually seemed to be extended by another chapter whenever I returned. (This time it was going to be different.) I'm not talking about furniture, décor and so on, though very little had been changed in that respect either; I'm talking about my parents' routines, the rites and habits dictating their day's timetable from minute to minute, which were all-embracing and, it seemed, immutable.

My parents sat in their familiar chairs, knocking back their customary drinks, conducting conversations that I could recite by heart:

Father: Do we really need more coal?

Mother: I can hear my teeth rattle.

Father: You could smelt iron in here.

And yet, despite the presence of so many time-honoured institutions, something radically new was present, something about my mother, which took me a while to identify. She looked different, more vivacious, perhaps even a pound or two plumper, which was to her advantage. Then I realised:

she wasn't smoking. An entire ten minutes had gone by, ten minutes of prime smoking time, without her lighting up a single cigarette. Furthermore, there were no ashtrays in the room, which lacked its accustomed pungent, acrid smell. I looked at my mother still more intently: she seemed to have emerged from black and white – perhaps I should say sepia – into what used to be called glorious Technicolor. She looked fresh and young. Like a painting, her skin appeared to have had all its grime and varnish removed, allowing her complexion to bloom.

'So,' she said, with more than her usual coquetry, 'how's your love life?'

The next morning I woke early and decided not to linger in my schoolboy bed. Ignoring Arthur's pleading whines, I left my parents sleeping and walked towards the river. Their house, bought by my father when my mother was pregnant with Rosemary, was a mock-Lutyens mini-villa built on the corner of a cul-de-sac which terminated at the gates of the city's riverside park. Soon after the Second World War, at ruinous and utterly worthwhile expense, the Corporation had glorified this park by building a paved promenade along the river's edge: furlong after furlong of smooth, cream-coloured concrete slabs that ran from my parents' suburb nearly as far as the docks in the heart of the city.

As a boy I often came to this park to use my roller skates. Did you roller-skate as a girl? If so, I'm sure you made a delightful spectacle. I wouldn't like to say whether I exhibited charm as boy skater, but once launched on my silver wheels I felt fleet and nimble.

The promenade was approached by a series of downhill paths paved in maroon asphalt, which dropped in serpentine bends down to the river, occasionally looping round big circular flower beds. I became expert at negotiating these Cresta Runs, crouching to speed down their curves and swerves, their straights and slaloms, then rising to burst onto the freedom of the straight and level promenade. Early in the morning when the park was almost deserted, or in the evening as the sun was setting over the cranes and silos on the Birkenhead side of the river, I would sprint along the concrete, head down, arms swinging behind my back, thighs pumping like pistons, until I had sufficient velocity to free-wheel, just maintaining speed with the occasional languid push of my agile ankles. I would throw aerodynamics to the literal winds and sail with my arms held out, my head upright, shouting with the joy of being weightless, lissom, unstoppable. With skates on my feet, I was Mercury, I was Superman, I was a bird, a plane, a train, the wind itself, anything but my usual earth-bound, blundering self. Joy! Joy! This was the childhood that belonged to me.

As I sped beside the river, my thrilling wheels would roll out a slow, rhythmic strumming on the tarmac joins between the concrete slabs. At the same time a different kind of rhythm was created by the railings that protected the public from the water flowing below. Strung between concrete stanchions, they formed an endlessly repeated succession that dwindled into invisibility whether one's eye followed their line upstream or downstream. At intervals they were interrupted by locked gates, blocking entrance to flights of stone steps leading to the river, their treads made slimy with an emerald weed that floated in strands like women's hair when the tide rose. This was water that no one would want to swim in, water that would persuade even suicides to think again when teetering over its foul-smelling depths, water that would poison as soon as drown you.

I loved the river. I loved it for being so huge and indifferent, for being an industrial highway not a pastoral dribble out of *Wind in the Willows*. I loved it for carrying the effluent and outpourings, the sewage and secretions of a great city that once ruled the seven seas. It was a powerful, uninviting river, and its traffic was strictly workmanlike and commercial:

dredgers, strings of lighters carrying sand or gravel, police launches, freighters, tankers and small cargo ships. You never saw a yacht or a rowing boat on its yellow waters. You never saw a cormorant diving into its oily depths, because chemicals and filth had long ago choked the life out of its fish. Only the rankest gulls fed off the detritus left on its muddy shore when the tide dropped. I loved those oozy, silt beaches which stank on warm days and showed the bones of rusting bikes. I loved the pungent breezes, said to be rich in salubrious ozone, that blew off its greasy waves. I loved it for being neither river nor sea, a leviathan that thrived on fresh and salt, that flowed one way then the other as it chose, a monster that was forever changing itself.

Too portly for roller skates, though not too old to long for their well-oiled liberation, I walked that morning along the promenade in the direction of the Garston docks. The tide was coming in, slapping water against the steps and throwing the occasional shower of spray and spume onto the promenade. The opposite bank was hidden in a smoggy mist and yet the sun had scraped the scum off the water in midstream, leaving a glittering, silvery graze. A dredger pushed upriver, making speed on the luxury of the tide. My father, walking briskly out of the mist towards me and accompanied by a long-bodied hairy dog pulling stupidly at its lead, turned out to be a stranger at close quarters, and to prove it he wished me good morning.

On my way home I found myself brooding over my mother's teasing question concerning what she was pleased to call my 'love life'. All trace of the dark forces (my father, surely) that had caused my mercifully short-lived breakdown, had been blown away for the time being by the river's rancid but curiously invigorating breeze. Was 'love' the word that now qualified my life? I desired Suzette, thought about her constantly and was gripped by an urgent need to be with her, but did that amount to love? Her recent refusal to see me now filled me with intense worry – another sign of love? Just as I had reached the point of feeling my life would be empty without the prospect of meeting her again, had she come to the contrary conclusion about her life? These anxieties became so acute that I broke my journey on the M1 at a service station (a preview of hell) to telephone her, but was forced to leave a strangulated message on her answer machine, in which I managed to invite her to dinner at my house yet failed, as I realised five minutes later with a sickening pang and a near-fatal lurch into the central barrier, to nominate the day. However, my torture was brought to an end when I got home, for I found a message from succinct Suzette on my machine. Even its appalling reproduction – the lowest fidelity – could not destroy the warm melody of her voice, which told me, 'Yes! Saturday? At 7.00?'

That evening I roasted a guinea-fowl and opened a choice bottle of Barolo I had been hoarding for a celebratory event. As I carved, I tried to give her an account of my return to the parental fortress.

Interrupting myself, I asked her, 'Leg or breast, Suzette? Or a bit of both? Do you have a preference?'

It was hardly a provocative question, but to my amazement she hung her head and shook it slowly from side to side, as if the bird and the fate I was inflicting on its poor carcass had overwhelmed her with melancholy.

'My name,' she said at last, 'is not Suzette. My name is Atalanta.'

I did not respond, not knowing how to do so.

'My father loved Swinburne's poetry. No one reads Swinburne these days, but he could recite it by the yard, especially *Atalanta in Calydon*. Do you know the story of Atalanta?'

It was my turn to shake my head.

'It's quite gruesome. My father was a classics scholar – an amateur scholar. He took my mother to Greece every summer and one year they went to Calydon, which I believe is near the place where Byron died. I've never been there. When they got home my mother discovered she was pregnant. With me.'

'"When the hounds of spring are on winter's traces,"' I began, but she looked at me forbiddingly and I stopped. 'That's all I know, except something about "the lisp of leaves" and "the ripple of rain".'

'I loved my father,' she said, 'but he was not an imaginative man. He thought he was bestowing a magical gift on me by naming his only daughter after a Greek heroine. And I might have been proud of being Atalanta if I hadn't grown . . . so big.'

She made a profoundly rueful gesture to indicate her magnitude.

'He couldn't have known that his daughter would become Miss Gargantua. His vision of Atalanta was a heroine who was a great hunter and athlete, but I was a schoolgirl with large feet and I thought my name would draw attention to my size. I loathed having a name that mocked me, so when I changed schools I began to call myself Suzette, which sounded as if it belonged to a smaller person. My father thought Suzette was a school nickname and I told my friends, the few who came home, that Atalanta was a family nickname.'

I didn't even smile at her admission – I knew too much about such futile stratagems – but within I was seething with excitement. At last the question of her immensity was out in the open: she had reciprocated my confidences about my bullish growth with an acknowledgement of her own adolescent ordeals. Nothing is more intoxicating than the mutual exchange of vulnerablity.

'What would you like me to call you?'

'I've come to hate Suzette; she's the name of my

cowardice, if you see what I mean. I've learnt not to be ashamed of my height, but I don't have the courage to rename myself again. And anyway Suzette is my professional name.'

She abruptly changed the subject, and never answered my question, leaving me with the dilemma, Suzette or Atalanta, neither of which seemed to be acceptable to its owner.

I walked my now unnameable friend home and then hurried back to my library where I looked up the legend of Atalanta in a schoolboy copy of Ovid's *Metamorphoses* (the Penguin translation; I have no gift for languages, dead or alive). I discovered that her version of the original Atalanta was prejudiced, to say the least.

It turns out that there are several stories connected with Atalanta, all containing some bloodthirsty element, though what 'my' Atalanta, if I can call her that, omitted to mention is that they all turn on the fact of her good looks. The title of the Swinburne poem refers to a boar hunt in which Atalanta ('Arcadian Atalanta, snowy-souled, fair as the snow and footed as the wind') distinguishes herself by firing the first arrow to hit the target after innumerable men have failed, including Jason and Theseus. By then the hero of the story, Meleager, has fallen in love with the huntress on sight. According to Ovid, she has features which in a boy would be called girlish, but in a girl are like a boy's; quite the modern woman, and no mention of Amazonian size. Atalanta was a beauty, not a giant. The hunt is a gory affair, but when the boar is finally slain Meleager presents its hide, head and tusks to Atalanta as a trophy and a reward for her skill. His gift is resented by the men, causing a terrible quarrel during which Meleager murders his two uncles and is shortly afterwards put to death himself by his mother. Atalanta is a *femme fatale* in the most literal sense.

Nor does the bloodshed end there. In a separate story that

my Atalanta had not mentioned the virginal heroine agrees to submit to marriage on condition that her would-be husband first beats her in a running race. The stakes are high, for her other condition is that she kills the suitors who are defeated. However, she is so beautiful, especially when stripped for her deadly races, that young men queue up to risk their lives. Ovid provides a rapturous description of the lovely girl as she darts away on winged feet; he sighs over her flying hair, her ivory shoulders, her flushed skin, her gorgeous figure exposed by the wind as she runs. She is beaten at last, but only because the winner, Hippomenes, engages the help of Venus, who distracts the dazzling athlete during the race by placing three golden apples in her path, which she pauses to pick up.

I could see that Atalanta was not an ideal name to impose on a self-conscious, shrinking violet sort of girl, but her father, a loving if wrong-headed man by his daughter's account, had presumably intended his choice of name as a compliment. Yet the more I thought about it, the less complimentary it appeared. Had he considered the consequence of bestowing on his baby the name of a heroine famous for her beauty, always a potentially cruel gift? And had her father taken into account the original Atalanta's singular approach to courtship? If so, was his choice the product of a perverse sense of humour? Or was he unconsciously declaring his fatherly possessiveness by pinning the name of a man-killer to his gal to warn off any rivals for her affection? Or had I been in therapy too long?

When next I saw Suzette (Atalanta?) I asked if she knew the stories attached to her distinguished name.

'Of course I know them,' she said irritably. 'You've been busy with your books, I suppose. Whose version did you look up?'

'Just Ovid's. In translation, I'm sorry to say. My Latin . . .'

She interrupted me: 'It's too late for me to take pride in it. I'm sorry I told you.'

However, she did not forbid me to use her true name and though as yet I didn't dare use it to her face, I had begun to whisper it to myself.

Atalanta, Atalanta, fair as the snow.

We had been to the cinema (the Baker Street Classic – alas, now defunct – to see Fellini's incomparable *8½*) and, in the tradition of our previous meetings, I had suggested a drink, but in my flat this time, and she had agreed with no sign of reluctance.

By way of a preamble to what follows I should tell you that, despite my ardent longings, Suzette/Atalanta and I had so far exchanged nothing more intimate than the social kiss I used to bestow on her cheek when greeting and leaving her, a practice we had soon abandoned because of the awkwardness created by our respective heights. I was obliged to stand on tiptoe, my aspirant lips reaching upwards, and she would lower her head like a giraffe preparing to drink. We made a ridiculous picture (unseen by anyone else) and as often as not achieved nothing fonder than knocks and air shots.

After discussing Fellini (admiringly in my case, disparagingly in hers), we (I) fell to talking about the work of Yoshitoshi, the Japanese print maker. His name is comical to our ears, though his life was anything but funny, poor man; I've read that at one point his mistress volunteered to work in a brothel to support him. I offered to show Atalanta a print I'd recently bought, a truly beautiful thing showing a white-faced women wearing a lilac hat that bloomed above her head like a huge, jungle flower.

As was my practice with new acquisitions, I had put the print on display in my bedroom so I could study (gloat over) it for a week or two before dispatching it to a place among the rest of my pictures where it could fight for itself, as it were. I left the sitting room to fetch it, but as I walked along the corridor I realized Suzette was behind me; she must have misunderstood and thought I had invited her to look at the print *in situ*. I turned the corner and she continued to follow as I approached the door of my bedroom, which was ajar. Without speaking, we entered the room.

The print hung on the wall immediately opposite the foot of my bed. In order to see it properly at a distance, Atalanta retreated a step or two into the space beside my bed, unwittingly choosing the side on which I generally slept. Keeping parallel with her, I backed into the space on the other side of the bed. We stared at the woman in her botanical hat, she smiled back at us, and though it was for me to say something by way of explication, I remained silent. I noticed that Atalanta's eyes had dropped from the picture to the sheepskin rug that cosseted my bare feet at nights.

A slight dizziness overcame me, and in order to steady myself I put my hand on the bedspread and she, mimicking my movement, did likewise on her side. Wordlessly and in tandem we took a corner each, drew back the bedspread a little and folded it down, thus laying bare the pillows, two on either side, in plain white pillowcases. Their virginal whiteness and bosomy plumpness made our stripping seem a shocking act of exposure, and we stared at them, appalled. In fact, we might well have covered them again, if at that moment the telephone had not rung.

Instinct pulled me towards the door, and then, recovering my self-awareness, I hesitated and stopped. However, I must have turned my back just long enough for Atalanta to slip into the bed, for when I faced it once again I was astounded to see that her head was lying on the pillow. She reposed like an effigy, eyes closed, chin raised, her shapely mass elevating the bedclothes. I kicked off my shoes, pulled back the bedding and climbed in beside her, still wearing my jacket, tie and trousers. Copying her, I lay on my back, chin pointed at the ceiling. I slid my arms down by my sides, and discovered her right hand lying palm upwards. I placed my left hand on it, palm down and missionary style. It was, I recall, deliciously warm. And that, dear, patient Anna, is how we passed the rest of the evening. We lay beside each other, fully clothed and, here I can only speak for myself, perfectly content.

Around two or three in the morning I was woken by her getting out of bed.

'Don't move,' she said. 'I'm going home.'

She leaned over the bed and placed a kiss on my forehead.

I would not hear of her returning alone, so we took to the street together. I put my arm round her waist, she put hers round my shoulders, and though we had spent the last six hours in bed together this position, not achieved without adroit manoeuvring, brought us physically closer than we had ever been. It was too late for taunting boys and as befitted the romance of the occasion we were observed by a benevolent, full-bellied moon. (Yet I couldn't help noticing the gross disparity between our moon-shadows, hers so elongated, mine blockish.)

From that evening onwards I never called her anything but Atalanta.

Later in the same week my happiness was made complete when Nick rang to suggest that I took him to lunch.

'By all means,' I said. 'Where would you like to go?'

'The Gay Hussar, where else? We're celebrating.'

The Gay Hussar (Hungarian restaurant in Greek Street – I'm sure I've taken you there, Anna) was a great favourite with us, largely on account of its matchless *quenelles* of pike, but in the past we had rationed our visits to special occasions.

'What are we celebrating?'

'You'll find out. It'll be worth the expense, that's all I'm saying.'

He rang off.

Most unusually, Nick was at the restaurant before me. He

had already ordered champagne, and was looking exceedingly pleased with himself. As soon as I saw the box file on the table beside him I knew the cause of our celebration: Nick had at last delivered his book.

For years I had been urging him to write a study of the carpets and rugs he imported from Pakistan, Afghanistan and Iran. Nothing lengthy was required, just an introduction to the subject and a series of extended captions to accompany the excellent photographs he had taken, mostly for insurance purposes, of the most beautiful items that had passed through his hands.

The waitress filled my glass and I toasted Nick.

'You've had this typed professionally,' I said as I opened his box, because inside lay an immaculate typescript, in two copies.

He nodded complacently.

'She's done a good job, hasn't she?'

I flicked through the text, which appeared to fulfil every expectation.

Turning back to the beginning, I was amused to see that his typist had conscientiously added the full complement of prelim pages: half-title, title, copyright and so forth. I was looking for the dedication, always an entertaining element. There is a monograph to be written about dedications, though you'll be relieved to know that I'm not going to do it here. They always hold a particular interest for me because they are sacred territory on which the editor's blue pencil may never trespass, and, as you know, they come in many forms, from the florid to the terse. The most abrupt formulation I have published was devised by an uxorious, but austere socialist of a bygone age, whose dedication consisted of no more than his beloved wife's initial – 'M'. Nick's dedication to Natalie was scarcely more forthcoming: it consisted of the bald phrase: 'To N., with love'.

'You needn't be so tight-lipped with your dedication. You can be as extravagant as you like. I'm sure Natalie will be thrilled.' I held up my glass to him again. 'Congratulations on the book. I can't wait to read it properly.'

'Natalie?' he said, with a crafty look on his face.

I'd put his unusual gaiety down to author's self-satisfaction, natural on such occasions, but now the true explanation was not hard to guess.

'Who is N.?' I asked him miserably.

'Her name is Nancy,' he said with disgusting pride and a smile that incriminated him by itself.

'I take it Natalie has no idea.'

He shrugged ruefully.

'And you don't think she's going to see through this infantile code?'

He leant forward, eager to embrace me in his happiness.

'The book is as much Nancy's as mine. I owe it to her.'

'You're pulling a cheap trick and it'll bring nothing but unhappiness. It's not too late to stop it.'

I was referring to the dedication page, but Nick interpreted my words another way.

'I could no more stop seeing her than stop breathing.'

Anna, I won't bore you with the details of his affair, which he furnished in abundance. The fact is that most of us lead lives whose plots are so banal that no novelist with a shred of imagination would use them, and such was the case with Nick. I don't have to tell you that Nancy was his junior by more than a decade (why couldn't he have defied cliché and had an affair with a woman *twice* his age?). The minx was single and unattached, though her tender soul was still bruised from cruelties inflicted by a brutish lover of the previous year, whom Nick moralistically vilified. She called herself a travel journalist and they had met in the bar of a hotel in St Petersburg or somewhere (it may have been St Asaph or Samarkand, for all I remember or care). Her hair was thick, long and auburn, the exact shade, in Nick's besotted eyes, of a certain *marron* fondant they had eaten together (one pot, two spoons). At first they had behaved honourably: he had fought his desire, she had felt sisterly loyalty to the wife she'd never met, but in the end they had been overpowered . . . They couldn't help themselves. And so on, and so on. You can make this tripe up for yourself. What did it matter whether she was tall or short, fat or thin, or whether she had three breasts? The fact was Nick had completely surrendered himself to her.

'You can't argue with love, can you?' he insisted fervently.

I was too depressed to answer. Nor could I enjoy my lunch. (My borsch might have been a bowl of blood for all the pleasure it gave me.)

Now that the moonstruck couple were back in London they were seeing each other whenever they could, either at his warehouse or her flat, a love nest somewhere in sordid Fulham. No wife could have been easier to deceive than Natalie, and no husband had more opportunities for infidelity than Nick, since he was by nature secretive and Natalie was used to his erratic hours and unexplained movements.

'For your own sake, as well as everyone else's, don't go on with this,' I begged him.

'The trouble with you, Bruno, is that you've never fucked your brains out with someone you adore.'

We left the restaurant and walked in silence down Greek Street. At that time striptease was undergoing a revival in Soho, and the so-called clubs deployed touts in their door-ways. Walking along Brewer Street and still silent, we were accosted by a striking young woman, who by an uncanny coincidence boasted a fine head of auburn hair. She had spotted what she took to be a pair of likely customers and pressed us to enter her club, even taking Nick by the arm. I shook my head and quickened my respectable pace, but Nick paused for a moment to give her a conspiratorial glance, a glance that sparkled with sensual complacency. (How do I know, my literal-minded Anna? Because I turned round and caught that scintillating signal as he flashed it to the woman, or rather to her plump bust.)

When he'd caught up with me, he said, 'I suppose you think it's just sex, with Nancy I mean.'

'I'm trying not to judge, but I can't bear the idea of you and Natalie separating. You know how I feel about Eddie. What would become of him – have you thought of that?'

'Don't be so naive,' he said. 'I'm just having an affair. It has nothing to do with my family. You don't think she's the first, do you?'

I returned to my office as despondent as I had been elated when I set out that morning to meet Nick.

I cursed him. Why had he told me? His puerile dedication, which he knew I would see and interpret before anyone else, was surely a signal that his relationship with Nancy, the torrid typist, was more than a fling, as he had insisted. But what could I do? A childish urge told me to hurl his book in the wastepaper basket and refuse to publish it, but how would I explain this to Natalie, who, being a generous woman, was probably proud of his long-awaited achievement? I had no choice but to cling to the hope that the affair would prove to be an infatuation and burn itself out before it destroyed Nick's marriage. Yet even as I conceived this hope I recognised its selfishness: I wanted Nick's marriage to prevail, not for Natalie's sake, not for the family's sake, nor even for Nick's, but for mine. As long as the Camberwell home was intact, my access to Eddie would remain assured and unimpeded. If Nick and Natalie separated, there was no predicting what rights I would be given or refused.

A month earlier I might have responded to Nick's shocking revelation by going back to my flat and rendering myself insensible with red wine. As it was, I sought the consolation of Atalanta's bed. Yes, Anna, her bed. For Nick had been wrong about my brains; I had indeed fucked them out with someone I adored, and very recently.

After several more dance-like approaches and retreats, with which I won't test your patience, Atalanta and I finally dispelled our shyness one evening at her house and lay naked in each other's arms.

Surrounded by a surf of sheets, Atalanta's body rose from her vast (sea)bed like an island, a beautiful, undiscovered tropical paradise, which I set myself to explore and colonise. I was Captain Cook to her Tahiti: I mapped her coasts, scaled her mountains, took refuge in her forest, pursued her river to its source. I frolicked over her geography like a happy castaway, and she, a dormant volcano, lay passively, allowing me to trek across the great, lush, rounded amplitude of her body. For once in my life, perhaps for the first time, I lost awareness of my own dumpy shape and gambolled across her like a faun, skipping here and there, lying down to rest wherever the fancy took me; I was a merry flea, light-footed, light-fingered, light-headed, light-hearted; I was the happiest maroon, for I loved every inch of my Treasure Island and never wanted to be rescued.

Later, the volcano stirred and after many ecstatic tremors finally erupted with such explosive force that when I had recovered my own senses I was amazed to see that the house was still standing and that I still had all my arms and legs. Instead of crying, I was overtaken with joy and a smile irradiated my face that did not fade until my lunch with Nick. To recover, I sprawled on the bed as if it were a raft, and as I dozed in a luscious half-way stage between waking bliss and blissful sleep, I heard Atalanta's voice. She was singing to me. At the time I didn't recognise it, clod that I am, but I know now that she sang Brahms's 'Cradle Song'. She sat on the bed beside me and crooned while stroking my hair, and her voice – this was the first time I had heard her sing – was light and airy and tender. It was a small, sweet voice, the very opposite of what you would expect to emerge from such a mighty instrument, but there she was, naked and majestic, trilling above my head like a lark.

Notebook 5

And now, Anna, I'm going to ask you to climb inside my bathysphere and descend with me into some very cold and lightless waters.

There are no horrors here, just ordinary failures, ordinary moments (never to be redeemed) of cowardice, ordinary miseries. I've always thought that the only point of Christianity, in which I zealously disbelieve, is that it promises remission of sins. Forgive us our trespasses. Forgive me; someone forgive me.

What is this thing called love?
This crazy thing called love.
Just who can solve its mystery?
Why should it make a fool of me?
I saw you there one wonderful day.
You took my heart and threw it away.

Not one of Cole Porter's best, perhaps, but surely he understood the ways of the heart better than most songwriters. (Do you admire the master, Anna? I hope so.) In any event, you can rely on Tin Pan Alley to ask the fundamental questions.

What did I feel for Atalanta? Was it love, and if so, what indeed was this thing called love? When I said I loved and was in love with Atalanta, as I frequently did (though only to myself), what did I mean by it? I was hardly the first to be baffled by these questions, and everyone has to solve them for himself, but at the undignified age of thirty-nine, with next to no experience of my own to draw on, I was perhaps unusually disadvantaged. Despite having read scores of novels concerned with the joys and agonies of love, and, furthermore, despite having advised scores of authors on how to make their fictional love affairs more credible, I suddenly discovered that naming, to say nothing of analysing, my own feelings was very difficult. After all, the exercise involves trying to give a rational account in coherent language to something that is irrational, or at any rate non-rational, and pre-verbal.

I can say this much, that what I felt for Atalanta was not what I had felt for Régine, the only precedent I had. My feelings for the Dutch queen had been determined by the prospect of losing her, and then by her loss itself. We did not have a love affair, for there was no time for love to develop; ours had been a grief-affair, grief anticipated, and grief endured.

(What became of Régine, you must be wondering. For many years I did the same and then, one fine day, I saw her in Knightsbridge. An unmistakeable figure – that neck had lost none of its swanlike length – she was strolling beside the windows of Harvey Nichols. Risking my life, I ran across the road, but by the time I reached the opposite pavement she had vanished, and I've never seen her again.)

I can also say that falling in love with Atalanta – if that is what had happened to me – produced all the symptoms of extreme happiness. I know that the concept of happiness is nearly as problematic as that of love, but I am talking about effects, not their baffling essence. Alone at home I found myself grinning and rubbing my hands; I also whistled, sang little snatches of song and broke into lumbering jigs. In the office, as you will recall (perhaps with a shudder), I was obnoxiously affable. I wore iridescent ties and drew your attention to the sun when it shone and the birds when they sang in our square. Out of sheer high spirits I took on books that should never have been published, dished out wildly extravagant advances that would never be earned, and – did

I ever tell you this? – even invited our office manager to lunch, an unprecedented gesture, which she huffily refused. In short, I made it obvious to everyone around me that, in the pungent words of our office boy, I was 'getting my leg over'. I heard him venture this observation to our receptionist, a young woman over whom, according to office gossip, he was eager to get his own leg. Her response, an indifferent 'So what?', could not have encouraged him.

I believe this lad enjoyed a certain fame in the office for his odiously accurate impressions of my walk. Am I right? In an effort to disguise my curious dimensions I had developed what I hoped was a mode of walking that was so svelte it would render me invisible. I don't have to tell you that the result, a kind of mincing scurry on the balls of my feet, was the exact opposite of what was intended. I made myself comically conspicuous, but the habit stuck and as I've grown older I've added speed to this singular gait in a further effort to obliterate myself. It horrified me to imagine the mirth our satirical office boy would raise if he ever saw my style of walking with Atalanta: the ape and his trainer.

Have you solved the mystery of love, Anna? I expect so; you seem to be a most wise and perceptive woman. Myself, I'm not even sure what mystery Porter's referring to; I suppose it's the puzzle of 'falling' for this person, rather than that; the arbitrary way these feelings come and go. Couldn't live without you yesterday. Can't stand the sight of you today. Who will it be tomorrow? Love squeezes the juice in your eyes, and you're ready to cut your heart out for someone you hardly know; then the juice dries up and suddenly you see his ass's ears. That's how love makes a fool of you. But Atalanta never saw the Bottom in me. It wasn't my heart that was thrown away.

In one respect at least our love was not at all mysterious, for in our leviathan fashion Atalanta and I became energetic love-makers. (The terminology of sex is problematic, isn't it? After all, you don't have to be in love to make love, though

151

by making love even couples who are indifferent to each other acquire the title of lovers.) We would often spend whole weekends aboard the great liner of her bed, where we behaved like guzzling cruise-goers and treated ourselves to every luxury in the way of food, drink and music. I recall we developed a particular taste for French sardines, of all things, which we consumed both hot and cold, and during the week I spent many a contented lunchtime searching the delicatessens of Soho, now, alas, all closed, for their distinctive yellow tins, bearing them back to our gourmet's bed with all the pride of a hunter dragging home a kill.

I don't want to force unwanted intimacies on you, Anna, but indulge me for a line or two.

My sight had been worsened by the intensive and continual reading that my job required of me, and as a result my spectacles in those days (before the ubiquitous use of contact lenses) were equipped with thick and powerful lenses. Without them the visible world was dissolved in a blur, and I was in effect blind. However, the spectacle of a lover wearing his spectacles was not, I assumed, an erotic one, so I took mine off in bed, or at any rate I did for sexual purposes, though I had to put them on again in order to open sardine tins, pop champagne corks and so forth. As a result I was condemned to making love to something I could barely see beyond the fact that it was pink and undulating (albeit wonderfully so). Atalanta was warm and soft to touch with many varieties of texture; she was deliciously perfumed to smell, again with several varieties of fragrance; but she remained formless and foggy to the eye. I have never discussed this problem with other short-sighted people, but I surely cannot have been alone in confronting it.

One afternoon, frustrated by addressing my passion to a mountain forever concealed by mist, I asked her, 'May I put on my glasses.'

'I wish you would,' she replied in her devastatingly blunt way.

I could scarcely believe what was suddenly disclosed to me. I had the same revelatory experience, though the analogy is quite inadequate, as swimmers when they first put their heads under water wearing a mask and snorkel. Even with the assistance of my spectacles my focal length was very short, and in order to examine my newly found wonders I was obliged to crouch over Atalanta, my nose almost touching her skin, as I rolled my eyes up and down the lovely details of her body. For the first time – I won't continue beyond this single example, but try to imagine the miracle that had been granted me – I saw what a truly extraordinary and beautiful thing a nipple is. You are a woman, Anna, and no doubt take nipples for granted, but consider them for a moment. Am I not right? Are they not phenomenal little organs, so robustly functional (Natalie feeding Eddie), and yet so productive of pleasure (if Atalanta was to be believed). To continue with the subaquatic trope, I was reminded of a sea anemone, a marvellously subtle and sensitive creature whose strawberry dimples palpitated with the to and fro of the current, or in this case my caresses, my playful pinches, the titillations of my tongue-tip, even the draught of my breath as I blew on the tiny, blond hairs – no, 'hair' is too coarse to describe these filaments of dandelion down – that were gathered round its rosy root. And, as if this was not enough, over there to the west, on the horizon of my field of vision, was another one of these exquisite creatures, throbbing in sympathy with its twin at my lips.

Extraordinary though it must sound to you, I spent many rapturous hours simply examining and palpating the great expanse of Atalanta's body, for so much of it was new to me – visually new, that is: the endearing crease that forms where arm and ribcage meet, the miniature maze of the navel, the sudden forestation after the belly's smooth tundra, the . . . Well, enough, enough. You get the point, I'm sure.

When not with Atalanta, I was out in the world. The company was then going through its most successful phase, and our building was crammed with staff. The editorial department alone had been inflated to a cadre of a dozen, not all of whom had functions I could have confidently described. Heady, dangerous times. My days were filled with meetings, lunches, conferences, telephone marathons, and my evenings saw me attending cocktail parties, dinner parties, book launches, receptions, awards ceremonies and premieres. I was frequently interviewed on the radio, acquiring a reputation as a literary pundit, though I refused all invitations to appear on television. My weekends could have been similarly hectic and sociable, if I had not reserved them for Atalanta and our bedroom adventures. I became something of a public figure, and was lampooned in *Private Eye*, an accolade of a sort. They referred to me as 'The Bruiser'.

By contrast, Atalanta seemed to live in virtual seclusion, sequestered in her flat, communicating with no one apart from me. She would often pass whole days doing nothing apart from listening to music; her house was never silent and she (we) would often fall asleep without turning off the radio (tuned of course to Radio 3). She had installed speakers in every room, allowing her to subsist in a womb (tomb?) of music, but her favourite spot was the barge-like sofa in her sitting room, where she lay with a glass and cigarettes at her side, her whole corporeal being metamorphosed into an ear. While I understood the joys of escapism more than most I was appalled by the hours she spent in this way, hovering on her magic carpet, travelling nowhere.

How, then, did my inamorata earn her daily bread? How could she afford the luxury of her musical vacations? For that matter, how could she afford the music itself, for though a formidable collector she did not stoop to buying cheap labels or second-hand records? Occasionally she did go out, and I assumed she visited the offices of *The Companion to Music* to collect her freelance assignments, but editorial work of this kind, as I knew very well, was not remunerative enough to support her languorous style of life. Perhaps she had what is decorously called 'private means'; perhaps she pursued a secret occupation, something so patriotic, shameful or criminal that she couldn't reveal it even to those most intimate with her. It didn't seem likely, but I was too busy with my own professional life and too content with the many pleasures that her strange isolation possessed for me to bring up the subject of her income and quiz her. In any event, the mystery was solved soon enough.

One of the few unsatisfactory aspects of my relationship with Atalanta was her inability to share my enthusiasm for jazz. Atalanta was not so churlish as to dismiss the whole genre, but I had the impression that my most beloved tracks left her, if not cold, decidedly tepid. (Rather late in the day I had just discovered the recordings Chet Baker made with the Gerry Mulligan Quartet for Pacific Jazz in the early 1950s.) She did, however, derive a disproportionate amount of impudent amusement from observing my pleasure. I relished the free-wheeling, uninhibited musicianship that makes jazz unique, and I would readily abandon myself, eyes blissfully closed, to an orgy of finger-clicking, toe-tapping and head-nodding. I was a picture of carefree surrender, but the moment the record came to an end I reverted to my usual disciplines. I could not bear to leave a disc idling on the turntable and was compelled to return it immediately to its sleeve and to return the sleeve to its proper alphabetical place on the shelf. (Barely suppressed laughter from Mademoiselle.)

I tried to explain my feelings about jazz to Atalanta one day, and as an example of a certain kind of rough-house spontaneity I made her listen to a live recording of 'Them Red Beans and Rice' by Roland Kirk, a lunatic player whose speciality was to blow three instruments at once. When it was finished I could see that she was unmoved.

'What I love about that piece,' I told her, 'is that there's a point somewhere towards the end when I get the feeling that time's been suspended and the music could go on forever. Even though I know perfectly well the track will only last seven minutes, I'm still transported to a kind of time-free dimension. Am I making sense?'

'For me,' said Atalanta, 'music does the opposite. It doesn't stop time, it fills it up. That's why I like operas – they last so long.'

And then, making one of those pronouncements that caught me by surprise, she sighed and said, 'The truth is my musical life is cut up into thirty-second bits.'

'What do you mean?'

'Haven't you ever noticed? Commercial breaks on TV are thirty seconds long.'

'You've lost me.'

'I'm a jingle singer. I sing jingles for a living.'

'Jingles? You mean for washing powder and all that?'

'Exactly. As it happens, I make quite a good living out of those idiotic little songs. I'm much in demand because, believe it or not, I sing them with passion and commitment, which is a rare quality. Most singers despise the work because they feel humiliated that they're not doing something more artistic. But I've learnt to take pride in it. No one would cast me in opera despite my training. You can guess why. My voice is too small for my body. I was told I looked laughable.'

She spoke defiantly, but a trace of unalleviated pain was audible in her voice.

'Ludicrous was the word one producer used. To my face, he said I would make a *ludicrous* Mimi.'

'Why can't you work as a studio singer?' I blurted, and wished I hadn't.

'That's the obvious question. And the answer's obvious too. It's childish really, but I don't want to belong to a world that doesn't want me. Nobody said anything about my' – she made a helpless gesture indicating her immensity – 'when I auditioned for work in advertising. They just listened to my voice, gave me the job and that was that. I've never been out of work since. We're all freaks in one way or another. I'm one of the lucky ones. I don't take drugs and I have no ambitions.'

We sat without talking any more while Gerry Mulligan played 'Makin' Whoopee'.

Not long after Christmas (an event Atalanta and I celebrated on a Lucullian scale, never leaving the mother-ship of her bed) my mother made one of her exceedingly rare telephone calls to the office.

'Your father will be ringing you, probably this evening, to tell you that I've left him,' she said, her voice huskier than ever. 'But it's not true. Nor is it true that I'm having an affair with another, er, chap, though he insists on believing it, despite all my reassurances to the contrary.'

She paused, evidently expecting me to say something in my turn, but I was incapable of speech. In any case, what could I say? I had no idea what she was talking about.

Sounding disappointed by my silence, she continued. 'I'm joining a retreat.'

'You mean, you're becoming a nun?' I said, stupefied.

'Don't be absurd. I'm simply joining a community of women.'

'You're becoming a lesbian.'

'It's not like you to be so crass. I'm joining a community of women who devote themselves to seeking peacefulness in their lives.'

'Forgive me. You've taken me by surprise. I'm trying to gather my wits. Do you pray?'

'Praying is not discouraged. I shan't be praying myself, since, as you know, I don't recognise a god I might pray to.'

'So this isn't a Christian retreat?'

'No. It's simply a place where one can be quiet. Where I won't be disturbed.'

'By my father?'

'By your father, by you, by anyone.'

What disturbance, I wondered, had I ever caused her?

'How will you occupy yourself there?'

'I intend to meditate, and since I won't be able to keep that up for long I also intend to work on their garden, which, by the way, is in a disgraceful state.'

'Meditate. You've never done that before. Anyway, what's this all this about? Why can't you meditate at home? If you're getting interested in religion, why don't you join a class or something?

'This has nothing to do with religion. I am simply seeking peace of mind. Don't we all long for peace of mind?'

I couldn't argue with that.

'What does my father think of your plan?'

(Note our terminology – 'my father', 'your father'. Strange, don't you think? As if we both wanted to hold him at arm's length.)

'He thinks I've deserted him, and that's what he'll say to you. But it's an unusual kind of desertion because I intend to come home each weekend and cook his lunch on Sundays. And I won't neglect Arthur.'

'Arthur?'

'Your father's dog. He'll have him for company in the evenings, but I'll walk him every afternoon. Our retreat is only round the corner. In fact it overlooks the river. You'd love it.'

She named the street and began to describe the house and its many idyllic qualities, but I was thinking about the hairy and affectionate Arthur, whose purchase, it was now emerging, had evidently been part of a long-range strategy. What was her ultimate goal?

'And don't let him tell you that I'm exploiting him. I'm paying for this out of my own money. I have more resources than you may imagine.'

Then, sounding confused for the first time, she added,

'Don't tell your father I said that. I need time to myself. For myself.'

She said goodbye abruptly and rang off.

What of my parents' spiritual lives?

My father was a primitive man, full of superstitions and fears to which in his unimaginative way he gave the name God, but he could not have been defined as a Christian, except in the most irreligious sense. He was a man who was happy to use the conventions at hand, baptism, marriage, burial, since they were the standard rituals for events that needed to be solemnised. If he had a spiritual life it was confined to a terrible quarrel with God on the single subject of his loss. Why had Rosemary been taken from him? Why had he been punished? Why had his happiness been destroyed forever? Why him? Why?

(He had other kinds of belief which he held with fundamentalist ferocity and would declaim in anyone's hearing. These he shared with rest of middle-class England whose bible was the *Daily Mail*, and whose convictions were in due course miraculously made flesh in the numinous form of Mrs Thatcher.)

And my mother? As usual she was an enigma. She had no truck with my father's Sunday vigil at the graveside, though I never heard her disparage or so much as comment on it, even when his habit persisted into a third decade, its obsessional strength undiminished. But how had she come to terms with her loss? From whom or what had she demanded an explanation, recompense, comfort? I had no idea. Perhaps she didn't want my father to find out that she was seeking to extricate herself from the prison they had built together. Did she feel that it was, at last, her turn to grieve?

My relationship with Atalanta was a winter affair, conducted under cover of darkness, so to speak. We fell into the habit of meeting most weekends, generally in Atalanta's house, and we tended to remain indoors, cooking for each other, reading, listening to music and – how can I put it? – *voyaging* on Atalanta's bed. We did occasionally go out to the cinema or a restaurant, but I usually contrived to delay these excursions until night-time.

The pleasure of being with Atalanta consisted in just what my mother was apparently seeking, that is tranquility and quietude. Silence, with which my father had beaten us, flowed from Atalanta like a balm. As you have discovered by now, dear Anna, so far from being a man of few words, I am in fact a man of many words. I am garrulous, a chatterbox – a windbag. In addition, I inhabit a world of words, the world you have joined. My business is words and it is conducted by means of constant verbalisation. When not talking myself, I am besieged by the words of those who work with me, all articulate people. Every one of us has his or her tongue in somebody's ear. And what do we talk about so expressively? Words, of course: literary words, misprinted and misspelled words, contractual words, rumoured words, gossipy words. I am exposed to words all day and most evenings as well when I go home to read for work or pleasure. The word is my beginning, middle and end. And if I can spare the time from this lexical lunacy I attend meetings to liberate persecuted writers so they can break their enforced silence and scatter more words.

My address is Babel, and yet the noise of those multitudinous voices, printed and oral, fell silent when I was with Atalanta.

I wouldn't have called her taciturn or tight-lipped, but when she had something to say, she said it pithily. She spent her words wisely, whereas I am a spendthrift. She was also an attentive listener, a virtue for which I can only strive, though she was by no means a passive listener, for her face often registered a quizzical look during my rants concerning the vanity of authors, the laxity of my colleagues, the nation's incorrigible philistinism. One other difference between us: unlike me, she was not anecdotal. I may be wrong, but it's my observation that women, notwithstanding the fact that women writers dominate the novel these days, are far less anecdotal in conversation than men. Is that your experience, Anna? I suspect the explanation is that men are more defensive, and nothing gives away so little while taking up so much conversational room as a story. There is a kind of anonymity to story-telling.

The point I'm struggling to clinch is that in Atalanta's soothing company I found myself falling quieter and quieter; following her lead, I adopted other ways of communicating and being companionable. Not that our homes were silent, far from it; like her I began to play music continually in my house, often different kinds of music in different rooms. In the past I used to switch on Radio 4 as soon as I was past the front door, if only to have a voice in the house (more words), but now I got into the habit of tuning to Radio 3 instead, leaving it to play, so to speak, all night. Atalanta attended to her music with rigorous concentration, turning the word *listen* into a very active verb. By contrast, I made use of music; it kept me warm and kept me company. Classical music is often said to help one *relax*, but, speaking for myself, I ask music to do just the opposite. I want it to give me a surrogate emotional life much richer than my own non-musical life. I throw myself into its arms hoping that music will overwhelm me with sublime and passionate feelings I couldn't possibly muster up by myself.

My father didn't call until two days after my mother, and then not until the evening. According to his code, and woe betide any employee of his who transgressed it, private calls made in office hours on company telephones were acts of theft, as well as virtual blasphemies, for to him the office was as hallowed as any church.

'I suppose she's told you she's buggered off,' he said.

'From what I can gather, she's only doing a spot of gardening round the corner.'

'Gardening!' he scoffed. 'Is that what they call it these days?'

'You can't believe that there's another . . . that she's . . .' I stammered.

'Shagging another bloke? No, I suppose not.'

This crudity was uncharacteristic, and I took it to be a sign of his anger.

'As I understand it,' I said, 'she's coming home at night, or at least at the weekends to cook and clean for you.'

'I should bloody well think she is,' he said. 'She has duties to me.'

As he spoke it occurred to me that for the first time in our collective lives our roles were reversed: I was playing the parent to whom the children in turn were breaking news of a 'muddle', to use my mother's word, they had got them-selves into. And yet, in spite of this reversal neither of them had used a tone of voice that made any concessions: they had both addressed me with their usual presumption of authority, which in my mother's case was flavoured with the note of exasperated amusement she reserved for *my* follies and foibles. We had changed seats, but nothing had altered. These two conversations were also classic examples of people saying what they didn't mean, and not saying what they did. In any case, why had either of them rung me?

I puzzled over these mysteries for many days afterwards, finally asking Atalanta for her opinion.

'Isn't it obvious?' she said. 'They're both trying to blame you.'

With a most uncharacteristic lack of professionalism I dawdled over the editing and production of Nick's monograph, hoping against hope that he would telephone one day to tell me he had finished his affair with Nancy, whom I had refused to meet. Alas, it was not to be. He did ring, but only to call my bluff.

'Forget the stupid dedication,' he said. 'Write whatever you think fit. In fact, you can forget the book altogether if you imagine delaying it is going to make me change my mind about Nancy.'

'You're still seeing her?'

He didn't bother to answer me.

I also procrastinated over introducing Nick to Atalanta, whom so far I'd kept in ignorance about his affair. Naturally, when we first met I told Atalanta all about Nick himself and the heroic shadow he had cast over the colourless chronicle of my past. I waxed eloquent on the subject of Natalie, little Nina and young Eddie, my swashbuckling favourite, but I her kept in the dark concerning this new, uncompleted chapter in Nick's story. Furthermore, I refrained from bringing us all together because I couldn't bear the idea of presenting Atalanta with a Nick who would be wearing a fake face: Nick the dissembling husband, Nick the counterfeit father. Not being able to unite the two halves of my life saddened me profoundly. I avoided going to Camberwell myself because I couldn't face Natalie; I felt disloyal enough, without having to look her in the eye and protect Nick's secret. I wondered if he had any idea of the ramifications caused by an affair, even one as clandestine as his. Not least of its ugly consequences was the fact that I was depriving myself of Eddie's company, a sacrifice I bitterly resented. And what sort of relationship was Atalanta supposed to make with Natalie? If she knew the truth about Nick but said nothing, it would be false; if not, it would still be false, a falsehood perpetrated by me on both the women. Did Nick's friendship give him the right to demand that I kept his nasty little secret from her? Surely not. Why had Nick told me? A secret is a virus that infects everything it touches.

On my way home that night I debated on the bus whether to tell Atalanta at last what I knew about Nick. By the end of the journey I had decided to do so, and I telephoned her as soon as I got home. Dialling her number, I was reminded that although she and I shared the intimacy of lovers, we were in many respects still freshly acquainted and knew very little about each other, as illustrated by the realisation that I had no idea how she would react to my news. In the event, her response was characteristic insofar as it was terse and unequivocal.

'What a shit!'

I was certainly not prepared for her next comment.

'I hate a liar. You must tell Natalie. If you don't, I will.'

'You've never met her.'

'I don't want to meet either of them at the moment.'

My world was crumbling around my ears. Would I remain trapped inside, imprisoned now by its ruins? We need the past, however gruesome, to remain steady so we can take our bearings and find our way in the present. Whatever I had achieved with Darling would be undone if my parents lost their mythological concreteness and began to change. What then would I cling to? Not Nick it seemed, for he too was metamorphosing into someone new and unreliable.

Why was Nick's loss so grievous to me? When I looked back over the years, now knowing that he was a deceiver, I could see that his behaviour was riddled with inconstancy and deceit. But for whatever reason he had always been loyal to me, or at least had provided me with such loyalty as I had called for. Admittedly, not much.

Love seems to be a thoroughly un-British word to use in

relation to men friends, but what other term applies? The fact was that I did love Nick; I had loved him since childhood. No mystery there. But what did I feel for Atalanta? What name to give it? My pleasure in her company was undiminished; with her I had achieved something approaching serenity, punctuated only by moments of ecstasy (and now one moment of misery). But was this love? I had discovered within myself a dark heart that loved, but only on its own terms. For Nick I felt an emotion that, until very recently, I had never stopped to consider, but my emotion for Atalanta was under continual consideration. If love was the word, it was love on certain conditions, which I had not revealed to her – nor yet to you, Anna.

I rang Nick at his warehouse.

'You can't ask me to lie for you any longer,' I told him. 'Why don't you give up Nancy and then there'll be nothing to lie about?'

'I'm not asking you to lie. I'm just hoping for a little discretion. No one knows anything about it except you.'

'I've told someone else.'

'You bloody fool. Who?'

'A new friend of mine. You don't know her. She's called Atalanta.' The second I said her name I regretted it. 'She's threatening to tell Natalie if I don't.'

'Who the hell does she think she is? I've never heard Natalie mention her. Apart from having a fucking pretentious name, what gives this Atalanta the right to pass judgment on me and destroy my marriage?'

'Natalie doesn't know her either. The point is you can't go on treating Natalie like this.'

'Are you trying to tell me you've got your hands on a woman at last?'

'I'm telling you that you're going to lose your wife and your children if you're not very careful.'

'Nancy's not just a casual fuck. I'm not sure I can live without her.'

'That's not what you told me when we had lunch.'

Nick fell silent and then said at last, 'It's a mess, I admit it, but I need time to sort things out. So keep that moralising bitch of yours in her kennel.'

'Don't be so bloody rude. Anyway, Natalie's bound to find out sooner or later, and then she'll hate you for deceiving her. Is that really what you want?'

'What I want is the chance to get my life in order without being betrayed, especially by a complete fucking stranger.'

'You're the one who's doing the betraying. Listen,' I said, attempting to conciliate him, 'Let's meet somewhere and talk about this. We've been friends too long to quarrel.'

'Apparently you've got a new friend. You'd better choose which one you want to keep.'

I didn't reply and Nick too fell silent. Finally he said, 'If you come to Eddie's party there should be time to talk then.'

I could not refuse him.

One afternoon around this time I invited an elderly author to my office to discuss the possibility of a manual on rose growing. I didn't know the man (dandelion-clock hair, Ronald Coleman voice, red spotted handkerchief blooming in the window box of his top pocket) and was only seeing him because I owed his agent a favour. As the conversation proceeded I decided not to take up his book, which would no doubt have been elegantly written and charmingly illustrated, but held no interest for me. I also decided to take the coward's way out and break the news to him by letter rather than tell him man to man. As far as I was concerned, rose, to parody the famous formula, was not a rose was not a rose . . .

To close the proceedings, I promised to discuss his proposal with my colleagues (publishers' equivalent of tipping you the black spot) and made to open the door for him. As he gathered his things together he said, 'You have an unusual name. I don't suppose that by any chance you're related to Carl?'

I told him that my father's name was Carl.

'When you next speak to your father mention my name and if he recognises it give him my regards.'

He picked up his hat, but at the door he stopped and said, 'Your father is a gallant man.

He nodded briskly and was gone.

The whole incident perplexed me. *Gallant* – what on earth could he have meant by that? It was not a word you would use loosely, for its applications were quite specific. I went to the dictionary to check. Yes, it had two meanings: 'brave, chivalrous' and 'markedly attentive to women'. Surely, the latter could not have described my father, even in his youth? It was inconceivable that he had ever been considered 'a ladies' man', still less 'a paramour'. *Gallant* was an archaic word, which I associated with soldiering ('he was a gallant officer'), though at first sight it was difficult to see its connection with my father. On the other hand, this rose-grower, though older than my father, could easily have served with him during the War; he might have been a fellow officer, or perhaps my father's commander, or at any rate someone in a position to witness my father's military gallantry. But if he was telling me that my father had made a courageous soldier, why did he immediately hurry from the room; why so eager to finish what he had begun so provocatively? After all, to tell a man that his father had been brave was surely something to be enlarged and savoured, yet this old soldier, if that's what he was, had postively legged it.

The more I thought about his declaration the more extraordinary it became. My father was one of those men who never spoke about the War. In fact, I had never heard either of my parents talk about those years. My mother would occasionally reminisce about her childhood, conjuring up a misty, mythical era through which she flitted like an elf, and it always surprised me that this hard-bitten, hard-headed woman should evoke a sugarplum fairy in plaits and party frocks when describing her girlish self. Yet again she proved to be a mystery.

My father's case was still more extreme: he offered no evidence of having been a child at all. To my recollection he never made mention of his boyhood or adolescence, nor his early manhood, which had coincided with the War. Indeed, apart from my mother's occasional dip into her fairy-tale book of memoirs, my parents behaved as if history had not existed for them prior to the year of Rosemary's death. Everything before that was silence, and everything after it was silence of another sort. I had once seen a photograph of my father in his army uniform, but it had told me nothing about his rank, his record, or even his regiment. It only told me that he had fought the enemy (Germans? Japanese?) with a moustache as deadly as a stiletto.

What could my rose-growing author have meant by his comment? It bothered me so much that I finally telephoned him, not an easy thing to do since I had just rejected his book, and asked him if he would enlarge. Had he known my father during the War? He replied only after a long pause.

'You're wrong about my book, you know.'

I didn't respond and another pause ensued that was so lengthy I thought he was going to ring off, but then he said, 'Your father had a special kind of courage, which does not win medals. He was never wounded himself, never saw any action in fact, but he lost a great many friends.'

He added nothing to this statement, though I could hear the rasp of his breathing, a disagreeably intimate sensation, as if his mouth was literally and moistly pressed against my ear.

'Your father was not a natural soldier, but he always did his duty despite his losses.'

Saying no more, he put down the phone.

These were astonishing revelations that evoked a barely recognisable picture of my father. Friends! Neither of my parents had friends worthy of the term; my father required nobody except my mother for his emotional needs, and my opaque mother gave every appearance of being self-sufficient. Yet I had just been shown a snapshot of my father as someone who not only had friends, but cared deeply for them, so deeply that the intensity of his grief had made his mere persistence in uniform seem heroic to one of his colleagues. This was a man I had never met, a man who had long since ceased to exist.

What had he meant by his remark that my father was not a natural soldier. What is that? A man who obeys orders readily, who is prepared to serve King and Country by killing other men nominated as the enemy. My father was a simple man, patriotic in his way and prone to following convention, so when the call came he had probably answered it dutifully. But wasn't a natural soldier someone to whom killing came, well, naturally? Even I, his least forgiving critic, couldn't say that I had ever discerned the killer in my father's bleak, unkindly nature. And why had the old man cut the conversation short; why did he insist on talking in riddles about my father?

I confided my confusion to Atalanta, who in her usual brisk way said, 'Talk to your mother.'

(A sour footnote: I was indeed wrong about the rose-growing manual. In due course it was published by another press, was universally hailed as the last word on its subject, and has remained in print ever since. A rose is . . . a thorn.)

During this period my spending, always profligate, became uncontrollable.

The best that can be said for my bibliomania, to which I alluded earlier, is that its expense was mitigated by the many gratis books that came my way through work, for I truly believe that otherwise it might have bankrupted me.

Are you a collector, Anna? If so, you'll know what I'm

talking about. If not, I must describe something to you which is probably incomprehensible and certainly unattractive.

I suppose we're all collectors to some extent, but you can be grateful if you don't suffer from what I call *accumulomania*. Whatever we have, we accumulomaniacs must have more of it, and this desire is expressed by gathering together series of things. Series are at the heart, supposing it has a heart, of collecting. To possess one of a thing is a bare beginning, a meaningless gesture if left undeveloped; a singleton is an offence against nature.

If I buy one of something, a Victorian wine glass perhaps, or a china figurine, no sooner have I got it home, unwrapped it and found a nice place for it to stand, than my pleasure is poisoned with longing for its pair. But the moment I have the twin, I pine for the triplet. And what's three, without four? In any case, three is half of six, which is the dealers' favourite number? What if one of the precious six should be broken (clumsy guest, never to be re-invited)? Best to get the seventh to act as a spare, and doesn't seven point the way to twelve, the round dozen? You see the path to madness, Anna. The permutations of collecting will expand to infinity. All the glasses in the world will not fill the void; more only wants more.

As I said, I lost all control over my spending, especially on records. But what was it I wanted from all those books, records, pictures, bits and pieces? They were feeding an insatiable appetite, which like a tapeworm consumed everything that came its way and still left its host hungry.

Whenever I opened a new book, regardless of its subject matter or genre, I always hoped it would reveal at last the truth that would illuminate my life and fill me with insight; I longed to discover that mystical something which would bestow on me what I can only call *spiritual poise*. I expect that sounds quite laughable to you, but it was (is) the case: from every book I pined to receive the blessing of *equilibrium*. How empty that must sound, a sign of how empty I was left at the end of each quest. I was a permanent failure in the search after enlightenment, forever glued to the lowest rung, forever peering upwards into a clouded sky.

Through music I hoped to discover the sublime within myself. Don't mock. I wouldn't be telling you this if I didn't trust you. Under Atalanta's influence I started to broaden my musical taste and within a week of her recommending a Schubert trio (D 929. Op 100) I had developed a passion, with collecting mania to match, for all sorts of classical chamber music. I thought I could fill myself with this music, as a church is filled with incense from a swinging censer. No less reverently than a priest placing the sacred wafer on an outstretched tongue, I would lay my record on its turntable and wait to feel the beauty of the music redeem the great empty space of my skull. To the god of music I prayed that I would be moved in every sense; that I would be uplifted, transported, transubstantiated. In short, I yearned for the replacement of what existed with something that was ineffable and definable only insofar as it was . . . *loftier.*

And yet even as I was on my knees, my hands clasped in supplication, my face upturned to the light streaming through the rainbow window, I would ruin the experience by a low desire to collect another record in the series, as if by owning two beautiful pieces of music I could double the intensity of my feelings. Say I was listening to one of Mozart's late string quartets, and music does not come much more sublime than that, a busy devil in the crypt of my mind would be checking the catalogues for the other quartets in the set, or the same quartet played by a different group.

My greed for ever more intense sensations was ravenous, all-consuming. I longed to consume, but was consumed by longing, which only left me feeling emptier. I was made hungry where I was most satisfied. What could be madder than that? And this was one of those periods. I could not go a day without buying a new LP. I was ashamed, and of course I did nothing to restrain myself. Instead, I tried to conceal my purchases from Atalanta, but since my collecting impulses were at their most obsessive I couldn't resist slipping the day's new discs (yes, I was buying in twos and threes at least) onto my shelves in their proper alphabetical and categorial places. I gambled that she wouldn't notice them (though I suspect she always did.)

Sometimes I would say to myself that collecting gave elegance and proportion to what would otherwise be vulgar acquisitiveness. But who was I trying to fool? In that private corner of the mind reserved for self-delusions I cherished the idea that a life devoted to heaping random objects together in orderly systems was a life magically protected. There was always one more item to be added to the series, and surely the grave could wait before adding another to *its* collection. If not to defy death, then what was the purpose of this greed? What emptiness was I trying to fill?

Atalanta did not relent from her hard line on the subject of Nick's infidelity; however, she agreed not to inform Natalie on condition that I persuaded him to bring things to a head one way or the other when we had our conversation at Eddie's party. I was relieved, but, privately, did not hold out much hope of swaying my old friend on whom I had never yet had the slightest influence. Nor did I seem to have any influence over Atalanta, whose strict, unbending disapproval, though morally correct no doubt, seemed to be invested with an additional anger that did not derive simply from principle. I wondered if in her past, a period still as obscure to me as the Dark Ages, someone, another man, a parent, a friend, had played her false, cutting her so deep as to produce this pitiless detestation of liars. I attempted to broach the subject, but she snubbed me with a terse, 'Surely you're not trying to justify his behaviour, are you?'

Eddie's party was billed as an outdoor affair, but in the event it demanded Spartan qualities from the celebrants because the weather was cold and damp. Word went round that Natalie had ruled that until it actually rained no child was permitted to withdraw into the house. Fresh air fun was compulsory, and so under a low canopy of grey cloud a dozen small boys milled about on the lawn at the back of Nick's house, kicking a football. To my inexpert eye it seemed an unusually quarrelsome game: it was interrupted again and again by arguments over the rules, interventions by partisan mothers, sulky attempts to leave the pitch and one or two actual fights. Eddie himself took no part in these bad-tempered diversions, for he was wholly engrossed by the present I had bought for him: a remote-controlled model car. This vehicle was not your ordinary, vulgar racing car, but a tremendous, open-top tourer, a miniaturised Hispano-Suiza with leather seats and brass fittings and a dozen other luxury features including a wicker hamper bound to the running board with a leather strap; in short, it was a motorcar that Charles Foster Kane would have been proud to own. (I had obtained it through Harrods at a price that might have caused even Kane to blanch.) Within minutes of wheeling the magnificent thing out of its box (I would not have been surprised to see a tiny mechanic tumble out of the packing, rag in hand ready to buff up the gleaming paintwork) Eddie was able to manipulate its movements with the skill and daring of Stirling Moss. He raced its considerable bulk up and down the garden paths and between the feet of the mothers who were miserably gathered on the patio, drinking white wine and trying to ignore their fractious offspring. Had this present not been mine, and had it not outshone all his other gifts, I would probably have been critical of the lad's neglect of his guests. As it was, I smiled indulgently and waved him on to greater speeds.

When I saw my chance I joined Nick in the kitchen, where he had retreated to open more wine. We stood at the sink, looking at the grim festivities outside. Before I could ask him about Nancy, he pointed through the window at Natalie.

'God! Look what I've done to her,' he said. 'Look what I've turned her into.'

As he spoke Natalie crossed the stage framed by the window from left to right, and I didn't have to ask what he meant. Over the last few months, without my noticing it, Natalie had gradually been losing the quality that had been so striking when Nick first met her. The light that had seemed to glow within her, a high wattage generated by her humane intelligence, had dimmed. In those days she positively shone with understanding, and it was expressed in a smile that was, I often told her, one of London's great smiles. I used to joke that people should book appointments to sit under its radiance; ten minutes under the sun lamp of her smile would be worth a decade's therapy on the couch. Just to watch her move around her office surrounded by her conservation books and campaign posters was to feel confident that if mankind left its affairs to the likes of Natalie, it might be saved from damnation after all. Graceful as a tree, she was one of those people whose beauty seemed to beautify other people.

But nowadays, where once she had floated, she trudged as if permanently shod in Wellington boots, head down, her smile dowsed. Furrows extended from the wings of her nose to the corners of her mouth, little trenches that seemed to suggest a battlefield where lives were being lost without the prospect of victory. She had cut her hair short.

We watched gloomily as she told Eddie to 'stop being childish' and look after his guests. I'm glad to say the dauntless boy did as she asked with good grace, carefully parking his car before running among the footballers with a whoop. His smile was as radiant as ever.

'You're going to destroy everything,' I said.

He shrugged. 'I love her, that's all there is to it.'

'How do you know?'

'Only you could ask such a dried-up intellectual question. Oh no, I forgot, you've finally popped your cork, haven't you? *Atalanta* (he pronounced her name with exaggerated politesse) must be quite a woman.'

'Don't bring her into this. Just tell me what it is you feel that has cancelled out your love for Natalie and your children.'

'I still love them. I love them all, that's the trouble. But I love Nancy with an intensity I've never felt before.'

'You have a short memory.'

'I can't explain it. Feelings are stronger than words; mine are at any rate. All I can say is that I think of her continuously, and when I'm not with her I'm tortured by a terrible sense of longing for her.'

'You're infatuated, my friend. Cure yourself, before you throw all this away.' I gestured towards the garden and its population of children, now glumly consuming cake and Coke.

As if responding to a cue Natalie crossed the proscenium of the kitchen window again, plodding right to left this time.

'They'd probably be better off without me.'

'Don't be stupid. If you leave them, they'll hate you. Eddie especially.'

'Nat will hate me for sure, but kids adapt.'

'You're talking as if you're planning to leave. I can't believe it. How can you be so sure of your feelings for this bird?'

'Her name is Nancy,' he said angrily.

'All right – Nancy. How do you know? What makes you so certain that this longing you have for her, this longing that tortures you day and night, is really love?'

Just as I said these words we were interrupted by one of the mothers, who burst into the kitchen and accused us of hogging the wine.

'It's bloody freezing out there,' she said. 'What's turned Nat into a sadist?'

Nick immediately picked up a pair of bottles and took them onto the lawn where I could see him playing host to the beleaguered mothers with his customary charm. The woman remained behind, warming herself and drinking a large glass Nick had poured for her on his way out. We stood next to each other for a moment, looking out of the window, both trying to think of something to say to the other, and not succeeding.

The birthdays of children should be celebrated. Every year of survival is a parent's victory and a child's achievement, in its way his greatest achievement. Looking at Eddie as he sprinted round the garden, engaged in some form of jocular warfare, I could not imagine that a life so vigorous and pugnacious could be at risk. No doubt, he would survive until his ninth birthday and, by the looks of him, until his nineteenth and probably his ninetieth, but survival was not everything. What flaws would be embedded in the boy's make-up if his father was foolish enough to desert him?

I would have left the party at that point if little Nina, Eddie's sister, who was by then aged six or seven and a delicious scrap of a girl, had not come in from the garden using her customary mode of propulsion, the somersault. She showed no sign of being affected by the cold, despite wearing a thin cotton dress and short socks.

'Hello, Bruno. Would you like to see our house?' she said, taking my hand and tugging it.

I allowed myself to be led and she took me to the far end of the lawn where another little girl was waiting for us.

'This is my friend Lucy. She draws cows.'

Lucy beamed up at me, evidently satisfied with this account of herself.

In a corner made by a low wall supporting a shrubbery they had arranged a miniaturised one-room house. A brick stood in for a table, another for a chair; they had pinned up a piece of wallpaper to decorate the wall; a handkerchief served as a carpet. A doll lay face down, arms by its sides, on a bed constructed from a cardboard fruit tray. A smaller doll was seated at the table and was engaged in drawing something (a cow perhaps?) on a tiny sketch pad with a piece of lead pulled out of a pencil.

'They're called Maggie and Aggie,' Nina said. 'Maggie's the mummy.'

She pointed at the doll prone on the bed.

'Does Aggie have a brother?' I asked.

'Yes. He's called Baggy,' said the other little girl, a remark of extreme wittiness to judge by their prolonged laughter.

'And where's their daddy?' I asked rather ploddingly.

'There isn't a daddy.'

Since I had nothing solid to report concerning Nick's intentions, I took the coward's way out and spared myself an uncomfortable interview with Atalanta by not seeing her that Sunday. However, on the Monday I discovered that the problem had been put into suspension, at least for the time being.

For the sake of editorial objectivity and to preclude any further dilly-dallying on my part, I had decided to place Nick's book in the hands of Ms N., whom you know well, Anna. As you'll recall, she was then new to the company and rumoured to have a passion for things oriental. Perhaps unfairly, I forbore to tell her that the author and I were old friends, and so I could hardly blame her for speaking insolently about him when, passing her in the corridor, I dropped a casual enquiry about his typescript's progress to the printer.

'The author's buggered off abroad,' she told me. 'There was a message waiting for me this morning. Apparently, he left last night for unnamed foreign parts and won't be back until he feels like it. Unless I get those revised captions by the end of the week, which looks highly unlikely, he can forget his autumn publication date.'

With a scornful sniff, she whisked into her office to attend to more deserving authors.

A typical manoeuvre: Nick had simply slipped away, solving nothing, confronting nobody. Natalie would not have been surprised by his departure since he often made sudden and unexplained trips abroad, returning just as unpredictably to receive the packing cases and bales that were delivered to his warehouse from Rajistan, Tajikstan, Kashmir, Uzbekistan, Azerbaijan and so on, places whose very names had brought an excited flush to the cheeks of his now disillusioned editor. But the question that I could hardly ask her, but dearly wanted to have answered, was whether Nick had departed on this impulsive expedition with or without the minxish Nancy.

The discovery that my father might once have possessed a streak of human feeling in addition to his capacity for grief, the only sensibility I had ever observed in him, had gradually expanded into an obsessive and irksome preoccupation. The fact that he had been capable of loving his wartime pals made it all the more galling that he had withheld even his affection from me. I struggled to dismiss these self-pitying anxieties and concentrate on the many blessings I had recently acquired. I tried to orient my thinking outwards rather then inwards, concerning myself with other people's difficulties, Natalie's for example, but my efforts were in vain. The shadow of my father, that gallant soldier, fell wherever my thoughts took root and withered everything in its darkness. To generate some light I tried to think mercifully about him. Had he been steeped in grief even before Rosemary died? Had he already lost so much that her death effectively killed the once loving person my mother had married?

I decided that I would take Atalanta's advice once again by paying my mother a visit – a surprise visit. I thought it would be amusing to call on her unannounced at her women's retreat.

In the event, I was the one who was surprised because I was told by an inmate that my mother could be found at home, having retreated, so to speak, from the community three weeks ago. I made a pleasantry to this effect, but my informant looked at me bleakly, and I was forced to add a third retreat by withdrawing myself, cringing under her basilisk stare. However, I retained sufficient courage to ask if I could stand for a moment in front of the house and admire the river. With manifest disappointment the woman said she couldn't think why not, and I walked through a pair of French windows onto the lawn, which sloped down to a low parapet marking the garden's edge. The house was built on a part of the bank that stood thirty feet above the water and was buttressed by a wall constructed of huge dressed sandstone blocks whose red skin was matted with black and green weed at the tide-line. I climbed onto the parapet and filled my lungs with fluvial air, which seemed to invade them like a vapour designed to give relief to asthmatics. The incoming tide slapped the sandstone below while a merry breeze turned patches of sunlight on the racing water into fish scales.

When she opened the door to me my mother simply said, 'Oh, it's you. Have a drink.'

I followed her into the house. Without looking round, she said, 'Have you told your father you're here? Are you planning to see him?'

I said, no, it was a spur-of-the-moment visit.

She poured me a whisky, mixed a powerful gin and French for herself, and perched in her customary way on the arm of a chair, a cigarette on her lip.

'I suppose I should be flattered,' she said, 'but I suspect your motives are not wholly filial.'

They could not be more filial, I told her. Babbling out of nervousness, I wondered whether there was a word to distinguish a son's devotion to his parents from a daughter's to hers.

'Don't play the pedant. Just tell me why you're here.'

And so I did. When I'd finished she asked the name of my rose-growing author. I told her and she said, 'Never heard of him!'

Nonetheless, I wanted to know if what he'd said about my father and his friends was true. Who were these friends and when had they died? And, anyway, where had my father served during the war? What had been his regiment and rank?

'You don't want to worry about all that stuff. It's in the past and long forgotten. I can hardly remember myself,' she added lightly, though I didn't believe her.

I was insistent and asked more questions. She grew testy and broke off the conversation to mix new drinks. She tried to distract me by making a ceremony out of getting the measures rights and going to the kitchen for more ice.

When she returned, I asked her again about my father's war record. Where had he enlisted? Had he seen foreign combat?

'Why on earth do you want to know? What difference does it make to you?'

I said it might help me to understand my father's behaviour.

'You're not going to tell me you've started all that therapy business again.'

I told her I was motivated by curiosity, nothing else. I couldn't bring myself to confess my fear that, like my father, or rather his current self, I seemed to lack an essential component in my emotional make-up. Could I truly love? If my mother could help me discover in him the man who had loved his friends, who had loved her and maybe other women before her, who had perhaps even loved his parents (a couple who had been expunged from the historical record with Stalinesque thoroughness), then there was surely hope for me? Nor could I confide in her that I feared my stunted body was itself a living metaphor of a stunted sensibility. After all, it might have sounded as if I was blaming her for my retarded condition.

'He lost friends in the war,' my mother announced abruptly. 'We all did. I don't think he lost more than anyone else. I don't think he took it harder than anyone else. I can't think what this man is talking about.'

She crushed out her cigarette with a finality that told me she was also crushing out the conversation. But now I was left with the suspicion that it might be my mother who was the insensitive one. Had she properly understood his grief?

'Anyway,' she said, with a sarcastic laugh, 'if it's so important to you, why not ask him?'

To change the subject, I asked her what had happened to make her leave the retreat.

'They were just a bunch of silly women who wanted to moan about their lives. Still, at least I cleared up their vegetable patch for them,' she said ominously, and I wondered what devastation she had left behind her.

My parents' house was darker than ever; the conifer hedges that enclosed it seemed to have grown higher, denser and more occludent, while inside the ceilings were yet more thickly yellowed with the nicotine from the cigarettes which my mother was once again chain-smoking. She was thinner than I had ever seen her. The proverbial puff of wind could have blow her away, though she seemed to have become a creature of places where the air was never fresh. Only the dog embodied any sense of liveliness, but he had fallen asleep, lying with both his back legs comically extended behind him. By leaving her women's retreat and its breezy riverside house, my mother had shunned the light, exchanging ozone for the ash and dead air that formed the atmosphere in her home; she had truly retreated by creeping back into the darkness that my father pulled round him like a sunless planet.

On my last visit she had offered a glimpse of a different woman, who had looked healthy and young, even sexy, and I had understood from our conversation about the commune that she had granted herself a kind of parole from my father's eternal night. But the light must have hurt her eyes, for she had dug her way back into the darkness; like a perverted Ariadne, she had followed a black thread, reeling herself into the coils of the maze where my father, not I, was the mino-taur, the dead heart at its centre.

I looked at this woman (did I love her?) and realised she was a stranger to me; we were estranged in the sense that she inhabited a world alien to me, where memory was forbidden and locked out. She and my father inhered a constant present; they behaved as if they had no past and were creatures of a single, narrow dimension in time that closed in behind them, leaving no wake, no mark on the paper, no perfume in the air, no negative that might later be developed. They did not reminisce, and their faculty for memory, insofar as they drew on it, represented a kind of steel cabinet in which, like the secret police, they kept the dirt on the peccadillos and shameful secrets of their acquain-tances. No sin was expiated in these merciless files, and they were never used to record achievements or virtues.

My mother was not being coy about my father's past, nor secretive. She was not deliberately hiding anything; the matter was of no interest to her, for it lay on the seabed of the past like the rest of history, and was therefore of no rele-vance to my father or me.

As I was about to leave she said, 'If you're really deter-mined to go down memory lane, I'll show you something.'

She led me upstairs to their bedroom and opened one of the drawers in the very chest where all those years ago I had found her colourful lingerie. From beneath a stack of scarves and handkerchiefs she pulled a desiccated envelope, which she opened with care to show me a black and white snap-shot of a little girl.

'She would have been a beauty,' my mother said. 'She had your father's good looks.'

Only then did I realise I was looking at a photograph of Rosemary. It must have been taken a few weeks before her death, which had occurred in the May of her sixth year. She was wearing a summer frock with what I believe is called ruching across the chest. Her white socks were trim round her ankles and dangling from her hand by its elastic strap was a hat of some sort, which had been rendered a grey blur by movement. Perhaps she had been twirling it mischievously; perhaps the wind had given it a spin at the vital moment when my father – I assumed the photographer was my father – had pressed the button of his box camera. No such indistinctness obscured her face, and she did indeed show every promise of being beautiful. Rosemary was a radiant angel: the sun had caught her blonde hair and it glowed round her head like a halo.

'Your father doesn't know I've got this,' my mother said.

With a shock that was accompanied by a most disagreeable clammy sensation I suddenly appreciated that I was looking at the only photograph I had ever seen of my sister. My father had prohibited every kind of reference to her, verbal, pictorial, or material. Her name was never mentioned; I had never come across a single garment or toy belonging to her; I had never seen a portrait of her in any album. In fact, there were no albums in the house relating to the era of my childhood, because my father had declared himself a hater of photography, and yet the truth, I now grasped, was that he had only abandoned his camera after Rosemary's death. All trace of her had been expurgated from the house, apart from the icon that my father had hung in his mind and draped in black. Had it not been for his Sunday morning pilgrimages to her grave, it would have been impossible for an outsider to guess that I was not my parents' first and only child.

I had no memory of seeing this or any other photograph before, and yet all these years I had preserved a mental image of Rosemary that exactly corresponded to the sunlit seraph my mother was already cramming back into its little coffin envelope. Had she shown it to me when I was a child? For that matter, why hadn't I discovered it for myself during one of my childhood searches of her drawers?

'Your father has no idea I kept it,' she said, hastily pushing the drawer shut as if she could hear his footsteps on the stairs.

I could hardly believe she had made this pitiable remark. Had my father's grief been so monstrous, so all-consuming and invasive, that she had been denied the chance to entertain her own modest feelings? Had she been reduced to hiding her relic in a drawer, like a schoolgirl? Was my father so tyrannical he had forbidden her to bury and mourn their daughter in her own way? Or was the sad truth of it that my mother's feelings, even for her daughter, were shallow, whereas my father's, however perverse and destructive, were undeniably profound? Had she suppressed an agonising maternal sorrow (and if so, at what cost?) or had she put aside a small sadness without difficulty, devoting herself instead to my father's colossal misery?

One last question, why had she shown me the photograph in the first place? As usual my mother presented me with an insoluble puzzle.

I wanted to offer her something, a word, a hug, a touch, but she had slammed the drawer shut and was already on her way to the door. The sight of her wiry body and self-sufficient manner were enough to keep commiseration at bay, and yet her straight back, encased in its armour of pride, must surely have bent with sorrow when her beautiful daughter died.

I followed her down the stairs and my hand hovered over her descending shoulder, closing with every step of mine, drawing back with every one of hers, but we reached the hallway without my making contact. At the foot of the staircase she turned quickly and, seeing my still outstretched arm, she shook my hand with a gesture that mocked and dismissed me in a single economic move.

In due course Nick returned from his foreign trip, something I learnt not from him, but from the acerbic Ms N. She sent me a memo to the effect that her author had graciously deigned to write his captions at last and had delivered them in person. Could I think of a 'selling' title for the book, for which she, 'personally' and 'frankly', could not see a commercial future?

Hurt that Nick had come to the office without seeing me, I telephoned him. He didn't apologise, but by way of tacit explanation told me that he was no longer seeing Nancy.

'Satisfied?' he asked bitterly and rang off.

My rejoicing was short-lived. When I blithely rang the Camberwell number and announced my arrival for lunch the following Sunday I was informed by a grim-voiced Natalie that I would not be welcome for the time being. Shattered, I rang Nick again, who said, 'She's probably pissed because I let it slip her that you knew about Nancy.'

(*Let it slip* – deliberately or by mistake, I wondered. And if deliberately, why should he do such a thing?)

'You told her about Nancy?'

'I did not. There's nothing to tell. She found an old letter.'

Anna, I won't bore you with the ins and outs of this wretched business. My doomed friends dragged each other along the *via dolorosa* that leads to the Golgotha of the lawyer's office. There were recriminations and reconciliations, lapses on Nick's part and forgiveness on Natalie's, second honeymoons and trial separations, attempts to keep it from the children and vehement assurances to the hollow-eyed victims that, despite everything, Mummy and Daddy loved them very much indeed.

During this miserable period I saw them together as a family only once (I was on my own) and I came away deeply concerned about Eddie. It seemed to my inexperienced eye that his playful pugnacity, his good-humoured terrorism, had lost its innocence, while his mock killings had acquired a new earnestness that smacked of genuine aggression, rather than boyish high spirits.

I was relieved to find that I could still impress him with extravagance, for he was flabbergasted when I gave him a *Times Atlas of the World*, which when upright in its splendid slipcase stood nearly as high as its new owner. He soon rallied, but then I learnt that my present had, after all, been ill-chosen. Eddie dragged the book over to Nick, saying, 'Show us were you've just been, Dad,' and from her acid expression I could see that wherever his most recent trip had taken him Natalie was convinced he had not travelled alone.

For his part Nick behaved like a visitor in his own home: he paced, lit cigarettes he didn't finish, drank greedily without tasting, checked his watch repeatedly and treated his children with unwonted indulgence. Only Nina acted as if untouched by current miseries, but then she seemed to have withdrawn deeper into her games and fantasies, perhaps protecting herself by becoming a refugee to a sunny world of her own making.

Not long after this doleful occasion I came home from work one evening and sat for the first time that year in Atalanta's garden, enjoying a glass of Chilean sauvignon blanc, then something of a novelty on the wine market. Relaxing on her garden bench and allowing the cares of the day to drop from me, I closed my eyes and felt the evening sun on my face, its warmth perfumed by the wisteria that Atalanta had trained to form a flowery bower over her patio. Its pendulous purple blossoms dangled round our heads like so many sweet-scented genitalia, or so I thought in Bacchic mood as I poured a second glass for myself. I brought the bottle to Atalanta's glass, but it was still full.

I was just about to mention the penile analogies to be seen in wisteria when she got to her feet abruptly.

'Let's go out,' she said.

'Where?'

'Anywhere. Just for a stroll. We could go down to the pub.'

I demurred – 'I'm tired. It's been a long day' – and began to tell her an anecdote about an unusually perfidious agent.

'You're ashamed of me, aren't you?' she said, still standing over me.

'Don't be absurd,' I said hastily.

'You're ashamed of me and too cowardly to admit it.'

She said this quietly, not in a challenging or bitter way, but in the voice of one who knew she was telling a truth that would not be denied or refuted. Nor was there anything in her tone that was sad or self-pitying. She had seen into my dark heart.

As she spoke she began to unbutton her dress. Made of some floral print, it was a dress I particularly liked. Nipped at the waist, buttoned down the front and cut low at the neck, it allowed her Junoesque figure to bloom, and that evening it seemed the very essence of spring, fresh and flourishing. She undid its buttons, shook it off her shoulders, and let it fall to the ground.

There she stood, quite naked, wisteria drooping to caress her shoulders, yellow roses climbing the pergola to tangle in her hair. The little garden was secluded, but I was by no means certain that it was wholly concealed from her neighbours' view. Head thrown back, eyes closed, saying nothing, Atalanta had positioned herself at a slight angle from me to face the setting sun, which cast a pink blush over her pale skin and set flowers of flame ablaze in her hair.

How was I to interpret this extraordinary gesture? My first instinct was to cover her and I struggled half-way out of my jacket, thinking I would throw it round her shoulders. But then, with one arm free and one still in its sleeve, I reconsidered. To cover her seemed a churlish response that would only confirm her accusation that I was ashamed of her. My heart, never one to shirk a cliché, was pounding like a jackhammer, for though embarrassed and flustered, I was filled with desire. I wanted to crush my lips on her rosy breasts, singe my fingers in her burning bush; yet I remained on the bench, enmeshed in my jacket, while she continued to stand, immobile, wordless, refulgent.

The picture she made was mythological: a naked goddess, she seemed to be intimate with the languishing sun, whose dying warmth drew the scent of honeysuckle and oriental poppies from her skin. The droning bees played round her towering torso as if seeking to sip nectar from her honeyed navel-bud; the very birds, roosting in the cherry trees, whose confetti blossom still littered her garden path, trilled a lullaby for her with their last song; and, for all I knew, a lovelorn hedgehog was strumming a ballad in the mulch beneath her rose bushes. Thus I, and I alone, obtruded, the only discordant element in Arcadia.

As she had no doubt intended, I was astounded, not only by her sudden nakedness, but by the spectacle of her body itself, whose stature was rendered still more titanic by the miniature scale of her garden.

'I cannot ask you to love me,' she said at last. 'But if you are embarrassed by me, you must say goodbye and never come back.'

I couldn't answer her, but risked a gesture of my own. I took off my clothes. As I did so, I was miserably conscious of the difference between her graceful disrobing in a single movement and my frenzied struggle with clothes that knotted themselves round my limbs, turning me into a laundry Laocoon. Motionless, apart from the decline of her face following the dwindling sun with sunflower devotion, Atalanta continued to stand while I hopped and cursed. Finally I kicked aside my underwear and was naked too. I was also flagrantly erect.

I placed myself behind her, a hairy, horny satyr, a priapic

gnome most improbably paired with a beautiful, all-powerful goddess. To hide myself, I put my arms around her breasts and pressed my face against her back, while my insistent truncheon pushed its way between her knees. Thinking I could put it to practical use, I attempted to prod her indoors, but she was immovable.

If I ever find myself in the presence of Christ or some other deity with the power to dispense forgiveness, I will beg him to forgive me, because, yes, yes, I was ashamed of Atalanta. I was not ashamed of her great size in itself, which I admired for its voluptuous proportions and craved in bed; my shame derived from fearing that her size emphasised my squatness in the eyes of others. Such was my selfishness, I did not consider that this must have been reciprocal; for, after all, my shortness drew attention to her height. She had correctly divined that I was finding every excuse to avoid being seen with her in public. When we did venture from the house, I made sure it was at night, and as often as not I took her to the cinema, concealing her magnitude in the dark. On the rare occasions when we ate out I chose restaurants in remote neighbourhoods, claiming that I had seen them reviewed, but where, in fact, I was confident we would not be observed by authors or tittle-tattling colleagues. I had become dependent on her company, I valued her astringent brand of wisdom and I was passionately addicted to her body, yet I could not bring myself to acknowledge our love affair to the world. That was the condition that ruled my love.

'Forgive me,' I said, drawing away from her.

'I can't forgive you unless you're sorry and you tell me you want to change the way you feel. But what you feel about me isn't going to change, is it? I can only forgive you once. More than once would destroy me.'

I sat miserably on the bench, clutching a sock as a foolish fig-leaf.

The temperature was dropping. The sun had slipped below the horizon of garden fences. The moon, once a smudge of chalk, was beginning to brighten.

'Atalanta, come inside. You'll get cold.'

'You must answer me.'

I poured another glass of wine and was suddenly struck by inspiration.

'The forecast says it's going to be a glorious weekend. Let me take you to Salting on the Norfolk coast. Have you ever been there? We'll stay in a hotel and go for walks and look at antique shops and bookshops.'

'Collect me on Friday evening,' she said, without turning towards me or moving at all.

So I gathered my clothes, scuttled indoors and went home, leaving her naked in the moonlight.

But Anna, I needed forgiveness more than ever. My invitation implied that I was taking her to a popular spot where we would be seen together. When she accepted she had presumably understood my meaning, but it was a trick and by no means a sign of reform in me. I knew from my childhood days that in truth Salting was remote and deserted, a fishing village that even fishermen had abandoned to the gulls and mud. By taking her on long walks across its salt marshes and bleak beaches, something I knew she would enjoy, I could continue to keep her out of the public gaze, while yet retaining our relationship. Such was my heinous plan.

As a result of strenuous research I managed to find a cottage that was close to the promised Salting but situated at the end of a long private track. Pleading pressure of work, I didn't collect Atalanta from her house until late on the Friday evening of our weekend, with the result that we arrived in the dark. Nonetheless, she was delighted with the place and insisted on an immediate stroll along the shingle beach, which lay at the very doorstep of our hideaway.

The moon, like a celestial sponge, had soaked up the last of the daylight, but we could see well enough to crunch our way along the pebbles, keeping parallel with the surf. Out at sea a variety of coloured lights winked and flashed, some close, some distant, none identifiable to us. On land all was darkness and silence: no music, no voices, no traffic, no metropolitan hum. We paused to sit on a log lying at the highest tide-line, which must have been in the water many months, for it had been stripped quite bare of bark and its exposed wood was as smooth and white as bone. The sea, exhaling a zephyrous, salty breath, was tranquil except for the restless furling and unfurling of its waves as they tried to find a comfortable position on the shingle. I put my arm round Atalanta and, as usual, was reassured by the great mass of her warm body, which seemed to yield to me and give me shelter at the same time. Adrift on our log in the darkness, we were contentedly shipwrecked; I slid my hand inside her blouse and found the sturdy globe of her breast.

In her light, melodious voice Atalanta began to sing one of my favourite Porter songs.

'Night and day, you are the one. Only you beneath the moon and under the sun.'

I could hardly believe my ears as she continued to sing.

'Whether near to me or far, it's no matter, darling, where you are, I think of you night and day.'

'When did you learn that,' I asked her, 'I thought the only songs you approved of were *lieder* – Wolf, Schubert, Brahms and that lot. Serious stuff.'

'You haven't preached jazz to me in vain,' she said. 'That day when I first came to your flat you played an instrumental version to me. Do you remember?'

'Ben Webster. But I didn't think you were that impressed.'

'It took me a while to get my ear in, so to speak, but in the end I bought myself a Billie Holiday record. She sings this so beautifully I thought I would learn it for you.'

She pressed my hand harder against her breast and sang.

'Day and night, why is it so, that this longing for you follows wherever I go?'

As you can guess, Anna, I was filled with joy that for my sake she had converted to jazz, to use her religious metaphor. At the same time my guilt over bringing her to this isolated, forsaken spot was made a thousand times worse. She loved me and I had rewarded her with deceit. My feelings were so contradictory that I experienced a kind of emotional over-load and simply fell asleep.

I've no doubt I only slept for a couple of minutes, but I didn't wake with a start, nor did I feel in any discomfort despite my crooked position; instead, I seemed to float slowly to the surface of a world where moonlight was life-giving and the wind a musical medium.

We returned to our cottage and lay in bed listening to the waves sucking and sluicing the stony shore.

'In the roaring traffic's boom, in the silence of my lonely room, I think of you, night and day.'

The next morning we drove a couple of miles down the coast, parked the car near a café-cum-shop that sold binocu-lars and field guides, and set off to hike across the salt marshes, one of the key sites of my childhood. It was typical of my father that he should take his family to what in those days, the late 1950s, was an utterly desolate spot where one could walk all day without seeing so much as a bird-watcher. It was no less typical of my mother that she relished such a place and turned its vacancy to advantage by becoming an expert on birds; in fact, so acute was her ear that she learnt to recognise species from their songs alone.

Have you ever been to that part of Norfolk, Anna? I'm talking about the north-facing coast at the top of the East Anglian hump that England carries on its back, a coast which offers some splendid sandy beaches, but in other parts crum-bles and dissolves into a geography that is neither land nor sea, neither earth nor water, but is, in a word, marshland. Or, in another word, mud. I've never seen mud to match it;

black, oily and thick, this Norfolk mud could be molasses if it weren't for its smell, which reeks of rotting matter and clings irredeemably to the fingers. After each holiday my mother would simply throw away my bathing costume and plimsolls.

This foul-smelling mire is the emulsion mixed by sea and soil, an unholy compromise between coast and ocean that produces a kind of perverted agronomy whose fertility depends on a twice-daily drowning in salt water. Far from being barren, the salt marshes are capped all summer long with a dense matting of flowers that drink salt: sea-purslane and scurvy grass, purple aster and lavender, fleshy glasswort and seablight, plantain and silver wormwood, the whole complex bound together by the roots of marram grass and saltmarsh rush. It was too early in the year for Atalanta and me to see most of these in full bloom, but the grasses were already dotted with sea pinks.

As we marched on I discovered that country hiking, in contrast with our rare pavement strolls, required my short legs to achieve one and a half steps, sometimes more, to each of Atalanta's Amazonian strides. I felt my heel chafing into a blister against my unbroken brogues. I was also aggravated to see that, so far from being the desert of my childhood, the area had become popular with a certain kind of rambler, the men distinguished by infantile bobble hats, the women by well-meaning, watery-eyed smiles that didn't fool me. I don't think it was paranoia that allowed me to detect mockery beneath those polite masks. Awed perhaps by our daunting size, one so tall, one so wide, these people made way for us long before it was necessary, shrinking to the edge of the pathway and waiting for us to pass with their eyes downcast. True, there were no sniggering boys among these pedestrian pedestrians, but I could sense their ridicule as surely as if they had shouted at us and thrown rotten fruit. In her queenly way Atalanta nodded graciously as we passed, bidding them, 'Good morning!' while I glowered.

At ground level salt marshes appear to form a dense matting, a kind of soggy meadow intersected by the odd channel, but if you were to fly over them you would discover that they in fact possess an extraordinary composition akin to a labyrinth. The sea has sculpted the mud into a convoluted system of spits, keys, reefs, atolls and hummocks, all topped with flowers and grass. At low tide their sheer banks show a foot or two of bituminous mud standing clear of the water, and it's easy to believe that the sea comes here to rest in these channels and lagoons, for the water lies in placid stagnation, rising and falling with the tide as though breathing in its sleep.

As a child I was timid and not at all prone to adventuring, but this mud-labyrinth held a fascination for me. Every sunny day of our holiday, when the tide was low, I would disappear into its foul-smelling coils to play games in which I starred as the unvanquishable hero of battles with pirates, Red Indians and Germans, often defeating their combined forces in a single anachronistic engagement. My mother used to provision me with a greaseproof parcel containing what she was pleased to call sandwiches, clammy chunks of cheese slapped between rounds hewn from a locally baked loaf. With my rations packed in a small khaki canvas bag (my father's?) I would march forth after breakfast and not return until late afternoon. It occurs to me now, though it didn't seem to worry my parents then, that I would have been quite beyond rescue if I had suffered an accident. Who could have located my blackened bull-calf's body among all that treacly sludge?

Our path took Atalanta and me to a melancholy spot at the edge of the marsh where a set of ruined steps fell from an old wharf into a brook poignantly named the Blythe that flowed from Salting village to the sea. A pair of iron bollards and a ring of Herculean proportions, pitted and flaky from rust, were all that remained of Salting's dock and its brief maritime glory. A moment of Victorian prosperity had been cut short one tempestuous winter when the Blythe's estuary had been clogged with silt and its mud flats restored once again to the mussel gatherers who had been plying their trade since King Cnut's time.

We sat on the wharf's edge and dangled our feet over the river, watching the tide swell beneath us while it drowned the fresh stream in its bed. The estuary gradually took on the lineaments of a shallow lake. A handful of boats that were moored along the river's edge and lay on their sides in the mud, prows pointing inland, were brought to life by the incoming seawater, slowly stirring and righting themselves. Once afloat, they swung round in the stream to the extent of their ropes and faced the sea, as if anxious to embark on a voyage.

Atalanta said, 'Every time the sea comes in, it brings a kind of second chance. It shows that second chances are possible, doesn't it?'

She sighed. It was a sigh the like of which I've never heard before, and hope never to hear again; a sigh that seemed to come from the very core of her being, dragged up like a bucket from the bottom of a deep well. And what did it contain, this bucket? Of all forms of human expression the sigh is the least considered, perhaps because it's the most difficult to interpret. In Atalanta's case, I thought it spoke of terrible sadness. It rose from within her and, like the tide, overpowered everything in its path. I looked at her. Here was a woman I knew, if not well, at least intimately, a woman who had sighed in my arms with pleasure, who was in the habit of sighing in exasperation over my foibles, a woman who sometimes sighed to seek attention. But this Salting sigh was different, unprecedented. I studied her great bulk beside me, a solid, warm, womanly bulk, and realised that the person within was a stranger to me. The interior of that familiar and beloved outward form was an obscurity, and I was appalled that sorrow flowed from the spring at its heart.

Atalanta stared across the estuary, watching the inexorable tide as it forced its flux of water between the estuary's thighs and flooded its womb. Forgive these obscene metaphors, Anna, but they swept into my mind as unstoppably as the water gushed into the river basin. I wished I were a tide that could overpower Atalanta and douse her misery in my balmy Gulf Stream. I wanted to love her. I wanted to love her.

Seated on the wharf we ate our lunch in silence. By the time we finished, the estuary was filled to its brim and the tide was neither ebbing nor flowing, but at rest. Between the wharf and the dunes on the horizon that held back the sea's breakers there now lay a vast expanse of still, silvery water. It seemed to be contained in a great shallow vessel that was in constant danger of tipping and spilling, yet remained miraculously stable.

Tied below us was an old clinker rowing boat, which like the other craft had risen from the dead and was now bobbing and scraping against the dock wall. A sign announced that it was for hire by the hour. There was no one in sight to pay, but since a pair of oars lay on the wharf I decided to make use of them. (One of my more improbable gifts, Anna, is the ability to row with the grace and vim of an old salt. I feel in harmony with this eccentric form of motion that requires you to face one direction, while driving yourself in the opposite.) I pulled the dinghy close to the steps and handed Atalanta down. Fearing that her height would cause her, literally, to rock the boat, I held out an oar for her to grasp, but she disdained it and trod dexterously along the boat's centre of gravity to install herself on the cushioned seat in its stern, a picture of nautical hauteur. I seated myself on the thwart facing her, thrust the oars into the water and pulled us onto the open estuary.

'This is your barge of beaten gold,' I told her. 'I have silver oars and will row you to the tune of flutes.'

Atalanta stared over my shoulder as I continued to scull us across the river's temporary marina towards the salt-marsh maze.

'We all deserve the benefit of the doubt,' she said, apparently still meditating on the tide and its redemptive powers.

I concentrated on keeping my strokes even and forceful, so that our course did not meander or zigzag, though I had no particular destination in mind. I rowed us across the estuary and then entered the wilderness of the salt marshes. The tide had flooded all the twisting channels that wound among the mud mounds, submerging everything but their upper flanks and the vegetation flourishing on their flat peaks.

I lowered the oars, allowing them to trail in the glassy water. Under the impetus of my last stroke we floated towards a small island, a bed of herbage standing clear of the surrounding water, and when we were within reach I placed my right-hand oar on its tufty crown, which was enough to moor our boat in the motionless tide. The hot sun drew out the scent of the sea lavender. Thirty or forty feet away, a pair of sleek white swans took their siesta in a backwater. We were enfolded in silence.

It occurred to me that it would be very pleasant to lie with Atalanta on the island's couch of herbs in this perfumed heat. The more I thought about it the more excited I became by the idea of unbuttoning her clothes and exposing her body on the very location of my childhood games; where once I had grappled with Red Indians, I would now be embracing a naked woman. Intoxicated by my alfresco fantasy, I pulled the boat close to the island's edge, stood up and stepped nimbly onto the island.

I was about to invite Atalanta to join me when she said, 'Let's eat at the Jolly Sailors tonight. We could book a table from that telephone box on the way back to the cottage.'

She was referring to a pub in Brancaster a few miles down the coast that was locally famous for its food and popular with the yachting crowd, a place shunned, needless to say, by my derisive parents.

I must have hesitated. Well, there's no point in denying it now, I did hesitate. I pictured the two of us entering the noisy dining room as rows of jolly sailors turned to stare at us, guffawing behind their menus, and I hesitated. What's more, I failed to disguise it.

With a deft movement Atalanta lifted the oar out of its rowlock and pushed our boat away, leaving me stranded with a yard or so of clear water between us.

'I love you, Bruno, but you're not available for love. You're still trapped in your parents' world.'

Grim-faced, she moved to the thwart and with a couple of vigorous strokes rowed herself still further from the island. I protested. I apologised. I pleaded. She said not a word and I was forced to watch while she hauled powerfully on the oars and skulled herself out of the maze of marsh tops into the estuary. She turned in the direction of the wharf, so I could no longer see her face, and then she and the boat disappeared behind a large mud bank.

I hallooed and waved, I danced up and down and shrieked, hoping all the while that she would take mercy on me, but after five minutes it was all too obvious that I had been marooned without reprieve and would have to rescue myself. Deserted and alone, I had no choice but to languish on my castaway's reef until the tide receded far enough for me to walk home across the oozy mud flats.

Many hours later, when the water finally dropped and the muddy flanks of the islands began to creep into view, I took off my shoes, rolled up my trousers and attempted to make my way to the relative firmness of the drying river bed. In my impatience I quit the accursed island far too early and was soon coated to my thighs with foul-smelling treacle. Once I slipped and fell on my face, taking a mouthful of filth; it tasted indescribably foul – bitter, gritty and feculent.

By the time I extricated myself from the marsh and reached the bird-watchers' café where we had parked that morning I looked as if I had been tarred from head to foot. Atalanta had taken the car, but it was standing outside the cottage when at last I reached the place in the moonlit darkness that had seemed so magical only twenty-four hours ago.

Atalanta herself had gone, leaving no note or trace of her presence, and I guessed she had called a taxi to take her to the railway station at Sherringham. I sat at the kitchen table in my stinking clothes and wept.

I didn't get in touch with Atalanta on my return to London; I didn't telephone, write to her or knock on her door, though I confess that I did lurk on the pavement opposite her house for a long, miserable evening, craving a glimpse of her, while torturing myself that I might discover her in the company of another man.

What did I feel about Atalanta? I struggled to analyse my emotions, a mental activity for which I possessed no gift. I felt loss, a terrible, grieving loss, but if my experience with Régine (may her beds be soft and her lovers tender) had taught me anything, it was to be profoundly suspicious of loss trading as love. In Atalanta's case, I feared that my sense of loss might be more acute than my sense of love. Did I miss her now she was gone more than I had valued her when she was with me? What a question! What else did I feel? Longing, yes, but longing for what, and was whatever I longed for the residue of love, or the product of sexual nostalgia?

I desperately wanted to see her, but knew it would be pointless unless I could bring with me a credible response to her parting remarks.

So far from being 'unavailable' for love, I was now achingly, pathetically available. I made myself available by waiting for the postman in the morning and hurrying back at the end of the day, hoping that the second post had taken pity on me. I made myself available by sitting in my flat every evening, listening for her mighty tread on the garden path and never straying five paces from the phone in case I missed her call. Available! How much more available could a man make himself?

Yet even as I made these protestations to my uncaring

kitchen walls, I knew I was too late. How could I have been so stupid, so self-centred? Now I was ashamed of myself, not her, and longed to expiate my sin. I would have given anything for the chance to take her to the pub or walk arm in arm with her (insofar as that was gymnastically possible for us) in the park. Too late. I had taken her heart and thrown it away.

If I could not love the amazon in her, she was no longer willing to love the monster in me – that, to coin a horribly apposite cliché, was the long and short of it. Look what she had given me! She had taken the minotaur into her heart; she had stroked his shaggy pelt, kissed his muzzle, caressed his horns. And how had I repaid her? By trying to lure her into my labyrinth, lock her up and keep her in the dark. She had given me a second and third chance, and in return I had offered her more tricks.

As for my being trapped, surely no one could have cut himself off more decisively from his parents' world. I had fled their house at the first opportunity, not allowing a week to elapse between my last day as an undergraduate and my first as a self-supporting resident of London.

I was being too literal. My labyrinth was still located in that prison of conifers, now grown into walls of solid green, that my mother had built to house my father's grief. My books, like a fleet of flying carpets, had whisked me out of the window and over the rainbow, but they had brought me back again, and now I had closed the gate on myself. It was true, I was trapped.

All I knew for certain was that I was in pain. I didn't sleep; I couldn't concentrate on my work at the office or read at home, though I bought books by the lorry load; I ate and drank like a pig; I indulged in lunches that began with solitary Camparis before noon and finished, long after my guests had returned to their dutiful desks, with solitary brandies in the late afternoon; I kept both television and radio switched on throughout the evenings, while maintaining my fruitless vigil by the telephone. And in the process I neither consoled myself nor discovered any insight into my condition; I learnt nothing except that I had no comprehension of my own life.

One other activity kept me occupied at night: I used to search my flat compulsively for a trace of Atalanta, a little reminder of the tremendous presence that had seemed to fill the place both physically and supernaturally, but she was a fastidious person and had left no intimate debris in the bathroom or bedroom. Nor was there any sign of her in the kitchen, where I had done most of the cooking. The cleaner, showing uncharacteristic zeal, had expurgated from the sitting room every last cigarette end and lipstick-kissed wine glass that might have borne a lingering memory of my vanished giantess. So huge, and now so utterly extinct.

The only relic I came across was a record she had brought round one evening, a particular version of Borodin's string quartets that illustrated some musicological point she wanted to make. As I recall, it was the first quartet that had interested her, but it was the second that I played obsessively, or rather its third movement, the celebrated nocturne. Do you know it? There could hardly have been a more heart-wrenching piece of music to hear under the circumstances, because it exactly evoked the balmy darkness we had shared on our first evening at Salting.

'Only you beneath the moon and under the sun.'

This quartet, which I could not stop playing, was a torture and consolation all in one: torture because it reminded me cruelly of what I had thrown away, consolation because it went a little way towards soothing and beautifying my grief. Night after night I listened to Borodin's music, hoping that its poetry would assist me to understand Atalanta's remarks, hoping that its oriental magic would float her spirit into the room to retract them.

But musical salvation was denied to me. In a moment of drunken clumsiness, I scraped my stylus over the nocturne's precious grooves and ruined the record.

Notebook 6

And this, my friend Anna, is when you had your finest hour (to date). If I didn't show my thanks at the time, and I'll bet I didn't, I'm about to redress things now.

I don't have to tell you that my behaviour in the office, during the brief periods of my attendance, became erratic and probably offensive. (If I was rude to you, I ask your pardon; you never deserved it.) Nor do I have to remind you that my delinquency coincided with the period when the Americans were plotting their takeover of our venerable but vulnerable house. I never thanked you for trying to foster the illusion that I was still functioning properly as editor and member of the board. It was a generous, albeit futile effort, and I respected your loyalty (are you suspicious of me in this ingratiating mode?), but in my heart of hearts I was not sure I still wanted to function, in any capacity.

I should have seen the debacle coming, but my guess is that I couldn't have salvaged the company's independence even if I had been at the top of my game. The kind of publishing I grew up with had become obsolete without my noticing, and modern management was killing off decadent old Bloomsbury. On the first day of his glorious reign our Philadelphian Führer proclaimed that the new order had no time for the saloon bar or the long lunch, and – *quelle horreur!* – it even frowned on the Garrick and its purple politics. Accountancy had become the boss and literature was now required to pay its way.

As it happened, I was at the very bottom of my game. My eye, so far from being on the ball, was too reddened and glazed to focus on anything, and when in due course the ball completed its predictable trajectory by smacking me on the head I was taken by surprise.

I am not a man of secrets, Anna, but here is one that I concealed from everyone in the office, including you. It was an error. If I had kept the Führer informed, my behaviour, which turned even more volatile and irresponsible, might have appeared explicable, though I doubt history would have been significantly changed.

On that Monday when the Philadelphian regime was installing itself in our hallowed precincts, I received a phone call from the mortuary attached to Liverpool's police station at Hope Street. (Hope Street! It's true.) A young man's voice apologised for intruding on me at this sad time, but declared that it was his duty to request my presence at the chapel of rest. Legal protocol demanded that the deceased be identified. The unfortunate victim's husband was not able to perform this distressing yet unavoidable task, but had provided my name and telephone number as next of kin. The ordeal would only take a moment, since he, the young man, could reassure me that the lady looked very peaceful and her face was quite unmarked.

Such was the euphemistic delicacy of his approach it took me a little while to realise that he was talking about my mother and that hers was the corpse that called for identification.

What had happened to her? How had she died?

It would be exceeding his professional brief to offer a forensic opinion. That was the function of the police. In any case, as with all tragic mishaps of this kind, a coroner's inquest would have to take place in order to ascertain the precise cause of death.

What kind of tragic mishap?

A drowning. He would say no more, except that the body had been retrieved from the Mersey. An ambulance had been called to the Otterspool Promenade. It was a very nice part of the riverside, he added, as if the information might console me.

I tried to ring my father at home, but there was no reply. His office told me that he was unavailable. I left my own office immediately, and drove to Liverpool.

Have you ever identified a corpse, Anna? I hope not, for your sake.

When I arrived at the morgue I was received by the diplomatic young man who ushered me into a small cubicle where the 'departed' lay on a trolley, her face concealed. My first sensation on entering the room was of a strong pervasive perfume, something my mother had never used, but which presumably had been applied to overlay another, less savoury odour. If what lay on the trolley was indeed my mother's remains, I was shocked to see how pitifully slight she had become. Her body hardly raised the sheet, which the young man folded back to expose her face. He retired from the cubicle, but a glance was enough to tell me that it was my mother. Her expression, as promised, was untroubled. The familiar waspishness had been smoothed away (by death or a cunning mortician?) to leave a bland serenity that was wholly uncharacteristic. This was and was not my mother.

I drew back the sheet a little further and detected another smell, the pungent and unmistakeable smell of river water. My mother appeared to be wearing her usual outfit, for I could see the shoulders and collar of a short-sleeved white shirt that might have belonged to a schoolboy. It was dry, but stained and streaked. In preparing her body the mortician had committed a little solecism because the two top buttons had been left undone, something my mother never did. A flash of silky colour in the gap below the second button caught my eye, and I couldn't resist lifting the collar an inch to see what lay beneath. I discovered the lacy trimming of a bra made of mulberry-coloured satin, a bra such as a young woman might have worn: sexy and chic. I pulled the sheet over her head and left these mysteries to rest in peace.

The young man of the morgue supervised me as I filled in forms to confirm that the body I had examined had once been the mortal shell of Mrs Vera H. of Riverdale Drive, Liverpool 19, housewife, aged 58. (Such are the salient points of identity; no mention of cigarettes, sarcasm, home-cut hair, inedible cooking, a dead daughter mourned in secret for thirty-three years. Did my father plan to dispose of her clothes and belongings, or was this another distressing but unavoidable task that would be delegated to me?)

When these procedures were completed I was referred to a policewoman, who told me she was authorised to outline the circumstances of my mother's death. Like her colleague, she was reluctant to anticipate the coroner's findings, but she was prepared to divulge that my mother had been blown into the river by a freak squall of wind. Without putting it into so many words, she implied that my mother had been foolish to venture out on a day when the local forecast had repeatedly issued warnings of violent gales. Gusts of sixty and seventy miles an hour had been recorded. Considerable damage to property had occurred all over the city that afternoon (more business for my father) as well as several injuries, though only one person had lost her life – my mother. Another woman, as foolish as my mother but luckier, had been hurled against the railings while walking her dog on the promenade and had suffered a fractured rib. (Had my mother been walking the effervescent Arthur? If so, what had happened to him?) The woman had seen my mother swept up by the same gust and flung over the railings into the river, where the tidal current, running violently under the storm, had dragged her body along the wall until it lodged against a set of steps and was thrown clear of the water. The river had swallowed her and spat her out. Someone had phoned the ambulance service, but they were too late to help my mother. In a low voice the policewoman confided that although the pathologist had not completed his analysis, it was his unofficial opinion that my mother had died instantaneously, not of drowning, but a blow to her head, presumably inflicted when she had first plunged into the river. Had I noticed the lesion at the back of her skull?

In the same confidential tone, she told me that the 'witness' had reported an odd thing: when the wind had pitched my mother into the air she had opened her arms wide, as if seeking to take wing. This detail comforted me; the vision of my mother flying to her death was greatly preferable to her being tossed into the river like so much jetsam. Then my policewoman, hitherto a touch maternal herself, showed a harder face. Had my mother been her usual self? Had she shown any signs of depression in recent weeks? I fended off the hint and assured her that, so far as I knew my mother had been right as rain.

But who was my mother's usual self? A stranger to me. I tried to remember if she knew how to swim. Had she gone willingly to her death? It was possible. Had she deliberately gone down to the river that day to place herself in the way of the tempest? I would never know, but the picture of my mother launching her bantam body into oblivion seemed eerily plausible; not so much suicide, as a kind of Russian roulette. Once the policewoman had proposed it, I could not get rid of the idea that my mother had wilfully abandoned herself to the four winds, putting her life in the hands of chance.

I tried to ring my father again, but there was no reply. I drove past the house, but there was no sign of him. The garage doors were closed, and I couldn't tell whether his car was inside or not. I drove on, deciding to proceed directly to London, not an intelligent move because I was in no condition to be at the wheel. Apart from being exhausted, I was consumed with rage. What did my father think he was doing by evading me? And what kind of coward was it that deputed his son to identify his wife's corpse?

I was angry because I didn't understand what I'd lost: I felt deprived of something I'd never really possessed in the first place. My mother, now a ghost, had always existed in a spectral fashion, forever disappearing with nothing to replace her but a dissolving question mark of cigarette smoke. I was at a loss to assess my own loss; perhaps my father, the loss adjuster, could evaluate it for me.

My feelings were unfocussed, nameless. Is that a definition of anger? I didn't know what to feel about her now she was dead, any more than I had known what to feel about her during her lifetime. I couldn't call my confused feelings grief, unless grief was the black suit worn by guilt. But what had I to feel guilty about? I struggled to put aside guilt and anger (unholy twins) in the hope of clearing the way to understanding, but I could only produce pairs of negatives: she had neither undermined, nor supported me; neither attacked, nor protected me; neither loved nor entirely ignored me. I had been fortunate that she had made so few demands on me; on the other hand, if she had set a more positive precedent, I might have been 'available' for love. I felt a great longing to have Atalanta in the car beside me; she would have unpicked these riddles.

One thought recurred with cold-blooded clarity: how would my father, who had relied so comprehensively on my mother, manage in her absence? Would he mourn her as he had done Rosemary? Had his reliquary acquired a new set of bones?

When I phoned my father at his office the next day he was willing to take my call; evidently, I had earned the privilege of speaking to him by doing my little chore at the morgue.

'Bruno,' he said. I did not know how to reply.

'Are you there?'

An urge to weep overcame me, which my father may have sensed, because he said, 'Bruno, this is not the time.' (There had never been a time, never would be.)

My voice shook, but I managed to ask, 'When's the funeral?'

'Cremation. Your mother asked to be cremated in her will. It'll be very practical, as she would have wished. The date hasn't been set, but it'll take place immediately after the inquest.'

I wanted to offer him a word of consolation; I wanted to discuss with him the extraordinary way my mother had died, this woman whom we had shared, whose loss mattered to nobody except the two of us; I wanted to listen for a hint in his voice that might confirm or quash the suspicion that her death had not been wholly accidental; I wanted to ask about his domestic situation, for this was a man who, as far as I knew, had never so much as boiled a kettle for himself or washed a pair of socks; and I wanted to hear from him some word of enquiry concerning my own feelings, for though he had lost a wife, I had lost a mother. However, I couldn't voice a word.

'I have work that must be done,' he said, clearly preparing to put down the phone.

'What about Arthur?'

I don't know why, but the creature had rushed into my mind as tumultuously as it had arrived on the doorstep when I'd first seen it.

'Arthur?'

'Your dog. Was he with her when . . . I mean, did she take him out that day?

'He must have run home on his own. I found him on the doorstep, soaking wet. His lead was missing.'

'Who's looking after him?'

'I've made arrangements to see that he gets a walk every day. I've made careful arrangements.'

His tone was defensive, which probably explained why for

the first time in the conversation he offered me something: 'It won't surprise you to hear that your mother's will is a little eccentric. In character, you might say. You're the chief beneficiary. Get in touch with the solicitor' – he gave me her name and the name of her firm – 'and she'll spell it out for you.'

He rang off.

I'm sure you recall these events all too vividly, Anna, but what you couldn't have known was their context, because for some perverse reason I continued to keep everything to myself. I should have confided in you.

When at last I turned my attention to company business it was to discover that the accountants brought in by our new owners from the city of brotherly love had decreed a regimen of severe 'pruning'. In the name of a 'leaner, fitter' budget, any forthcoming book that looked unlikely to bear golden apples was to be lopped off and burnt on the bonfire of 'dead wood', which had, apparently, been obstructing our profitability. Nick's book, whose colour illustrations were just about to be printed (at princely expense – such books cannot be produced on the cheap), was one of many titles I had commissioned that had been selected for elimination. I stormed into Ms N.'s office, demanding to know what efforts she would be making to rescue it from the firing squad.

'Let's face it,' she said, 'it was never going to make money. It was one of your pet projects.'

'Surely you don't approve of this butchery,' I shouted, waving the list of victims in her face. 'Doesn't literature count for anything in this place nowadays?'

'Calm down, for Christ's sake. First of all I don't think your pal's book had much claim to being literature. Secondly, I've got a kid at home and a nanny with expensive tastes in food and drink. If it's a toss-up between literature and keeping my job, literature's going to have to look after itself.'

'Have you told Nick yet?'

'I haven't got round to him yet. He's in the queue.' She gestured wearily to a heap of files on her desk.

'I'll do it.'

I telephoned Nick at his warehouse, but a woman answered whom I didn't recognise.

She asked if I was Bruno, and when I confirmed it, she said, in a voice that shocked me with its animosity, 'This is Nancy. Yes, that's right Nancy, "the little whore". I think those were your words.'

Had I described her that way? I had no memory of it, and said so.

'It hardly matters now, but for your information Nick has finally left Natalie and he'll be living with me when he gets back.'

I asked where Nick had gone.

'What difference does it make? I hardly think he'll want to speak to you, unless you've managed to get his book printed at last.'

With a sinking heart, I explained that the opposite was the case: to my great regret, the book was being dropped, but Nick would be compensated and I would do my best to find another publisher for him.

'You vindictive creep! Is that your idea of revenge? How pathetic! Well, don't think it's going to win you any brownie points with saint Natalie. She can't stand you either.'

I went to Camberwell that evening, where I was met on the doorstep by Natalie, who did not allow me into the house. She had lost so much weight I hardly recognised her. I could hear Eddie and Nina inside the house, shouting at each other. Natalie pulled the door shut behind and stood on the step, her arms folded across her chest.

'I'm sure you meant well, Bruno, and I know how you feel about Eddie, but for the time being it's all too painful.'

She lowered her head and spoke in a quieter voice.

'I can't tell you what a shit he's turned out to be. He doesn't even talk to the kids.'

It appeared that she could not bring herself to pronounce Nick's name, but her hatred for the man was all too audible in her hissing enunciation of his pronoun.

'I don't see how anyone could be loyal to such a bastard.'

She made a move to go back into the house, then relented for a moment and smiled quickly, a flash of the old radiance.

'Goodbye, Bruno.'

The inquest into my mother's death was held a few days later. My policewoman friend had promised me it would be a straightforward affair, no more than a formality, and that I need not attend. I don't know if my father went or not. The verdict was death by misadventure, and though the local papers inevitably dwelt on the melodramatic nature of her passing – 'Killer Gust: Housewife Drowned' – no suggestion of suicide was introduced by police or press.

I drove back to Liverpool for the cremation, which was due to take place in the old crematorium at Anfield cemetery, not half a mile away from Liverpool's football ground. I don't know what sort of funeral I would have arranged for my mother if I had been responsible for it, but I assumed that my father would play safe by leaving everything to the undertaker. I was therefore shocked when I saw the coffin lying on its catafalque in the crematorium, for it was a plain, unadorned box apparently made of unstained deal. If it had not been for its distinctive shape, the thing could have been mistaken for a piece of industrial packaging, a container for tools perhaps, or guns. Whatever else my father could be accused of, he was not tight-fisted, and he always spent freely when convention demanded it. Was this simplicity another of my mother's posthumous whims?

As I entered the – what do you call the main area of a

crematorium: nave, auditorium, hall? – I could see my father seated at the front, head erect, back straight. I walked down the central aisle, making for his pew. When he heard my footsteps ringing on the tiled floor he turned and cast a furious look in my direction. Before I was able to sit down next to him, he made an agitated gesture with his hand, which he was forced to repeat because its instruction was evidently not understood the first time. Four men in black suits emerged from the rear and, marching in step, slowly approached the coffin. Again my father waved his arm, this time clearly urging them to speed up. They did so, but lost their solemn rhythm. They lifted the coffin onto their shoulders without effort – my mother cannot have weighed seven stone – and marched it forward a few paces to lower it onto a platform that stood before a set of purple velvet curtains. One of the men, evidently the undertaker himself, looked again towards my father, who nodded his head with an impatient chopping motion. A signal, unseen by me, must have been transmitted to a hidden colleague, because the coffin, mysteriously propelled by faintly whirring mechanism, trundled towards the curtains, which simultaneously parted. Once the coffin was nosing its way through the gap my father got to his feet and, without a glance to me, strode down the side aisle in the direction of the door. My mother had been disposed of without ceremony, without a note of music, without a word said by anyone, without a flower to relieve the starkness of her box, without a witness except my father and myself.

I chased after his hurrying figure and caught up with him as he was unlocking his car. Before I could speak he said in a harsh voice, 'You must understand I'm alone now. Entirely alone.'

Not looking at me, he climbed into his car, slammed the door and started the engine. I had to stand back to allow him to drive away.

If he had slapped me in the face he could not have

surprised or hurt me more. Indeed, I think my face reddened and tears sprang from my eyes as if I had been struck. Reacting instinctively I got into my own car and with a furious mangling of the gears drove after him. I could see his stiff-necked profile three or four cars ahead, looking neither to left nor right, and certainly not looking behind him. And where did he drive? I didn't have to guess. Not south towards his home, but west towards his office, now perhaps his true home. The man was going to his desk. He would only have lost an hour's work, and you could be certain he would make it up later in the evening.

Driving recklessly I overtook two of the vehicles that separated us, but then as we reached the centre of the city and he turned into Exchange Street I realised I had no idea what I wanted to say to him. I abandoned the chase and drove towards the river, parking near the ferry terminal at the Pier Head.

Do you know Liverpool? If you're looking back from the river its waterfront is truly majestic, but in those days the Pier Head was a favourite spot for the unemployed, the unhinged and people like myself who had become uncoupled from their ordinary lives. They loitered on the open space overlooking the river, and their private dramas were given a flamboyant backdrop by the Port of Liverpool Office, a domed and marble extravaganza that seemed to have floated up the Mersey from Renaissance Italy.

One of the ferries, the *Iris* I believe, was about to leave on its river-crossing voyage to Birkenhead, and I boarded her, climbing to the upper deck to watch as she churned away from the landing stage and made a tight half-circle into the mainstream. Like professional mourners, gulls swooped round my head, shrieking and moaning.

In what sense was my father alone? Now that my mother was dead and I was materially independent, he obviously felt free to repudiate me at last. In effect, he had orphaned me. But should I care? I was, after all, a grown man. Here was one of those paradoxes that pernicious parenthood throws up: who wants to be loved by someone unloving? Answer: the unloved children of unloving parents. They crave what they will never get. What had I lost in being rejected by a parent who didn't want me? Manifestly, I was better off without him. His severance should have been the source of mutual relief, yet such is the nature of these relationships that, although he was the one who was behaving monstrously, I felt guilty.

To hell with him! I threw my cigarette into the wind. I cursed my father and I cursed myself for failing to bring my flask.

A milky mist had descended on the river like a veil, making me regret leaving my coat in the car, and as the ferry straightened her course and made directly for Birkenhead's Woodside pier the doomed pomp of Liverpool's riverside profile gradually faded. The Liver Buildings, the Cunard Building and the Port Office, sometimes given the fatuous sobriquet 'The Three Graces', were draped and then screened altogether by vapour. My father's office block standing behind them had already disappeared. Meanwhile, Birkenhead's humdrum silhouette of cranes and warehouses was also invisible, masked in a denser mist. The ferry rumbled forward, heedlessly pursuing her customary course, and entered a world without borders, where there was nothing to be seen but the mist and the encircling brown water. We could have been at sea or on a lake, for there were no landmarks, no stars to guide us, no albatross to hail. Impossible to believe that this placid, tea-coloured fluid had been my mother's killer.

From where I was standing I could see the deck below, where a set of varnished wooden benches faced the stern railings. It was still mid-morning and the ferry was not busy. A trio of women with their shopping bags huddled in a corner, lighting cigarettes. A young man was reading a book, which he closed for a moment to stare into the chilly white void, and I could tell from the jacket that it was, of all things, *Moby-Dick*. I recognised the jacket from our own 'Classics of the Victorian Age' series.

A small girl was holding on to the railings, her blonde hair fluffed up by the breeze. An old-fashioned school hat made of grey felt, secured by an elastic band round her neck, danced on her shoulders. In her summer dress and white anklet socks she seemed underdressed and strangely misplaced, suggesting an uncanny resemblance to the figure of Rosemary in the secret photograph my mother had kept all those years. (Would my father find it at last?) Standing with both feet on the lowest rung, she rested her elbows on the handrail and leaned over, watching the frothing wake as it receded into the mist. I watched her closely, afraid that she might lean too far, but she stepped down onto the deck.

The girl lifted her head and stared intently across the water, apparently straining to see something in the white emptiness that enveloped the Liverpool bank. She made a shade for her eyes with one hand, and continued to search the invisible dockside. The sight of the child, who was so urgently seeking her unguessable object in the fog with which my mother's smoke was now perhaps mixed, released in me a spring of emotion. My heart was suddenly filled with tenderness for the child, a feeling I had only known once before when the newly-born Eddie had been placed in my arms. I felt as if a spring of love had been released within me.

The steady chug of the ferry across the misty vacuum and the association of my mother with the river that had run past my parents' house all the years of her marriage combined to let loose a flow of emotion that had been buried until then in a deep aquifer of my heart. I felt that in some profound way, which defied articulation, I had been set free – not wholly free, but generously paroled – and that my freedom consisted in gaining access to a new dimension of love.

I had lost Eddie and my grief had been intense. There is no word to describe the adult who loses a child: wives are widowed, children are orphaned, but what is the term for the adult who is deprived of a child? Of course, Eddie had never been mine to lose, and thankfully he had not died, but he had been the only child in my life. I would never forgive Nick for taking him away from me. On the other hand, my love for him had not died; it had survived his absence. Nor, I suddenly realised, was my capacity for loving exclusive to Eddie. Just as I had loved him, I could love another child. I was available for love.

I had lost Atalanta, and my love for her . . . but had it been love? Surely it had been love?

I was using terms I didn't understand to describe a medium that, like music, was perhaps indescribable; and yet the feeling that had been released within me seemed utterly concrete and vigorous. I can only tell you, Anna, that I felt as if some new resource had been bestowed on me, an extra chamber of the heart.

When I looked back on it, I saw that my 'love' for Atalanta had been something I had tried to do to her, to put into her, almost as a penetrative thing, like sex. We were adults, but in these matters I had been an adolescent. Now I could see that love was not a missile aimed at the other's heart, not a deluge, however sublime, in which to drown the other person, not a drug to induce ecstasy in the beloved. Love was opening the heart and a willingness to receive the other. Love was compassion, the ability to see another person clear, without letting your own shadow block or distort your vision, and this required a dispensation of the heart not the mind. In their different ways my parents had done their duty by me, and my mother had even shown me a kind of strangulated love, but she had not opened her heart to me. In Atalanta's phrase, she had not been available for love.

It seemed cruel that her death should have provoked these

insights, and yet they were a kind of gift she could not have bestowed while she was alive.

Love is not an absolute and it probably comes in as many forms as there are people. In my case, love required me to break free of my childhood labyrinth and its obsessions. The time had come to leap beyond them. My parents had lived in a prison of their own making, and my father carried the key. Perhaps my mother had taken the only escape route open to her – flying for freedom – only to drown in the moat that encircled their Alcatraz.

I carried my prison with me: my bull's body, my bull's soul. Who had the key to that? It seemed that any insolent boy could lock me up with a joke – *Little and Large!* But who could set me free?

I now saw that I had been blind, stupidly, obstinately blind. I had kept my eyes myopically focussed on the darkness that lay within my maze, not seeing that all the time the gate had been standing open while Atalanta waited for me in the sunlight, flowers of flame ablaze in her hair. Atalanta, O Atalanta!

The ferry docked at Birkenhead and I stayed aboard while her passengers disembarked. Fresh passengers came up the bouncing gangplank, and the *Iris* set forth once more into the mist, which was now clearing.

As a teenager I had often made this meaningless trip. Though she was only a river bus, I relished the nautical feel of the ferry, with her companion ways, brass fittings and varnished wood. I was fascinated by the business of tying up at each destination: the sound of her massive ropes as they stretched and creaked against the bollards, the agonised squeezing of rubber tires that protected the hull, the seething water in the narrowing gap between ship and dock, the rattle of the ramp as it was lowered onto the pier.

I found it reassuring that this ludicrous ship made her

pretend passage across the ocean of the Mersey a dozen times a day, from west to east and back again, from one toy continent to the other. It was fitting that a sea-faring city should provide a convenient, hourly adventure to its citizens, reminding them of braver voyages to stranger shores. Surely, it was also fitting that sons should grieve their mothers and widowed fathers should turn to their sons for comfort?

My own voyage came to an end and I walked into the city via Brunswick Street, passing between the Cunard Building and the Port Office. My mother had loved the river, and there was something about the mutable, insubstantial quality of water that she had shared. My father, on the other hand, was at home in that most substantial of elements, the office block. He worked in Dock Way, a long, narrow corridor of a street striding away from the Mersey and bringing with it a salty wind smelling of money, shipping and competition. The city's dockside streets were his kingdom. Other people ran their business in these buildings, but my father's business was these buildings; they were the labyrinth in which he had entombed himself, king and monster at once.

I pictured him seated at his desk, dressed in his habitual suit and dark tie. (Since he was in permanent mourning for my sister, no funeral could take him by surprise.) Was the loss of his wife just another dimension to the loss of his beloved daughter, the loss that had taken the vitality out of his own life? My mother had been his confidante, his co-conspirator, his only friend; she had invested his grieving for Rosemary with a kind of heroic quality by abnegating her own needs. Had he loved or used her? How would he grieve now that he was alone, 'entirely alone'? The fact was that these and all other questions relating to his emotional welfare would have to go unanswered, because they were no longer any of my concern. He was on his own, and I was disowned.

I confess I wept. Don't ask me why. Not for my mother, not for my father, not for myself; after all, what had I lost? I wept over the sheer folly of it. I wept as much as anything because there was nothing to weep over. I couldn't love him, but I couldn't hate him either.

I returned to the Pier Head to collect my car. The mist had lifted, leaving the river to sparkle under the noon sun.

When I got back to London I discovered that I had been sacked.

You know the rest, Anna.

One detail: when the Führer told me the company was obliged to 'say goodbye' to me (a dainty locution for a bloody act) he finished the interview by reaching over his desk to shake hands. Out of sheer instinct I responded, but once my hand was in his grip he held on to it, staring me in the eye.

'No hard feelings, eh?'

I told him I had no feelings at all.

I then went round the corner to the Museum Tavern and under the noble gaze of the British Museum's portico proceeded to do the gentlemanly thing: I drank myself into a vile temper.

Presumably you witnessed my return to the office; if not, you must have seen the devastation I wreaked. My recollection of the episode is uneven, but a handful of moments are lit with hectic clarity. As you know, I trashed my room (did you have to clear it up, or did the job call for carpenters and decorators?) and I recall stamping in a kind of war dance on the heap of rubbish I had created: books, files, letters, jacket designs, posters, manuscripts, typescripts, all ripped and strewn. Very childish and very satisfying, or so it seemed at the time. I have a worrying memory that I roared like a bull to match the bullish strength I seemed to have acquired. The chairs, desk, bookcases and other bits of furniture yielded to me as if made of balsa-wood. A nosegay of appalled faces was crammed into the doorway as the staff gathered to behold my disintegration (a touch of theatre to relieve the day's monotony). Did I succeed in bloodying the office boy's nose? I'm sure I tried. Finally, I remember being 'escorted' from the building by the newly employed security officer, resplendent in his Ruritanian uniform, who flagged down a reluctant cabbie to take me home. Thus, my fifteen years with the company were brought to a glorious termination.

Will you ever believe that I was not trying to kill myself that night?

Yes, I spent the remainder of the afternoon and most of the evening drinking as drunks do: in solitude, solely concerned with quantity not quality. (However, since I am nothing if not a snob in such matters, I might add that the whisky concerned was Talisker single malt from the Isle of Skye, 45% proof and £20 a bottle. This liquid gold is said to have an aroma of sherry and kippers and a flavour of burnt butter; in addition, the stuff gets you royally pissed.)

Yes, I took a *couple* of sleeping pills, because booze never puts me to sleep. It always wakes me an hour after I have managed to nod off, leaving me both insomniac and horribly hung-over. Yes, the bottle of Mogadon you found on the bedside table was nearly empty, but only because I am a regular user of the little fellows (so small and yet so powerful), as my doctor will readily confirm.

Yes, I took the phone off the hook. I gave it the night off and left it to purr like an idle cat on my desk. There was no one, not even you, my solicitous colleague, I wanted to hear from or speak to; I wished to be alone and undisturbed.

What would Atalanta have thought if she'd known that despite my ever advancing intoxication I played Shostakovich's eigth string quartet over and over again, without inflicting the slightest scratch on the record? Do you know it? Grim, but consoling.

Yes, I probably took too many pills, especially when

combined with whisky, and, yes, I did feel horribly low, low enough to think of consulting Dr Darling in the wee hours. (In an earlier stage of drunkenness I considered ringing a certain number in Maida Vale; don't they say that funerals make a macabre aphrodisiac?) This time my depression was quite different from the black hole that had once consumed me and driven me to Darling's room to save my life. So far from being the victim of emptiness and futility, I was engulfed by an emotion too acute to be borne, and for an evening at least I craved anaesthesia.

It's a measure of the strength of my feelings that it took a bottle of Mogadon cocktails to render me comatose. I was not in despair, I was in pain. My mother, Atalanta, Eddie and his father, and now my job; all lost. (I had been married to my work, and now I was summarily divorced, cast aside in favour of a younger rival: the politic Ms N. Good luck to her!) Loss is an emotional dead end; there's nothing you can do with it except endure the grief and wait it out.

Yes, I wanted to stop feeling for a night. No, and no again, I did not want to kill myself. If I sought suicide, it was only on a temporary basis, so to speak; I was looking for the respite of no more than an evening. And I most definitely was not making a cry for help. Whose help? What help?

My return to consciousness the following morning brought me face to face with you, Anna, so angry and solicitous at the same time.

By the way, how did you get into my flat without causing any damage?

You slapped my cheek, slapped it harder than first aid required, but then you surprised me by the intensity of your relief when I rose from the dead, looking and, no doubt, smelling like a corpse. You scolded me and put me to bed, where I remained for the rest of that day. I woke when a doctor, whom I did not recognise, presented himself at my bedside to make sanctimonious remarks about the perils of alcohol. When I woke again in the evening, there you were, still ministering to me, still upbraiding me for my foolishness. Finally, you arranged with Cynthia for me to recuperate in her Pyrenean chalet. (It pains me to confess that once again I am shamed by Cynthia's kindness.) And it must have been you, Anna, who booked my train ticket and filled my wallet with francs, allowing me to flee the country in dignified secrecy.

I failed to show my gratitude – embarrassment makes brutes of us – but let me express it now. We don't know each other well, and you owed me nothing in the way of loyalty or friendship. How long had you worked for me? No more than six or seven months. Indeed, now I come to reckon it up, you joined me the week after I met Atalanta (holy day), which was in October last year, at the time of the Frankfurt Book Fair. You have a family to care for, you have difficulties of your own (you see, I'm not so egocentric after all). You are certainly not paid to nurse your disgraced and defrocked boss. You acted out of sheer kindness, and I thank you.

I don't know whether you will consider it a further abuse of your good will, but I'd like to put a proposal to you.

During my month here I have compiled this memoir partly because I felt you were owed an explanation for my behaviour. It was unfathomable unless you knew about extramural events, which I had confided in none of my colleagues, not even you. They don't make my hooliganism any the more forgivable, but at least they show that it had a comprehensible cause.

I also wanted to demonstrate to you that, notwithstanding recent crack-ups, I have an essentially resilient and steady character that is powered by my dedication to books and writers; in a word, my bibliomania, which like all obsessions has the strength (ruthlessness) to overcome most difficulties in its path. (Obsessional personalities, by the way, do not make suicides: there is always another record to collect, another enemy to vanquish, another species to spot.) I'm sure you didn't think I was going to accept my fate meekly and hide my ignominy behind another desk in another company. No, excellent Anna, I have been hatching a plan here in Cynthia's French nest and now the chick is beginning to crack open its egg.

I'll come to the point immediately. What I have in mind is a new company, my own imprint, which I propose to call Minotaur Books. What do you think? I am sure that a number of authors, whom I brought to the list, will not find the Philadelphian regime congenial and can be persuaded to march under new colours. I'm talking about authors whose 'bottom-line performance' has probably put them on Ms N.'s hit list in any case. I feel confident of recruiting enough good writers to make up a publishing programme that would earn a modest livelihood, if overheads and expenses were kept to a minimum (always excepting lunch, of course – some corners cannot be cut).

My dear Anna, would you do me the honour of joining me in this daring enterprise as manager and factotum?

Let me anticipate your first, utterly reasonable question. I would not formally invite you into my employment unless I could guarantee your salary, to say nothing of a pittance for myself and funds for all the other inevitable expenses and costs, but at the moment, sitting here in deepest France, I can't do that. However, I happen to know that my dubious friend Oliver Breakspear, whose acquaintance you have been fortunate not to make, is entertaining proprietorial longings now that he is a merry widower. I may have shirked my duties at the office, but I was not so steeped in folly as to neglect my interests at the Garrick Club. Breakspear has inherited a fortune and is now in a position to indulge both his publishing pretensions and his hatred of conglomerates.

I will be speaking to him as soon as I return to London.

Before I leave here I will write you a separate letter, describing my plans in detail and putting my offer to you, but I'll urge you not to accept or refuse me until you've read these notebooks and allowed me to introduce myself, so to speak. I am not the man you brought back to life a month ago; nor am I prisoner any longer in my father's dungeon.

A last word. My mother's will turned out to be as idiosyncratic as my father had promised. She left me all her capital, which came to a tidy £20,000 (her mysterious 'resources'), but the legacy was subject to conditions. According to the lawyer's letter, a masterpiece of sobriety that was sent to me here in France, my mother had instructed that the 'monies' should be lodged in an account to be administered by the executor (the lawyer herself and not my father, interestingly enough). I was required to spend my inheritance on foreign travel to specific destinations, but was only permitted to claim against the account after the completion of my trips. I could redeem my expenses from the executor by submitting hotel bills, ticket receipts and any other material evidence of disbursements made in, or en route to, one or more of the prescribed destinations. A further condition stipulated that money spent on books or printed matter of any sort, such as guides, handbooks, histories, travel journals, maps, atlases, gazetteers, dictionaries, phrase books, foreign language newspapers and magazines would not qualify for compensation from the legacy. (This was a mother who understood her son.) The destinations she had nominated were: Archangel, Duluth, Gdansk, Hamburg, Kobe, Marseilles, Piraeus, Rotterdam, Vancouver, Vladivostok. What a list!

It was clear that my mother had derived an enormous amount of entertainment from drafting this whimsical document and teasing her po-faced lawyer. But, as ever, her motives were impenetrable. It took me several days to discern that the places on her seemingly random catalogue did have a common factor in that they were all ports, but otherwise there seemed to be no point to their choice, apart from the fun of despatching me to some of the world's grimmer waterfronts. Gdansk, for God's sake! And where exactly was Duluth? Surely, there was no reason why she couldn't have given me the money outright, without playing games. On the other hand, perhaps her intention was no more baffling than a mother's ordinary desire to see her son 'get out of the house', the injunction she had so often used when driving me from my library-bedroom and down to the river with my rollerskates. Translated into adult terms, her will might have been a way of urging me to experience the world beyond book-bound Bloomsbury and the Charing Cross Road. (She wasn't to know that I had in fact been expelled from my bibliopolis, and that the price of readmission would be considerably more than £20,000.)

If her desire was simply to ensure that I got some cultural fresh air, why had she specified these ten, apparently unconnected ports? What was her purpose? To make mischief, or perhaps to create deliberate obfuscation for her own posthumous amusement? Anything was possible.

And then, one afternoon as I was walking on the valley ridge above Cynthia's chalet, I recognised that the significance of her designated places was precisely that they were ports. No particular meaning was to be read into their selection, for they had probably been picked arbitrarily and without much reflection; geography had never been her strong suit. It was sufficient that they were ports, like Liverpool, because this in itself linked them to my mother and me. We had shared a love of the Mersey and its estuary (which in the end had claimed her for itself) and so, by inciting me to explore these other sea cities, she was perhaps trying to widen my circle of pleasure? It was an appealing theory and I decided to adopt it.

I reached the topmost point above the valley, which was

marked with a cairn amassed by walkers. Snow glittered on mountain peaks in the far distance. Thirty miles to the west was Biarritz and the Atlantic. To the south, not five miles away, lay the Spanish border where the valleys lost their pastoral mildness and turned jagged and barren. Within sight was a pass that pilgrims had been using since the middle ages to travel from France to Santiago de Compostela.

My mother's personality, like her cache of underwear, would remain forever inscrutable. Did she have a lover; did she seek her own death; did she ever think of me with a warm heart? Who was the person behind that mocking mask, with its scarlet lips and inextinguishable cigarette? Since these, and all questions about her, were unanswerable, I let them go, releasing them to soar above the valley and join the vultures, graceful, majestic creatures that circle these Basque valleys in effortless gyres, waiting their chance to turn death into clean bones.

My father's shadow would fall on me until the day he died. The past does not let us go; we are who we were. But my mother's will took the two of us beyond the confines of the old prison, with its conifer walls and single vista of my sister's grave. By being so typically enigmatic, it gave me room to construe her personality as I chose. In my mother's honour I added a stone to the cairn and made my choice. I would interpret her last wishes as an expression of love, a benign gesture of farewell that allowed me to think kindly of her. If there had been any malice in her last wishes, I didn't want to know about it. Or, to use Atalanta's phrase, which was finally beginning to mean something to me, I would make myself available for love – my mother's version of love.

Postscript

I expected to be in London by now, engaged in discussions with you, Breakspear and anyone else who might be persuaded to take an interest in Minotaur Books, but I have been delayed. I telephoned Atalanta. (You didn't imagine I would abandon her without an attempt at redemption, did you?) She had heard about my dismissal, but not my mother's death. I told her about the will and did my best to explain my vision on the mountain top. When I'd finished she was silent and I feared she was going to cut me off.

'Would you be willing to meet me?' I asked her. 'I have a thousand things to say to you.'

She remained silent.

'I know how to love you, Atalanta. Please give me that second chance you talked about.'

'I'll come to France,' she said, taking me by surprise. 'Where shall we stay?'

I was tempted to suggest Marseilles, where we could have squandered some of my newly inherited fortune and lived like royalty for a week or so. But I dismissed the idea, fearing that Atalanta would see it as a sign of my continuing imprisonment within my parents' world. Instead, I proposed Biarritz, a place I had never visited, though Cynthia had often recommended it.

'It's only an hour from here and according to Cynthia a very amusing spot. I'm looking at the guidebook, which tells me it was "once a playground for monarchs and their mistresses" . . . Good lunch to be had at the Port des Pêcheurs. Sounds irresistible, doesn't it? Oh, and the Grande

Plage has been called "the queen of beaches and the beach of kings". That clinches it, surely?'

'I'll catch the next train,' she said in her abrupt way.

I was about to tell her that we could see Maurice Ravel's birthplace in Ciboure just down the coast when I heard the line go dead.

I met Atalanta at the station in Biarritz and took her in a taxi to the Hotel du Palais, where I had spent the previous night. A shyness, reminiscent of the earliest days of our acquaintanceship, prevailed in the car as we drove through the town towards the sea, yet its cause was quite different. In those days we had both been hobbled by inexperience, which had at least put us on an equal footing, but now the old symmetry was gone. I was contrite, hoping for that second chance, if not forgiveness, while she, the injured party, was reserving her judgement, unwilling to jump into a hasty reconciliation. Atalanta stared persistently out of the window, unwilling to meet my eye, which, in any case, was continually shying away from the risk of meeting hers. Yet the sight of her, so immense, so shapely, produced in me a familiar stab of desire and a deep longing for us to be reunited.

The driver whistled admiringly at the opulence of the limousines and sports cars, mostly British, parked along the gravelled approach to the main entrance of the hotel, and he carried Atalanta's suitcase into the hall with the air of a man happily anticipating a munificent *pourboire*. He was disappointed.

I had given a great deal of anxious thought to the delicate matter of our bedroom/s. I wanted to be close to Atalanta, and of course I had hopes of sharing a bed with her once again, yet I didn't want to appear presumptuous and destroy our new entente before it had begun. What, then, was the answer? A suite? (Too vulgar.) A twin-bedded room? (Worst of both worlds.) I took courage from the fact that the Hotel du Palais, despite being the size of a chateau, had once been the holiday love nest of Emperor Napoleon lll and his precious Eugénie, a memory enshrined in its matchless address: 1, Avenue De L'Impératrice. Without confiding in the manager, an exquisite in a bow tie whose English was better than mine, I must have communicated a sense of my confused needs to him, because he proposed a solution that neatly matched romance with etiquette: a pair of rooms, *chambres de luxe (face mer)*, that were separate but inter-connecting. (They were also the most expensive rooms in the place; the man knew his job.)

I took Atalanta into her room, opened the shutters and ushered her onto the balcony, where with a theatrical sweep of my arm I showed her a beautiful crescent of beach that stretched from the hotel to a rocky promontory on the far side of the bay.

'Behold, Biarritz!'

Meanwhile, following my instructions to the letter, a flunkey entered, rolling an ice bucket on wheels from which emerged the neck of a champagne bottle, swathed in a white cloth. He uncorked it, poured two glasses and, bowing low – so low in fact that I wondered if there wasn't a touch of satire in his manner – closed the door behind him. I toasted her.

'Welcome, and thank you for coming.'

I left her alone to rest and take a bath before dinner.

While Atalanta relaxed, I passed a fretful couple of hours in my adjoining bedroom (our mutual door unlocked, but sealed by a much steelier bolt) and was driven to order a second bottle of champagne for my own use. Though she had taken the trouble to journey the length of France to see me, and had done so at very short notice, she had said nothing so far to indicate whether or not she was inclined to absolve me. I comforted myself with the thought that she was more a woman of gestures than words. Taking my cue from her, I planned a gesture of my own.

I reserved a table at a restaurant in the *vieux port*, which lay on the far side of the bay. To get there we would have to stroll along the seafront and then round to the next cove, which gave shelter to the town's dilapidated little harbour (port was too grandiose a term). Have you ever been to Biarritz, Anna? A preposterous place – Miami Beach in bed with *la belle époque* – but delightful. The beach, an expanse of fine, yellow sand, was fruitily described by our hotel brochure as *la dune à l'embonpoint confortable*, and from my balcony I could see that it was oily with young bodies. Since they were French, they were both beautiful and half-naked, but I longed to see Atalanta stretched out under the same sun, putting them to shame: a woman amongst girls, an Amazon among elves, a goddess beside puny mortals. And I longed to lie beside her (a god in my own bullish way), showing these skinny youths that I was her Olympian partner. However, I knew we had a long way to go before Atalanta and I could share in such conspicuous intimacies.

Famous for its titanic waves, the bay is also a place of worship for surfers, strange youths with bleached hair and rubber suits who gaze devoutly at the horizon, eternally waiting for the transcendent wave. These breakers roll across the great prairie of the Atlantic before smashing on the defenceless *embonpoint* of the beach, and it takes a swimmer far brawnier than I to brave the maelstrom when they explode in their final convulsion.

The seafront is bordered by an elegant, paved walkway running along the edge of the beach from the Hotel du Palais to the casino at the other end. This promenade, so different form its counterpart in Liverpool, is lined with cafés, bars, ice-cream stalls and boutiques selling negligible bikinis at momentous prices. In the evenings it becomes a kind of catwalk where the *jeunesse dorée* (and others who are gilded if not so young) parade themselves, their newly bronzed skin glowing in the twilight. It was my plan to make an unequivocal gesture of atonement for Norfolk by walking Atalanta the entire length of this front when the promenade was at its busiest and swarming with people whose only purpose was to see and be seen.

When Atalanta finally knocked on our connecting door. I could hardly believe she had not telepathically apprehended my plan, for she looked magnificent in a white suit made of some filmy material that showed off her gentle British tan. In contrast with the alarming kipper colour achieved by so many French women under the fierce southern sun, the hazy radiance of West Hampstead had baked her no darker than an entrancing shade of pinky-brown, just the colour of certain hens' eggs. In this outfit, and looking as healthy as she did, she seemed, if anything, taller than when I had last seen her.

I had not neglected my own appearance (straw boater, two-tone shoes, double-breasted scarlet jacket; I'll say no more) and the pair of us made a remarkable sight, though I say so myself. When we emerged from the lift the manager hurried from behind his desk to escort us personally to the door, a rare token of respect. After Atalanta had passed through he caught my eye and put his finger tips to his lips in a fervent kiss of appreciation.

Out on the promenade we attracted universal attention. Some people frankly stared, some stepped out of our path as though we were royalty, and one man went so far as to call out 'Bravo!'. In short, we were an event – un événement. As was her way, Atalanta neither acknowledged nor appeared to notice these attentions, but maintained a stately pace, holding her head high and her back straight.

I was proud to walk beside her, and I told her so.

We sauntered to the end of the promenade, climbed to the top of the rocky outcrop that overlooks the bay and admired the sun as it sank into the horizon out at sea. In the twilight a constellation of lights began to mark out the coastline below us. We walked down to the harbour and claimed our table on the pavement outside the restaurant. A few boats bobbed idly in the harbour, and the air was perfumed with that characteristic bouquet of fish and gasoline, with a hint of sewage, that always seems to hover over such places. I ordered a bottle of Jurançon, a local white wine that is slightly honeyed and not everyone's choice, but had become my favourite over the last month. Without consulting Atalanta, I also ordered sardines, salad and *frites*. If nothing else, I knew I'd got that much right.

During the afternoon, while pacing my monkish hotel room, I'd carefully devised an agenda for discussion over dinner, topics which I hoped would encourage Atalanta to review my prospective behaviour in a tolerant light. I had also taken a stern vow to keep my tongue on a leash, but like an untrained, wilful dog it promptly slipped its collar and ran away. Instead of asking Atalanta about her life since our separation, I rattled on compulsively, talking about my mother's crazy will, the horror of confronting her corpse, my epiphany aboard the ferry, my feelings about my unfeeling father, the agony of losing Eddie and so on. I even spoke about you, Anna, and my plans for Minotaur Books. Finally, as my tongue wearied and limped home, I tried to tell Atalanta about my new understanding of love.

When I'd finished she put her hand on mine for a moment. I ordered a second bottle, and allowed myself to entertain fantasies of setting sail with her in one of the imperial beds that lay anchored in our rooms, waiting for us to climb aboard and cast off. I wondered if she would sing to me again.

'You made me very angry in Norfolk,' she said, 'and I swore I'd refuse to see you again. But then I realised that your shame of me was only an extension of your own shame – your self-hatred.'

I hadn't anticipated this; my blueprint for our conversation had not included the possibility of her replying, still less taking the initiative.

'I realised as well,' she continued, 'that in a perverse way you had restored my pride. Even though you hid me away, you paid me so much attention you convinced me I must have a value. No one else had ever done that. So I have something to thank you for, which is why I came here.'

She stood up and left the table, wandering across to the harbour wall, where she studied the fishing boats and their nets piled up on the slipway. I paid the bill and joined her.

We walked in silence back to the promenade and stopped for brandies, sitting outside in the balmy night air. Next to the café a jazz band was setting up its instruments on a makeshift open-air bandstand, and I pointed out to Atalanta that its unusual combination was the same as the famous quartet led by Gerry Mulligan in the 1950s: saxophone, trumpet, bass and drums. My reference was pertinent because, despite being young and French, the four players drew on a repertoire of venerable American standards by Porter, Berlin, Gershwin, Khan and the like. They made a very agreeable sound.

When we'd finished our brandies I said she must be tired after her long day, but Atalanta didn't stir. We listened to another couple of numbers, in my case with mounting but disguised impatience, in hers with immoveable concentration. Finally, I showed my discontent and suggested that we leave. She rose to her feet, but ignored me. Instead, she walked over to the band, which was taking a break, and spoke to its leader, the saxophonist. The conversation was prolonged and I was forced to order another brandy.

When the band picked up their instruments again I expected Atalanta to join me, and was amazed to see her take up a position in front of the quartet with a microphone in her hand. 'Anything Goes,' she said. The band struck up with a brush of the drums and she began to sing: '*In olden days a glimpse of stocking was looked on as something shocking. Now, heaven knows, anything goes.*'

At the end she was applauded, but she immediately began a raffish rendering of 'Makin' Whoopee'.

In her white dress, with the summer breeze playing round her statuesque figure in a way that Ovid would have relished, Atalanta was both beautiful and impressive. People on the promenade were slowing and stopping to listen to her, and by the time she had launched into her third song, ''S Wonderful', a considerable crowd had gathered, forcing the few who wanted to get past to walk on the beach. It wasn't long before I lost sight of Atalanta in the press of bodies round the bandstand. Unable to reach his customers, the waiter became enraged, but was told to keep quiet.

I walked a little way down the promenade and stood on a table belonging to the next-door café, now deserted, in order to see Atalanta over the heads of the crowd. The café lights caught the lustre in her chestnut hair which she had arranged in a chignon, the very style, I remembered, she had worn when I had first seen her all those months ago in our doomed art class. But this was a very different person from the inhibited Amazon who had crouched self-effacingly over her easel. Atalanta, the torch singer, was confident and upstanding, provocative and voluptuous. I ached with desire for her. She had taken off the jacket of her suit to reveal a flimsy décolleté blouse supported by shoestring straps, which in turn displayed her stupendous bosom and heroic shoulders. Without diminishing the impact of her noble height, she leant forward a little to confide in the micro-phone, a visual effect that created a seductive intimacy with her rapt audience. She marked the beat by a subtle undula-tion of her hips. For me, the most extraordinary feature of her performance was the voice itself, which was as sweet and beguiling as ever, but invested with vigorous, witty projection. Of course, I had never heard her sing profession-ally before, but there seemed to be something about this Atalanta, the vocal, physical and emotional Atalanta now entertaining a positive throng, that was altogether newborn.

For the second time that night I was proud of her, though it was not the way I had hoped to hear her sing.

After completing a set of half a dozen songs, she announced (in French, another hidden talent) that she must stop since she had come to the end of her voice and her repertoire. She begged the forgiveness of her audience, explaining to their disbelief that she was only a tourist. She wished everyone '*bonnes vacances*' and returned the microphone to the saxophonist. He whispered something urgently into her ear while the crowd clapped and shouted '*Encore! Encore!*' in vain.

'*Elle chante très bien, la géante,*' a woman standing near me said to her husband.

'*Bien sûr! Bien sûr!*' he said, clapping heartily.

Atalanta bowed and bowed again, and finally quit the bandstand. The crowd broke up and I pushed forward to congratulate her on her triumph, though in my heart I felt sore.

We walked along the promenade, and though she said nothing I could tell that she was both exhausted and thrilled. We returned directly to the hotel, where news of her triumph had travelled even to that august precinct, for the doorman raised his top hat to her and said gravely, '*Félicitations, Mademoiselle!*' as he opened the door. '*Encore du champagne?*' was the night manager's gallant enquiry, but a glance at Atalanta answered his question: she was yawning mightily as she trudged up the stairs.

She went to her own bedroom, but did not lock the door. Later, dressed in silk pyjamas, she came into my room, sat on my bed and with her gentlest voice crooned in my ear Cole Porter's song, 'Just One of Those Things' – '*one of those bells that now and then rings . . . just one of those nights, just one of those fabulous flights, a trip to the moon on gossamer wings . . . our love affair was too hot not to cool down . . . goodbye, dear, and amen; here's hoping we meet now and then . . . it was great fun but it was just one of those things.*'

'Thank you, Bruno,' she said and kissed the top of my head, before returning to her own room. I took this to be her farewell, and wept in my pillow as I had not wept since the days of my prep school.

Atalanta slept late the following morning. When she finally rose, she joined me on my balcony, still in her pyjamas, and announced, 'I've arranged to have lunch with Johnny, the saxophonist from last night.'

'Johnny!'

'Don't be pompous. That's his name. You know, like Johnny Halliday, or Johnny Hodges, if you prefer it.'

'What does he want?'

'He's asked me to sing with his band for the rest of the summer season. They've got dates in various places up and down this coast, and in August they're playing on the Côte d'Azur. We've got to sort out arrangements. For a start, I need to build a repertoire.'

'You can't make a living with this Johnny character,' I said.

'I'm not looking for a living, Bruno. I want a life. You heard me last night. I can do it.'

She leaned on the balcony and looked out to sea; with a breaking heart I looked at her.

'Come on, I'll help you pack,' she said. 'You must catch the next train to London. You have a company to launch and great books to publish. You have your destiny, just as I do.'

I knew it was the end; there was no appeal, no third chance. I put my head in my hands.

Have you ever suffered a great disappointment, Anna, and then found that, rather than feeling miserable and defeated as the occasion warrants, you are overtaken by a sense of release? Fate has done its worst, you think; now I can move forward. The future, instead of looking black the way it should, glows with a kind of hectic promise. That was my experience. I lifted my head, saw the sun, the beach, the young women laying out their towels and I knew Atalanta was right. We did have destinies to pursue, splendid destinies, even if we were bound to fulfil them apart.

I was suddenly filled with crazy exhilaration. My heart, though bruised, was not broken. Atalanta was now a diva, which might never have happened if we had not disported ourselves on Biarritz's promenade. And in losing her I was not losing the power to love, which I might yet acquire in full. The door out of the labyrinth still stood open; surely there would be another woman and one more chance to escape?

'Let's swim,' I said joyfully.

'I'm no swimmer, and nor are you. It's too dangerous.'

'Too hell with it! Nothing can defeat us now.'

And I persuaded her.

We bought Atalanta a sensational bikini and I wore an old-fashioned costume in the style of a circus strongman's outfit, with a strap over one shoulder. Hand in hand we walked down the beach, where a crowd collected, saluting *'La Grande Chanteuse'* as we plunged into the tumultuous waves. We were gods and the sea itself could not destroy us. We subdued the surf and broke the white horses; we turned back the tide and sent the rollers running home to Newfoundland. We washed away the mud of memory. We were innocent again, parentless children bathed in the sea's grace, frolicsome as dolphins.